"The voice-y, hilarious, and unique rom-com I've been waiting for. Reality TV fans and animal lovers will go wild for its off-the-charts tension and whip-sharp banter. Last, it beautifully captured the struggle of overcoming the past, broadening one's horizons, and pursuing joy to the fullest. Perfect for fans of Christina Lauren and Kerry Winfrey."

—Amy Lea, author of *The Catch*

"No monkeying around: I'm wild for Kerry Rea's latest. *Lucy on the Wild Side* is a hilarious journey of self-discovery featuring a steamy romance, a unique zoo setting, and, of course, lots of gorillas. I would tune into the Lucy and Kai show any day of the week."

—Amanda Elliot, author of *Love You a Latke*

"A perfect meld of humor, heart, and romance. It's a beautiful story about busting out of your comfort zone to find the joy that you deserve. Kerry Rea will make you laugh, cry, and swoon, and you'll love every minute of it."

—Sarah Smith, author of *Twelve Steps to a Long and Fulfilling Death*

"Rea elevates the enemies-to-lovers trope with crackling chemistry, light humor, and genuine emotional nuance. Rom-com lovers should snap this up."

—*Publishers Weekly* (starred review)

"Readers looking for a fast-moving, spicy novel with a dash of wildlife education should enjoy this one."

—*The Columbus Dispatch*

"Hilarious, heartwarming, and absolutely delightful. I was as invested in Lucy and Kai's relationship as I was in the gorilla drama, all because of Kerry Rea's whip-smart prose and masterful storytelling. It's impossible not to fall in love with Lucy the hot-mess zookeeper as she journeys to overcome the wounds of her past."

—Kristin Rockaway, author of *Smart Girl Summer*

"With its perfect blend of humor and poignant moments, this is a rom-com that will capture your heart. Kerry Rea is quickly becoming one of my favorite authors!"

—Kerry Winfrey, author of *Faking Christmas*

"A compelling romantic comedy with a refreshingly unique storyline. . . . Rea's heartfelt, well-paced novel with realistic and well-developed characters is elevated by the parallel storyline of the gorilla troop."

—*Booklist*

THE
JEWEL OF
THE ISLE

KERRY REA

BERKLEY ROMANCE

NEW YORK

BERKLEY ROMANCE
Published by Berkley
An imprint of Penguin Random House LLC
penguinrandomhouse.com

Book design by Katy Riegel

Library of Congress Cataloging-in-Publication Data

Names: Rea, Kerry, author.
Title: The jewel of the isle / Kerry Rea.
Description: First Edition. | New York: Berkley Romance, 2024.
Identifiers: LCCN 2024008166 (print) | LCCN 2024008167 (ebook) |
ISBN 9780593815649 (trade paperback) | ISBN 9780593815656 (ebook)
Subjects: LCGFT: Romance fiction. | Novels.
Classification: LCC PS3618.E213 J49 2024 (print) |
LCC PS3618.E213 (ebook) | DDC 813/.6—dc23/eng/20240223
LC record available at https://lccn.loc.gov/2024008166
LC ebook record available at https://lccn.loc.gov/2024008167

First Edition: November 2024

Printed in the United States of America
1st Printing

To Riley,

who found adventure everywhere.

Happy trails, sweet boy.

THE
JEWEL OF
THE ISLE

ONE

EMILY

Jason dumps me while I'm wearing a bucket hat.

When I look back on this someday, I think that's the detail that will haunt me the most. Not that he broke up with me halfway through our weekly out-and-back hike, meaning we had to spend three very awkward miles together on the way back to the trailhead. And not that he dumped me for a professional dog walker named Piper who somehow wears overalls and a fanny pack without looking like a harried mom at Disney World. I won't even be most disturbed by the fact that he broke up with me three weeks before we were scheduled to take a very important, very nonrefundable trip to the most remote national park in the lower forty-eight.

It'll always be the bucket hat.

It should be one of the basic rules of being a decent person. Like *don't wear white to someone else's wedding* and *don't date somebody who's rude to the waiter, don't dump your girlfriend while she's wearing a hat with an adjustable chin cord* seems like basic manners.

I knew the hat was a bad idea. When I studied my reflection in the REI changing room, it practically sparkled under the harsh fluorescent lighting. It had a sun-protective neck nape and a reinforced brim that could best be described as nauseating, with tiny blue fish stitched onto the yellow canvas. It was horrifying, and I looked horrifying in it.

"I can't tell if I look more like a large toddler or a grandma on vacation," I told my sister Brooke, who squinted at me as she, too, tried to figure it out.

"Both, I think," she said finally. "I can't decide. But buy it anyway. You don't want skin cancer."

So I bought it. But now, as I'm sweating my butt off in the ninety-degree heat and listening to Jason explain that it's him, not me, but it's also kind of me, I regret my choice. It's like the time I went on a midnight ice-cream run wearing a tunic and sweatpants tucked into snow boots only to run into my handsome ex and his new girlfriend. They spotted me carrying four cartons of cookies 'n cream to the checkout, two tucked under each arm, and today is still worse. Because at least then I had dessert.

Today started out like every other Saturday for the past six weeks: I woke up, second-guessed my life choices while I hastily ate a protein bar, and drove with Jason to Hocking Hills State Park, where we strapped on our backpacking gear and hit the trail. By *hit the trail* I mean that he pranced over tree roots and muddy puddles with the grace of a nimble deer, and I tried my best not to slip on a wet leaf and break my leg.

Before we reached the first mile marker, however, I knew something was up. Jason, who rowed crew in college and gives off Tony Perkis from *Heavyweights* vibes when engaging in athletic endeavors, usually doesn't mind that I hike at the pace of a decrepit turtle. It's not that I'm lazy—my sixth-grade PE teacher wrote, *Emily tries hard, so that's something!* in the comments section of my report card—so much as wildly unathletic, and Jason usually peppers me with encouragement that borders on grating. But today, he didn't remind me that *The longest journey begins with a single step!* when I tripped on a rock and landed on my ass. Nor did he cheerfully inform me that *Nothing is impossible; the word itself says I'm possible!* when I mistook an Eastern milk snake for a rattlesnake and watched my life flash before my eyes. He just hiked silently, not even whistling as we started the steep ascent toward the turnaround point.

If I had oxygen to spare, I would have asked him what was up. But because cardiovascular exercise robs me of my breath and my general will to live, I focused on pushing through the burning ache in my muscles. Turns out I didn't have to ask anyway.

"Emily," Jason says once we reach the trickling waterfall that marks the turnaround point. "I need to tell you something."

I freeze. Hardly anyone calls me Emily; it's always Em or Emmy or Dr. Edwards. Even Jason's mother, who once snidely described my taste in living room decor as *Cracker Barrel gift shop, minus the subtlety* doesn't call me Emily. That's because she calls me Emma, but still.

"Um, okay," I say, wondering if he's about to announce that Taylor Swift died or something. The last time he went this many hours into the day without humming "Eye of the Tiger," he was about to tell me that Bed Bath & Beyond was closing forever. And Bed Bath & Beyond was my happy place. "Shoot."

He takes a deep breath, as if steeling himself to drop a bomb. "I can't go to Isle Royale with you. Because, well, because I want to break up."

I would have been less surprised if he told me he drank deer blood and sparkled in the sunlight. "Huh?"

"I know how important the Isle Royale trip is to you, and I can't go," he says, nudging a rock with the toe of his hiking boot. "It wouldn't be right."

I blink at him as my brain tries to assemble the sounds coming out of his mouth into something that makes sense. Isle Royale National Park, a jagged stretch of island in Lake Superior so remote that it can only be reached by ferry or seaplane, is my emotional and physical Everest. It's also the site of the super important backpacking trip Jason and I are scheduled to take in T minus twenty days and counting. The super important trip that he's bailing on, apparently.

"Em?" he asks, waving a hand in front of my face. "Are you okay? Can you hear me?"

His voice sounds muffled and tinny, and I wonder if the suffocating early September humidity is making me hallucinate. Surely my boyfriend of two years isn't dumping me right before the one week I'll desperately need his love, support, and ability to carry a shit ton of camping gear on his back.

"Water, please," I croak, rubbing my throat and pointing to the canteen fastened to Jason's day pack.

He passes it to me hurriedly, watching with wide eyes as I lift the canteen to my lips and gulp like my life depends on it.

"I, um, I know this is probably difficult for you to hear," he says, his eyes going even wider as some of the water goes down the wrong pipe and I break into a coughing fit. "But I think it's best for everyone."

I sputter again, so loudly that I startle a family of robins from a nearby oak tree. It's definitely not best for everyone for me to attempt a solo backpacking expedition in a national park that lacks potable water and cell service but has plenty of wolves and moose. It's certainly not the best thing for *me*. The closest I've ever come to camping is watching *Troop Beverly Hills* on repeat as a kid, and I single-handedly ruined Wilderness Day for my entire fourth grade Girl Scout troop in a hapless attempt to make daisy chain necklaces. (Note to self: if you can't find any daisies in the forest and sub in a leafy green plant instead, make sure that plant isn't poison ivy.) Unlike Jason, I am not built for surviving a week in the great outdoors. I'm built for appreciating a good pair of cashmere socks and reading Nora Roberts books by the fireplace.

"The thing is, you haven't been yourself this last year," Jason continues, studying me with mild alarm as I frantically dig through my day pack for a granola bar. "You've been really distracted, which is understandable. Considering, you know, what happened."

My fingers locate the bag of peanut M&M's that are supposed to be my post-hike treat, and I tear it open so roughly that half the candies fly out. *What happened* is that on a chilly October afternoon eleven months ago, my dad died. One second Jason and I were eating Chinese takeout on the couch, and the next I was answering a frantic call from the tearful bookstore owner who watched Dad collapse in the checkout line. Roger Edwards Jr., a bearded, bear-hugging guy who still listened to baseball on the radio and never watched a World War II movie that didn't make him misty-eyed, had suffered a sudden massive heart attack. He died next to a cardboard cut-out of Clifford the Big Red Dog, the Jesse Owens biography he wanted to buy on the ground beside him.

Of course I haven't been myself since; losing your best friend will do that to you.

"Is this because I left your mom's party early?" I ask, crinkling the candy bag with my fingers. "Because I stayed as long as I could."

Last week, I'd left Judith's sixtieth birthday brunch long before she even opened my present, a rose gold pendant necklace with her and Jason's initials that took me three painstaking attempts to wrap. But after she gave me a pointed eyebrow raise for ordering a second mimosa and sharply corrected me for using the fancy forks out of order, I cried in the bathroom and peaced out. It wasn't her criticism that reduced me to tears, even though it hurt. I cried because of how hard it was to watch Judith, who called Jason's assistant *the help* and tried to sit me at the kids' table at Thanksgiving, ring in another year of berating waitstaff and terrorizing managers while my dad was gone.

It's not that I wanted anything bad to happen to Judith,

even if I had spent two years trying to (not literally) kill her with kindness. I just missed Dad so much that it ached, and running off to the bathroom to listen to one of the *Hey Emmy, just your old dad here* voicemails saved on my phone hadn't helped the situation. So I left before I could ruin the fancy vibes of Judith's party with my fun little mental breakdown.

"Not at all," Jason says. "I know how hard you've tried with my mom. It's just . . . we barely connect anymore. You're always at work or on your phone. And when you do get a day off, you seem way more interested in going to HomeGoods than spending time together."

I take another sip of water, mostly to ward off the tears swelling in the corners of my eyes. As much as I want to protest, he isn't wrong. After Dad's funeral, in addition to the grief, I felt a restlessness that made it impossible to relax. Working double shifts in the ER kept my mind and hands busy, and with every chest compression I performed or chest tube I placed, I felt like I was helping some other family avoid the fate that befell mine. And in an attempt to make my inner world cozy and soft when the outside world was anything but, I spent entirely too much money on handwoven accent rugs and cute ceramic planters shaped like pineapples. When Brooke came over for dinner last week, she took one look around my apartment and warned me that if I hung one more piece of wall art with a cutesy phrase like MOODY FOR FOODY or MORE ESPRESSO, LESS DEPRESSO in my alcove kitchen, she'd stage an intervention.

"HomeGoods had a lot of steep markdowns last month," I tell Jason quietly. "I got those watermelon hand towels half off."

He lets out a long exhale. "I know this year has been rough on you, so I've tried to be patient. But at some point, you have to start moving on, you know? You can't keep living in the past."

I chew my bottom lip, letting his words sink in. I don't think Jason, a thirty-eight-year-old man who screamed at the ref when his adult kickball team lost the league championship, has any right to accuse me of living in the past.

"I am moving on," I insist. "That's what the Isle Royale trip is all about. I'm going on my dad's behalf so that I can say goodbye properly. The way he would have wanted."

I pause and shove a handful of M&M's into my mouth, hoping a blood sugar boost will get rid of the woozy, light-headed feeling that just washed over me. "Besides, we'll be in the literal woods for six days with no work or phones to distract us. That's basically a couples retreat!"

He blinks. "With all due respect, I don't think spreading ashes is part of your standard couples retreat."

I take a deep breath, trying to calm the pounding in my chest. If Jason backs out of the trip, I'll be forced to go into the wilderness alone. And considering that I don't know the first thing about filtering drinking water or starting a campfire, my chances of being mauled by a wolf or accidentally swallowing a brain-eating amoeba are greater than zero.

"I can't go alone," I say, practically shouting to hear myself over the hum of buzzing cicadas. "We've been together for two years. Shouldn't that count for something?"

He sighs and passes me a second canteen from his hydration belt. "There isn't a linear relationship between time and love, Em. I think you and I both know that. Besides, do you hear yourself? You said you can't go alone, not that you can't go *without me*. There's a big difference, and it's time we stop pretending otherwise."

I press the canteen to my forehead to cool my burning skin. Jason's words are harsh, but maybe he's not saying anything I don't already know deep down. Since we met at the complimentary breakfast our hospital hosted for National Doctors' Day, our fingertips brushing as we reached for the same basket of stale blueberry muffins, our relationship was driven more by convenience than chemistry. By the time I realized it, though, I was planning Dad's funeral, and it was easier to keep laughing at Jason's mediocre jokes and dragging myself to monthly dinners with his family than create another disruption in my already blown-up life.

So I nod, even though I wish I could argue. "Maybe you're right."

He wipes sweat off his brow and breathes a sigh of relief. "I'm so glad you agree. And look, I know my timing sucks, but you can just push your trip back until spring, right? So Brooke can go with you."

I pull the canteen away from my forehead. He might as well have said, *You can dye your hair green and become an Oompa Loompa, right?*

"No," I say. "No, absolutely not."

Dad, who died exactly one month before he was set to retire from his career as the editor of a small-town newspaper, had a mile-long bucket list of things he planned to do with his newfound free time. Some of his dreams were goofy—sample every fried delicacy sold at the state fair, convince Brooke and me that *Abraham Lincoln: Vampire Hunter* was a cinematic masterpiece—while others, like solve an Amber Alert and fish with Jeff Goldblum, were patently ridiculous. But the goal he was most excited about was visiting the national parks. After raising two stubbornly indoorsy daughters who made him attend countless teddy bear tea parties and suffer through every Mary-Kate and Ashley movie in existence, he was ready for fresh mountain air and crackling campfires. Don't get me wrong, he loved being a girl dad and could paint nails and French braid with the best of them, but he'd earned the chance to follow his own passions.

The national park Dad was most excited about was Isle Royale, and he asked Brooke and me to join him on a hiking trip in celebration of his retirement. We couldn't say no to the man who taught us to tie our shoes and do long division and love beyond measure, and so he'd booked our ferry tickets and planned our backpacking route months in advance. It was going to be the official kickoff of his national park adventures, and Brooke and I promised to be good sports and not complain about being briefly separated from air conditioning and our ten-step skincare routines. But then Dad died, leaving us heartbroken and haunted by what-ifs, and my sister and I vowed to go on the trip anyway. We'd stick to his planned itinerary and spread his ashes and pay tribute to the dude who loved donuts, *Indiana Jones*, and us. And when Brooke got pregnant and understandably backed out, we agreed that I would still go on our behalf. We'd made a promise to Dad, and I intended to keep it.

I still do.

"I'm not postponing," I say firmly, both for Jason's benefit and to quiet the nagging voice in my head warning me that this is a terrible, horrible, no good, very bad idea.

"Well, what about asking a friend to go?" he suggests, as if any of my friends would sacrifice a week of PTO to sleep on the ground and possibly contract Lyme disease. "I mean, you run to your car every morning because you're scared of your neighbor's Pomeranian. I'm not sure you should be going into wolf country on your own."

I stare at him, wondering if he's suffered one too many kickballs to the head. "Of course I shouldn't go on my own. That's why I invited you! And everyone's afraid of Tipper. He's unhinged! Besides, I don't run to my car. I walk briskly."

My boyfriend—no, ex—shakes his head and reaches into his pocket, pulling out a folded piece of paper. "I really am sorry for leaving you in the lurch. But I made you a list of reputable tour guides that work in the national parks. Promise me you'll look into them?"

I consider tearing the paper into bits and sprinkling them over his head like confetti, but I'm more mature than that. Besides, it's very wrong to litter.

"I promise nothing," I say dramatically, but I take the list from his outstretched hand. He is a meticulous researcher, even if he mostly uses his skill for looking up *Zelda* cheats.

"I'd go with you as a friend, if I could," he tells me, which is the exact same thing my high school lab partner said when he politely rejected my invitation to the Sadie Hawkins dance. "But I have, well . . ." Jason trails off and points at something on the ground, clearly trying to distract me. "Hey, look at that ant!"

"You have what?" I ask, wondering what's so important that it's worth leaving me to my own devices in the untamed wilderness.

"Well. I made, um, plans. Other plans."

"Other plans?" I repeat, watching a profusely sweating Jason fan himself with a trail map.

"I . . . well, I'm going to an EDM festival," he admits, his words barely a croak. "With Piper."

I don't know which bit of information baffles me more: the idea of Jason, who's terrified of porta potties and stans hard for Michael Bublé, willingly going to an electronic dance music festival, or who he's going with.

"Piper?" I ask, perplexed. "Isn't that your neighbor's corgi?"

His cheeks burn scarlet. "*Posey* is my neighbor's corgi. Piper is the dog walker."

When I look at him in bewilderment, the flush spreads down to his neck. "Posey escaped her leash while I was getting the mail last week. I helped Piper catch her before she peed on the Wilsons' hydrangeas, and we started talking. Turns out we have a lot in common."

"Oh," I say softly, dropping an M&M. "Oh."

"I really am sorry."

I nod and massage the hard ball that's formed in my throat. It's not the breakup that's making my teeth clench, or even the revelation that he's dumping me for an early-twentysomething whose complete lack of a capsule wardrobe will give Judith an aneurysm.

It's that I now have to say goodbye to my dad alone.

"For what it's worth, I'm sorry for having this conversation in the middle of a hike," Jason adds, slipping on his polarized sunglasses. "I've been meaning to talk to you for a few days now, but I hoped sunshine and endorphins would make the news go down easier."

I don't bother explaining that I get endorphins from bubble baths and color coding my bookshelf, not from hiking. Instead, I catch a glimpse of my bucket-hat-wearing reflection in his sunglasses, and just like that, I have the answer to the question I asked Brooke in the REI changing room.

"Grandma on vacation," I whisper.

Jason stares at me. "Huh?"

"Never mind." I tear my hat off with a grumble, cursing my sister for letting me buy it.

"Are you okay?" He raises his sunglasses to get a good look at me. "I really do want you to be okay."

It's an odd statement coming from someone who just said some very not okay things to me, and I don't know what to tell him. I don't know if I'm okay, or if I will be, and I really don't know how I'm going to manage hiking fifty miles across a remote island when just this morning I was outpaced by a group of sprightly senior citizens. Wiping my palms on my shorts, I try to imagine what Dad would say if he were here right now.

You're acting like a fool, son, he'd tell Jason, his voice booming but without malice. *Don't act like you've never seen a damn ant before.*

The thought eases a fraction of the heaviness in my heart, but it's not quite right. Because if Dad were here, he wouldn't worry about Jason. He'd pass me my water bottle and encourage me to take another drink, then tell me the same thing he did when I was a gap-toothed kindergartener nervous for the first day of school or an over-caffeinated twenty-year-old panicking about the MCAT.

You got this, Emmy, he'd say, showing me how to place my hand on my heart and focus on steadying the beat. *Just breathe. I'm here. You're okay. I'm here.*

Once I calmed down and wasn't teetering on the edge of a panic attack, he'd nod and give me his signature toothy grin. *See? You got this. Adventure awaits.*

I'm here. You're okay. I'm here. I breathe in and out, closing my eyes until the pounding in my ears subsides.

"Good luck, Jason," I say, not bothering to respond to his question as I slip my pack onto my shoulders. "And a word of advice, if I may? Never make Piper move to the back seat so Judith can sit shotgun."

He opens his mouth to say something, but I don't wait for his reply. I just start hiking back the way we came, reminding myself that I might be the furthest thing from a wilderness girl, but I can do this. And if not, I have to at least try.

"Hey, Em?" Jason calls, jogging to catch up. "Don't forget, we drove here together. Can I still catch a ride back with you?"

I'd like to tell him where to shove his polarized sunglasses. "Seriously?"

He shrugs and holds up the bucket hat. "You forgot this."

I glance from him to the hat and back to him before sighing and taking it from his hand.

"Come on," I mutter, gesturing in the direction of the trailhead.

Then I pull the hat down over my hair and quicken my pace.

Because whether I look like a large toddler or a grandma on vacation or just a sweaty thirty-three-year-old trying to piece the jagged edges of her broken heart back together, I have nothing left to lose.

Adventure freaking awaits.

TWO

RYDER

Someone is licking my face. It's not the weirdest thing I've ever woken up to—that honor goes to the squirrel I found cuddled up inside my sleeping bag during a camping trip to Estes Park—but it is unexpected. And since I haven't shared my bed with anyone since my ex-girlfriend Hannah called me an asshole and stormed out of our apartment with a box of her stuff, the tongue currently caressing my forehead definitely isn't human.

Jesus. I spring out of bed, wiping a trail of drool off my cheek. I haven't exactly been living my best life lately, but if I've reached the point where rats are infesting my apartment and greeting me with morning kisses, things are way worse than I realized.

Ruff! A cold, wet nose nudges my hand, and relief floods me when I realize the licking culprit isn't vermin but Daisy, the friendly collie I'm dog-sitting for the week.

"Hi, girl," I say, giving her a scratch behind the ears. She wags her tail and sighs in contentment. "You're in a good mood this morning, huh? Well, that makes one of us."

Instead of going to bed at a decent hour last night, I stayed up watching all four *Jaws* movies and drinking an entire six-pack, and now I have a raging headache to remind me of my stupidity. I also have a pile of beer cans and Hot Pocket wrappers cluttering the nightstand. I riffle through the mess to find my phone and wince when I register the time.

"Shit, Daisy, it's not morning at all," I mutter, grabbing the first pair of boxers I can find. I'm not entirely confident that they're clean, but it's twelve minutes past noon and I'm late for a TaskRabbit gig. Again.

With Daisy panting at my heels, I take a cursory swig of mouthwash, swipe a deodorant stick under each arm, and make a rushed cup of coffee while I feed Daisy her kibble—plus a handful of treats for waking me up. TaskRabbit isn't exactly lucrative, and performing random odd jobs for strangers isn't anything to write home about, but rent's going up again, and I need all the cash I can get. Dog-sitting isn't a huge moneymaker, either, but at least I get paid to hang out with cool girls like Daisy.

She finishes her kibble and glances up from her bowl with a question in her eyes. It's probably *Hey, are you just gonna stand there, or can you get me more food?* but I interpret it as *Why did Mommy and Daddy leave me in the care of a thirty-four-year-old man who wears pizza-print boxers and subjects me to* Jaws 3-D*?*

"Good question, Daisy. I, too, doubt your parents' judgment. Let's go."

I put on her leash and haul ass to my truck, where she jumps into the passenger seat without hesitation. When I pull up my navigation app, I see alerts for a missed call and a voicemail from my former almost-sister-in-law Tara. I delete the alerts and hit the road with my tires squealing. Talking to Tara brings back memories I'd rather forget, and it's too early in the day for that kind of gut punch.

It's always too early in the day.

I pull up to a sprawling Colonial in Cherry Creek, only a handful of miles from the townhouse I rented before my life went to shit and I was forced to downgrade to a squat apartment with low ceilings and nonexistent natural light. I ring the doorbell while Daisy seizes her chance to pee all over a neat row of yellow rhododendrons. When a man in a dark blue suit opens the door to find her mid-squat, he scowls at us.

"No solicitors, please," he says coolly, already halfway to shutting the door in my face.

"Oh, I'm not a solicitor. I'm Ryder Fleet." I give him my best sorry-for-the-dog-pee smile, but the introduction doesn't seem to register.

"Ryder from TaskRabbit," I clarify. "You requested help mounting a TV?"

He turns away to call to someone inside the house. "Lexi! TaskRabbit Ryder is here!"

When he disappears down a hallway, leaving the door ajar behind him, Daisy and I exchange a look. If someone told me two years ago that I'd be referred to by that title, I'd have thought they were crazy.

Daisy gives a soft bark that sounds a bit like *Whatever, Don*

Draper! and leaves a wet kiss on the palm of my hand. We step inside a foyer with vaulted ceilings and an enormous painting of a Revolutionary War soldier on horseback, and I try to guess how many odd jobs it would take for me to afford a single inch of the canvas. I'm estimating somewhere around a hundred when a dark-haired woman in yoga pants and a loose sweater waves at me, a silver bracelet jingling from her wrist.

"It's a Foxamura," she says.

I'm not familiar with that brand of TV, but I sure hope it doesn't require any fancy mounting equipment.

"Foxamura," she repeats, pointing at the painting. "The Canadian artist featured in the *New Yorker*? This is from one of his early collections. He's examining the intersection of coercive diplomacy and the human-equine relationship."

I don't know much about coercive diplomacy—it looks to me like a messy doodle of a fugly dude riding a horse—but I'll take her word for it. My expertise lies more in playing *Skyrim* and disappointing people than appreciating highbrow art.

"Foxamura, sure," I say with a nod. "Hey. I'm TaskRabbit Ryder."

"Hi there, TaskRabbit Ryder. I'm Lexi." She smiles, giving me a lingering once-over as she shakes my hand, and I find myself wishing I'd worn a looser-fitting T-shirt. Even though I haven't hit the gym in a while, good genetics and frequent manual labor mean I still have relatively toned biceps, and judging from Lexi's appreciative glances, I've still got the tall, dark, and handsome-ish vibe that all the Fleet men are born with. I'm not particularly concerned with my looks, but there was a period last year when I used them to my advantage, turning to pretty women and casual hookups in an attempt to soothe the unrelenting ache in my gut.

It didn't work.

"Mind showing me where you want the TV set up?" I ask.

Lexi leads me into the living room, swaying her hips more than necessary. She shows me the giant Smart TV she wants me to mount above the fireplace, and I thank her for the instructions and slip in my AirPods, hoping she'll get the hint that I prefer to work alone. She seems to, and I've finished locating the wall studs and am halfway through marking my drill holes when my phone buzzes. It's Tara again, and I shake my head and set my phone on the coffee table. The universe is working hard to screw with my head today.

"Lemonade?" Lexi returns just as I'm attaching the mounting bracket to the wall. She's abandoned her loose sweater in favor of a thin tank top that leaves little to the imagination, and I force myself to fiddle with my drill instead of looking directly at her.

"I'm okay, ma'am, but thank you very much." At somewhere in her early forties, Lexi's probably only a decade older than me, and with her pretty brown eyes and cute dimples, I'd be lying if I pretended like the me of six months ago wouldn't have happily accepted the drink and engaged her in flirty banter.

"No need to call me ma'am. Lexi will do just fine."

I nod and give her a closed-mouth smile. "You got it."

"So," she says, crossing her arms over her chest and watching as I grab the mounting plate. "How'd you get to be so good with your hands?"

I cough, and a series of buzzes from my phone saves me from having to reply.

"You sure are popular," Lexi observes.

I'm actually wildly unpopular, seeing as how my own mom dodges my calls these days and my ornery next-door neighbor Lulu is my closest (and only) pal. I make a noncommittal noise and grab my phone to see another incoming call from Tara.

"It's my sister-in-law. Mind if I answer this real quick?"

Lexi waves a hand at me. "Go for it. You never know if it's an emergency."

I'm not too worried about an emergency, seeing as how the worst has already happened, but I thank Lexi and step out to the back patio with Daisy to answer the call just in case.

"Hey, Tara," I say, closing the sliding glass door behind me. "How's it going?"

"And here I thought you dropped your phone in a toilet." Her Southern drawl lands thick in my ear, and the warm cadence of her tone could take me back to happier times if I close my eyes and let it. I don't.

"Nope, just busy with work." I wink at Daisy, who curls up in a patch of sunlight next to a teak bench.

"Still bartending?" Tara asks.

"Yep. Still tending bar, still on the dog-sitting app, still donating plasma when the budget gets tight. What can I say? I'm a winner, Tar."

She laughs, and I can picture her in the sunlit kitchen she used to share with my brother Caleb, her phone tucked between her ear and shoulder as she spoons fruit into her yogurt.

"So," I say, "is everything okay? Or did you just call to listen to me brag?"

Her heavy sigh speaks volumes. "We have a problem, Ryder."

"Uh, yeah," I say gently, thinking that *problem* is a nice way to describe the unthinkable tragedy that ruined both our lives. "I'm aware. But if you're trying to drag me to that grief support group again, I told you, it's not my thing."

"I'm not. But just so you know, there's a really great new facilitator, and he hardly ever lets Simon dominate the whole meeting by talking about his pet iguana," Tara says. "May she rest in peace, of course."

"I'll keep that in mind," I tell her, even though I definitely won't.

"Anyway, I'm not calling to wrangle you back to the support group. I'm calling because I can't sleep unless I get monthly verbal confirmation that you're alive and somewhat well, and also because . . . look, there's no good way to say this. Look at the text I'm sending you and you'll see what I mean."

I pull the phone away from my ear and frown at it, wondering if Tara's about to tell me that she's dating again; that she's moved on from Caleb with someone named Mike or Dave or Christopher, a good dude from a good family who I'll dislike simply because he's not my big brother. Maybe she's sending me a picture of the new guy, and I'll have to pretend that I'm happy for her. But when her message flashes across my screen, I see something much, much worse.

"Goddammit," I mutter.

It's a screenshot from an app called Boat Trader, and I instantly recognize the vintage turquoise bow rider listed for sale. *Fully repaired 1976 open bow Sea Nymph*, the text beside the boat reads. *Lovingly restored and ready to get back out on the water!*

"Dad's selling Caleb's boat," I say in disbelief, rage coursing through my veins. I blink at the spotless wood paneling and pristine leather seats that my brother spent countless hours restoring in our grandfather's old barn, and it takes everything in me not to fling my phone across Lexi's backyard.

"I couldn't believe it when I saw the listing," Tara says. "Your dad promised he wouldn't."

I kick an invisible rock across the deck. "I can believe it."

When Caleb and I were kids, our father's obsession with the racetrack and betting on the Packers was as constant as his bad moods. Luckily, Caleb was two years older and about ten years smarter than me, and he quickly figured out how to outwit Dad's sticky fingers. When my birthday approached, Caleb taught me how to race to the mailbox and check for a card from our grandparents in Tulsa, because if we didn't get to it first, Dad would tear open the envelope and pocket the cash inside. Caleb kept our best baseball cards hidden safely in an old coffee tin in the attic, and when I won a KB Toys gift card at field day by smoking the other fourth graders in the sack race, he taped it to the underside of my bed until I figured out which Super Soaker I wanted to spend it on. Even as a boy, he always found a way to protect the people and things he loved.

And I'll be damned if I let Dad sell Caleb's most prized possession like it's a Nintendo 64 he swiped from underneath the Christmas tree.

"We have to stop him," I say firmly.

Tara sighs. "Trust me, I've tried. I yelled and begged and pleaded, but your dad says he's fallen on hard times. He wants it sold ASAP."

I snort. "The only hard times he's fallen on are the Packers' shitty season. Anyway, screw him. *The Little Adventure* should be yours."

When Caleb and I were teenagers, we spent most summers visiting our grandpa Tim in Michigan. Grandpa Tim ran a bait and tackle shop during the day and restored old boats at night, and while I spent most of my time flirting with cute girls and going to bonfires on the beach, Caleb loved tinkering with the broken motors and collapsed metal fittings. He and Grandpa Tim spent an entire summer fixing up a worn-out old boat they found at an estate sale, and though I pitched in here and there, it was Caleb who repaired a thousand hull cracks with gelcoat and made regular trips to the hardware store, bringing back paint samples until he found the perfect shade of turquoise blue. By mid-August, the boat had a shiny new exterior and a motor that purred like a kitten, and Caleb whooped with glee when Grandpa Tim let us take it out on the lake. When Grandpa died a few years back, he left *The Little Adventure* to Caleb in his will.

When Caleb died, he didn't have a will. He hadn't planned that far ahead; he was only thirty-four.

"Legally, I have no right to it," Tara says, her voice hollow. "I called a lawyer to ask, but since we weren't married—"

"You were three weeks out from your wedding," I cut in. "That's practically the same thing."

"It might as well be three hundred years in the eyes of the

law," she explains. "The legal system isn't exactly known for its nuance."

I nudge a potted plant on the deck with my toe, fighting the urge to kick it. "So what can we do? I'd say we steal it, but a boat's kind of hard to hide."

I don't say what we both already know—that I sure as hell don't have the funds to buy it. Not unless Lexi has another few thousand TVs she needs mounted.

"I can use my savings," Tara says, "but I'm a few grand short. I think I found a way for us to close the gap, but I need your help to make it work."

I'd sell every spare organ in my body on the black market if it meant keeping the boat from ending up in a stranger's hands, and she knows it.

"Anything."

"I hope you really mean that," Tara says. "Because you got a submission on the Fleet Outdoor Adventure website, and I responded to it. There's a woman in Ohio who needs a guide for a trip to Isle Royale National Park, and, well . . . I sort of told her you would do it."

"Tara," I say, shaking my head like she can see me, "have you lost your damn mind?"

"I know, I know. It sounds crazy, on the surface. But—"

"Oh, it doesn't just sound crazy. It sounds crazy *dangerous*. Crazy irresponsible. Crazy d—"

She sighs. "Just hear me out, okay? Her name is Emily Edwards. She was supposed to go to Isle Royale with her boyfriend, but they broke up, and she has no camping or backpacking experience. She's in desperate need of help."

"Well, Emily Edwards will have to figure something else out," I insist. "And so will we. There's no way in hell I'm taking on a guide gig. And there's no way anyone would want me to. That was Caleb's territory, and you know it."

Almost a decade ago, Caleb got the idea to start a business offering private tours of the national parks and other wild places for tourists who wanted to explore nature with the security of an expert's guidance. Caleb, who'd never met an adventure he wasn't up for, had extensive training in backpacking, wilderness survival, and every outdoor activity you could think of. I, on the other hand, had extensive training in browsing Tinder, winning beer pong tournaments, and parroting Dwight Schrute's lines from *The Office* until Caleb wanted to slap me. But I also had a degree in marketing, and despite my twenty-something immaturity, Caleb saw enough promise to invite me on as his co-partner. We created Fleet Outdoor Adventures in the living room of his apartment, me building the website and handling advertising and promo while Caleb did the grunt work of leading the tours. Within a year, we had a waitlist of clients wanting to go everywhere from the Grand Canyon to the Rocky Mountains, and within five, Fleet Outdoor Adventures had a roster of expert tour guides and a glowing write-up in *Outside* magazine. Tara, who Caleb fell for when she brought her class of first graders to a community adventure day the company hosted, had helped with the administrative side of things.

But that was then, and this is now.

"Come on, you can set up a tent, can't you?" Tara asks. "And help Emily carry her luggage? Because that's all you'd have to do. It's a simple six-day backpacking trip from Windigo to Rock Harbor, and she has her itinerary planned down to the hour. You couldn't ask for a smoother gig."

"First of all, nobody should bring *luggage* to a national park," I tell her. "You bring a backpack and a day pack, max. And did you miss the part where I'm no good in the wilderness? You were on that camping trip in Big Thicket where my dumb ass decided to shortcut through a swamp and almost got killed by a cottonmouth."

"You'd do just fine in the wilderness if you learned to trust your instincts," Tara says, cutting me off. "You'd do just fine in your personal life, too."

I'd argue that following my instincts is the reason I'm an underemployed slacker with too much emotional baggage and too little 401(k). Caleb was the planner, the thinker, the one who knew exactly what a venomous cottonmouth looked like and where one might be hiding. He wasn't just the brains of the company but the brawn, too; I was merely the goofy little brother who lucked out with good genes and a knack for wooing the right social media influencers.

"Look, I want to save Caleb's boat as much as you do, but we both know I'm in no shape to take on a gig," I reason. "And are you forgetting how I ran the agency into the ground? Frankly, that cottonmouth should have done us all a favor and finished me off way back then."

"Come on, Ry," Tara says softly. "You can't possibly mean that."

I'm half joking about the cottonmouth, but I'm dead serious about everything else. I tried to keep Fleet Outdoor

Adventures going after Caleb died, but in true Ryder fashion, I failed spectacularly. I screwed up tour dates and pissed off employees and completely ruined a sweet elderly couple's fiftieth anniversary trip by booking their lodging at Yellowstone instead of Yosemite. Honestly, Emily Edwards is better off without me.

"Listen," Tara says gently, "I know this is a big ask. I'd do it myself if I could, but between my work obligations and my mom's health, I . . ." She sighs. "I won't pressure you to do anything you don't want to. But I think you should consider the possibility that this is a chance for you to have a reset."

"A reset from what?" I ask, letting Daisy lick my palm. "A carefree life where I work when I want and do what I want, with no strings holding me back?"

I don't need to see Tara's face to know she's rolling her eyes.

"*You're* the string holding you back, Ry. I know you insist you're doing okay, but we both know that's not true. I mean, you haven't dated anyone since Hannah or held a stable job in almost two years. You're one of the best guys I know, but you're drinking your days away instead of living the life you deserve."

"I'm drinking my nights away, technically," I say, gulping in air to loosen the tightness in my chest. "And I'll have you know that when it comes to minor home repairs, I'm one of the most sought-after Taskers in the Denver metro area."

"You used to be happy, Ryder." The gentleness of Tara's voice cuts right through my bullshit. "You used to have goals and hobbies, and you used to care about things. And I know how much it hurts you that Caleb's gone, because I miss him every second of every day. But it's like . . . it's like you're gone, too, even though you're still here, and I don't want that for you. Caleb wouldn't, either."

Her voice cracks, and the sound is a stab to my heart. Everything about this is wrong. I should be living in a nice Colonial like Lexi's right now, maybe engaged to Hannah and certainly the proud fur dad of a good girl like Daisy. Tara and Caleb should be married and trying to keep up with a chubby-cheeked, sticky-fingered toddler, or at least have a baby on the way, and Fleet Outdoor Adventures should have expanded abroad, just like Caleb planned.

The business shouldn't be in shambles. Caleb shouldn't be gone.

"Please don't cry," I tell Tara. "I'll figure something out, okay?"

But even as I say it, I know she's right. I don't have any spare cash laying around, and it's not like I can get a loan with my shitty credit score. I'm sure Mom doesn't have the money, and even if she did, I couldn't get her to pick up the phone so I could ask to borrow some.

"Maybe this is a chance," my sister-in-law says. "A chance for you to realize that you're way more capable than you think. And I know you don't believe in fate, but doesn't it seem weird that the website goes months without a request, and then as soon as we need an influx of cash, someone needs our help? Maybe it's meant to be, you know? Maybe this is supposed to happen."

"It's a coincidence," I say flatly. Tara can subscribe to the notion that things happen for a reason if it brings her comfort, but I know better. I know that shitty things just happen, and good things do, too, and we all just have to do our best with whatever comes our way.

"Oprah says there are no coincidences."

"Yeah, well, I bet Oprah's sister-in-law never signed her up for a job she has no business doing."

"You can do it, Ry," Tara insists. "We both know you can."

I sigh, wishing she'd pin her hopeful belief on someone worthy of it.

"So, this Emily person," I say. "She's really in a hard spot?"

"She's in an impossible spot," says Tara. "She said she's going to Isle Royale whether she has a tour guide or not, but she'd very much prefer not to wander through a wolf-infested hellhole on her own. And that's verbatim."

I scratch the back of my neck, wondering how much longer I have before Lexi loses her patience and I lose my excellent TaskRabbit rating. Why would a woman with zero camping experience be so committed to venturing into the wilderness that she'd risk her own safety to do it?

"Did she say why she's going?" I ask Tara, knowing that I should say no regardless.

"She just said she needs to unplug and enjoy nature's beauty for a while. Given her recent breakup, I'm guessing it's an *Eat, Pray, Love* kind of thing."

I'm busy doing my own cope / mope / self-destruct kind of thing, but I don't love the idea of somebody out on their own and exposed to the elements. I'm not sure I'd be much help— I didn't even take good care of the Chinese money plant

Hannah gave me, a fact she threw in my face when she broke up with me—but there's safety in numbers, right? And I'm not the expert Caleb was, but I have been camping, haven't I?

"Between my savings and what you'd make from the gig, we could buy *The Little Adventure* from your dad," Tara says, her voice hopeful. "We could have a little piece of Caleb back."

I close my eyes for an instant, and what I see is Caleb at twelve or thirteen, no more than a boy, his dark hair bleached with comically frosted tips and his wiry arms sticking out of a yellow Green Day T-shirt. He squats in front of a disembodied motor in Grandpa Tim's garage, biting his lip as he lifts the muffler cover and reaches for a wrench.

"You just gonna stand there, Ry, or are you gonna help me?" he asks, nodding toward his toolbox. "C'mon. I'll share my Funyuns if you find my missing screwdriver."

I can almost hear the shaky pitch of his deepening teenage voice, almost inhale the thick scent of motor oil and paint. It's a deeply ordinary memory, a happy Caleb moment made significant only by the fact that there will never be any new ones. But it's enough to stop me from saying no.

"When's the gig?" I ask Tara, knowing I'll probably regret this.

"Two weeks from tomorrow. I know it's not much time, but—"

"I'll do it," I tell her.

Because I owe this to Caleb. I let him down once, a fact that I'll spend the rest of my life regretting. But now I have a chance to make something right, to return the boat he loved to the woman he loved even more. I can't bring back what's gone, but if I can stop *The Little Adventure* from sailing out of Tara's life forever, maybe I can hang on to a small piece of my brother.

"Really?" Tara cries in disbelief, her excitement radiating through the phone. "Oh my goodness, Ryder, thank you! You're going to be happy you said yes, I promise! Okay, I'll send you an email with Emily's itinerary and all the trip details, and you'll want to review Caleb's old tour guide handbooks and make sure the gear's in working order . . ."

I don't really hear her as she launches into a long list of what I'll need to do to prepare for the trip. Because all I can see is two boys fiddling with a broken boat, one laser-focused on his work while the other pounds Funyuns and daydreams about Pamela Anderson. All I can hear is Caleb's reedy teenage voice. *You just gonna stand there, Ry, or are you gonna help me?*

No matter what Tara says, I know this is a bad idea. I'm in no shape to hike and camp in an unfamiliar island, let alone lead someone else through one, and to answer her earlier question, I'm actually pretty shit at reading maps. But I can't say no to that good-natured, farmer's-tanned kid asking for my help. I can't lose another piece of Caleb.

Let's just hope, for Emily Edwards's sake and mine, that there aren't any snakes on the island.

THREE

EMILY

There are certain jobs you probably shouldn't fill with a rando you find on the internet. If you need a plumber or a handyman, sure; it makes sense to hop on Google and call the first promising candidate you find. But when it's something more personal—like, say, hiring a guide to help you navigate the backcountry so you can spread your dad's ashes in the national park he never got to visit—settling for the first person available doesn't seem like the best idea.

Then again, I didn't have much of a choice. When I got home after an excruciatingly long car ride with Jason—during which he took a call from Piper and informed her that the breakup had gone *Really well, actually!*—I drank a glass of wine in a bubble bath and realized that I could not, in fact, do this. There's no way I could spend six days on a remote island alone without losing my sanity and possibly a limb or two, and so I uncrumpled Jason's stupid list of tour guides and got to work calling them. Unfortunately for me, most reputable tour guide agencies don't just have on-the-spot availability, and I made forty-two phone calls before I found an agency with an opening. I almost cried with relief when Tara from Fleet Outdoor Adventures responded to my website inquiry and told me that thanks to a cancellation, she could match me with a guide.

"You'll love Ryder," she said brightly. "Everybody does."

I don't particularly need to love my tour guide so much as trust that he's capable, and according to everything I could dig up online, Fleet Outdoor Adventures is the real deal. I knew Jason wouldn't put the agency on his list if it weren't truly reputable, but I was impressed by FOA's glowing client testimonials and raving Yelp reviews. I'm less impressed, however, that an hour after Ryder Fleet was supposed to meet me in the marina parking lot, there's still no sign of him.

Tara told me that Ryder had brown hair and would be wearing a hunter green Fleet Outdoor Adventures T-shirt and a big smile. I told her that I'd be wearing a purple life jacket and a slightly terrified expression. She'd laughed, assured me all would go well, and sent me a copy of our signed contract, and I'd slept well for the first time since Jason dumped me. But now, standing alone on the deck of the *Voyageur II,* the passenger ferry that will transport us to Isle Royale, I'm feeling much less confident.

Trying to keep my growing anxiety at bay, I scan the crowd of passengers in case I missed the arrival of a G.I. Joe-looking dude in a green shirt. Of course, I don't actually know that Ryder looks like a G.I. Joe. But when I imagine the kind of person who becomes a national park tour guide—or an *ambassador of adventure*, as the contract so describes him—I picture a lean, mean, hiking machine with the stern buzzcut and permanent sunburn of someone who spends every waking hour outdoors. I bet Ryder Fleet has a fanatical devotion to ice baths and loves scarfing down flaxseed granola bars in between tirades about cardiovascular fitness and the many evils of screen addiction.

Maybe that's why I didn't tell Tara the true purpose of my trip. The Fleet website showed hi-res images of happy people jumping off waterfalls and bungee jumping in the Grand Canyon, and *Hi, I'm Emily, and I've got cremains in my backpack!* wasn't something I was eager to share. So when she asked me if I had any goals for the trip, I gave her a throwaway line about unplugging from the rat race and left Dad and his bucket list out of it.

"Attention, passengers!" a voice warbles over the ship's PA system. "This is your final call for boarding. We'll depart for Windigo Harbor at Isle Royale National Park in T minus one minute. There's a strong eastward breeze coming in at ten miles an hour, so brace for choppy waters."

Whatever choppy waters we'll encounter on Lake Superior are nothing compared to the waves of panic crashing around in my stomach, and my heart races as I make another lap around the deck in search of my no-show tour guide. I press my phone to my ear, making a third call to the number Tara gave me in case I needed to get ahold of Ryder, but it goes straight to voicemail again. I scan the ferry desperately, but there are no smiling men in green T-shirts milling about. In fact, because it's Isle Royale's late season, there aren't many people on the boat at all. There's only a small but enthusiastic Girl Scout troop on a day trip, a couple of college-aged guys tossing around a football like we're on a campus quad instead of a creaky watercraft, and a cluster of couples wearing matching glum expressions and THIS MARRIAGE RETREAT CAN'T BE BEAT sweatshirts.

I wince as I adjust the straps of my incredibly heavy backpack and try to come up with a game plan. When I'm working in the ER, my first rule is never to panic, but that's a hard one to follow when I spent the whole drive from Ohio to Minnesota listening to *Bloodsport: The Ripper of the Rockies*, a terrifying podcast about the unsolved murders of solo hikers in Wyoming.

"Announcing our departure to Windigo Harbor," the captain declares. "Off we go, folks!"

My pulse skyrocketing, I take a deep breath and imagine what Dad would say if he were here. He believed—or at least made me think he did—that I could do anything I set my mind to, whether it was get into med school (which panned out) or marry Zac Efron (which has not). So if he could talk to me right now, he'd probably A) tell me that he never liked Jason ever since he heard him call caramel *care-uh-mel*, and B) sling an arm around my shoulder and assure me that I could navigate Isle Royale on my own.

Sure, it'll be tough, but so are you, he'd say, adjusting the brim of the blue Cleveland Guardians cap he always wore. *Adventure awaits, Emmy.*

Right. Adventure awaits. I can do this. I *will* do this. Isle Royale is in Michigan, not Wyoming, and the likelihood that the Ripper of the Rockies has decided to continue his stabbing spree there seems slim to none—

"Raising the ramp!" a deckhand calls out, signaling for passengers to move away from the railing. "Farewell, Grand Portage!"

And that's when I come to my senses. Because he's not really saying goodbye to Grand Portage so much as he's saying farewell to running water and Starbucks and any chance of getting help from the proper authorities should I accidentally stumble across a deranged serial killer who keeps his victims' pinkie fingers as a fun memento. Dad might have spent his whole life thirsting for adventure, but I've spent mine going out of my way to avoid it, and there's no point trying to change that now. I'm no Lieutenant Ellen Ripley or Sarah Connor or any of the other fearless protagonists in the action movies Dad raised me on. I'm Emily Edwards, a thirty-three-year-old emergency medicine doctor who wears elbow pads while bicycling because I'm afraid of breaking a bone. I am not a warrior or a fighter; I'm just a worrywart in an ugly bucket hat, and I'm getting off this boat.

Now.

I grip the straps of my pack and hurry toward the deckhand, waving to get his attention.

"Excuse me, sir! Wait, please! I need to get off the boat!"

"Pardon?" The deckhand, who wears a weary expression and a name tag that reads TERRENCE, wipes his hands on his shorts and frowns.

"I need to get off, please," I repeat, pointing toward the dock. "I've decided not to go."

Terrence shakes his head. "I'm sorry, ma'am, but it's too late. Once we pull up the ramp, we're officially in transit."

"Okay, but can't you, like, hit the brakes or something?" I ask, panting from my brief attempt at hustle. "Please?"

"Boats don't have brakes, ma'am."

"Oh. Then, um, batten down the hatches, please!"

He blinks. "That doesn't apply to this situation. At all."

"Stop the rudder?" I ask. "Drop the anchor? Shift the gear into neutral?"

Terrence crosses his arms over his chest. "Is this your first time on a boat?"

I blush. "Look, can you *please* put the ramp thing down so I can get to the dock?"

He groans in exasperation. "No, ma'am, I cannot put the 'ramp thing' down. I also cannot make a dolphin jump out of the water, or look the other way while you try to smuggle an entire case of liquor onboard. This is a passenger service vessel, not a damn party boat."

I squint at him. "Are the college guys giving you a hard time or something?"

"No. The Girl Scouts." He sighs. "Look, it's company policy that once the ramp is up, nobody boards or disembarks until we reach our destination."

My heart sinks. "I understand. I guess I'll just buy a return ticket when we get to Win—"

"Wait! WAIT!" a booming voice shouts.

"What in the world," Terrence mutters as we both turn to see a man sprinting down the dock toward the ferry.

"Hold the boat!" the man yells, gesturing wildly. "I have a ticket! Hold the boat!"

"Frickin' people, man," Terrence grumbles, shaking his head. "Nobody gets how boats work."

"WAIT!" the runner shouts again, jumping over a small flock of seagulls as he races down the deck. As he comes closer into view, I squint to see that he's got chin-length dark hair, a long stride, and a broad torso stuffed into a dark green T-shirt . . .

Wait.

"Fear not, Emily Edwards!" the man shouts, breaking into a dead sprint. "I'm coming!"

Holy shit. It's ambassador of adventure Ryder Fleet, and he's barreling down the deck like his life depends on it.

"HOLD THE BOAT! I HAVE A TICKET!"

The ruckus draws the attention of my fellow passengers, who flock to the railing for a better look.

"I HAVE A TICKET!" Ryder repeats, his chest heaving with exertion.

"Hey, Terrence?" a baby-faced Girl Scout says, blowing a bubble of bright pink gum and then popping it loudly. "I could be wrong, but I think that guy has a ticket."

Terrence lifts a whistle to his lips and blows it sharply, waving Ryder back. "Sir, this ship is already in transit! You cannot board!"

Unfazed, Ryder dashes farther down the length of the dock, and I gawk, riveted, as he leaps over a cluster of seagulls pecking at a french fry and sails through the air with impressive athleticism.

"Sir, you have missed the ferry!" Terrence hollers. "Turn back now! Any attempt to board would be a flagrant violation of Safety Code 28.5a, and I refuse to allow—"

"Catch, man!"

Ryder, who clearly does not give a rat's ass about Safety Code 28.5a, shrugs off his backpack and swings it backward to gather momentum. Then, letting out a guttural noise that practically sends the Scouts into convulsions, he flings it toward the boat with all his might, where it lands with a thud at Terrence's feet.

"Sir!" Terrence chastises, piercing the air with shrill blasts of his whistle. "Let me repeat: you have missed the boarding window! Just let it go, dude!"

But my ambassador of adventure will not let it go. Picking up speed, he eyes the ever-increasing distance between the end of the dock and the ferry and lengthens his strides like he's a long jumper at the Olympics.

"Oh-em-gee, he's gonna jump!" a Girl Scout says in a tone of pure delight. "No freaking way! This is awesome."

"No, no, no," I whisper, covering my eyes. Because I know how this could end. I've treated too many grown men who watch a single episode of *American Ninja Warrior* and suddenly think they're a professional athlete. Their ridiculous stunts turn into concussions and compression fractures that take eons to heal, and I've had my fill of cocksure dudes who decide that eschewing safety equipment or snorting paprika makes them a badass.

"Jump!" a Girl Scout shouts, cheering him on. "You can do it! Jump!"

"Do not jump!" I counter, earning glares from the Scouts. "You can catch the next ferry!" He won't be any help to me if he breaks his legs, and I don't need Terrence suffering an aneurysm on my watch. "Think of the risks! Think of Safety Code 28.5a!"

But Ryder does not think of the risks, or if he does, he decides to jump anyway. And boy, does he jump.

"PARKOUR!" he cries, leaping off the dock in what seems like slow motion. His hair billows out behind him like a short but magnificent cape, and I hold my breath as he soars over the sea green waves of Lake Superior, his jaw clenched in fierce determination and his arms extended.

"Aha!" he cries triumphantly when he clears the railing, and a pint-sized Girl Scout lets out a screech and scurries out of the way as he crashes onto the deck, his tan boots smacking the ground with a thud.

But Ryder doesn't seem to notice that he nearly squashed a small child, or that he came within two feet of landing on a terrified-looking elderly man clutching his trekking pole for dear life. Because the ambassador of adventure raises two hands in a celebratory V, eliciting a round of raucous cheers from the crowd.

"Who *are* you?" a middle-aged woman asks breathlessly, marveling at Ryder as he places his hands on his hips and surveys the ship like he's a regular Jack Sparrow.

"I'm Ryder Fleet," he says, beaming at the woman. "And I'm here for Emily Edwards."

"Who's Emily Edwards?" a Girl Scout near me whispers to one of her friends.

"I don't know," the friend whispers back. "But she's one lucky bitch."

"Excuse me," I mutter, "that kind of misogynistic language is highly inappropri—"

But the girls don't hear me, because they're too busy gathering around Ryder with the rest of his admiring fans. I watch as he high-fives a couple people from the marriage retreat group, and, okay, I sort of get what the Scouts were saying. Because Tara neglected to mention that Ryder, who is indeed wearing a hunter green shirt with the Fleet Adventures logo on it, is completely fucking gorgeous. He's got the broad frame of a rugged lumberjack and the musculature of a Marvel stunt double, with sandy brown hair that looks perfectly touchable and skin that could best be described as sun-kissed. He's what my late grandma Jean would have called *A real looker*, a compliment she reserved for super hotties like Kurt Russell and the jacked EMT who rescued her when she fell and broke her hip.

So yeah, Ryder Fleet is handsome as hell. But he's also completely effing reckless.

"Is Emily here?" Ryder asks, puffing out his chest like he's cosplaying Gaston at a Disney World character meet and greet. "I'm looking for Emily Edwards, folks!"

There's nothing I hate more than being the center of attention—the time I was "randomly chosen" from the crowd to be the magician's assistant at my seventh birthday party still haunts me when I close my eyes—and I feel myself shrinking into the background.

"Emily Edwards, anyone?" he repeats, his voice full of bravado.

"That's me," an older woman in a visor and a retreat sweatshirt replies. "I'm her. I'm Emily Edwards."

The woman, who is assuredly not Emily Edwards barring some very strange coincidence, beams at Ryder. "Has anyone ever told you that you look like a young Paul Newman?"

"Seriously, Loretta?" a man in a matching visor says, shaking his head. "I'm right here!"

"I was joking, Stan!" Loretta-not-Emily hisses as Stan's eyes shoot daggers at Ryder.

"Um, okay," Ryder says, looking like he doesn't quite know what to do with this interaction. "Is anyone here actually Emily Edwards?"

"You jump like a ninja," one of the younger Girl Scouts tells him, staring up at him admiringly. "Will you sign my backpack?"

I wait for the grown adult man to explain to the small, impressionable child that jumping onto a moving vessel is a stunt that belongs in the movies, not real life, and that she should never try this at home. But instead, Ryder smiles and pats her on the head.

"Sure thing, jelly bean. Anybody got a Sharpie?"

That's it. Visions of Girl Scouts with crutches and full-body casts dance in my head, and I step around the kids to confront him.

"Excuse me," I say, sounding more like Judith than I mean to, "but you do realize you could have been badly injured, right?"

Ryder blinks at me in surprise. "Uh, I guess? But I wasn't, so. All good." He grins as one of the guys from the college group claps him on the back.

"Right, but you *could* have been," I insist. "What if you'd jumped and missed?"

"I wasn't going to miss." He crosses his arms over his ridiculously broad chest and smiles at me magnanimously. "You'd have no way of knowing this, but you're looking at the former sixth-place finisher in the Colorado high school long jump championship." He winks at Loretta-not-Emily. "I would have gotten first, but I sprained an ankle in the warm-ups."

I scan the crowd to see if I'm the only one who hears how absurd he sounds, and except for the positively fuming deckhand Terrence, it appears that I am.

"I'm sorry, is that supposed to be impressive?" I ask. "There's nothing laudatory about peaking in high school. And sixth place doesn't even medal."

"Well, joke's on you, because I didn't peak in high school," he retorts. "I didn't even do that well there."

I press a hand to my chest, confused. "I'm sorry, how is that a joke on me?"

"And I may not have gotten a medal, but I did get a very large ribbon," Ryder adds. "And that's plenty loudatory."

"*Laud*atory," I correct him, enunciating the first syllable.

He rolls his shoulders back in a devil-may-care gesture. "Exactly. That's what I said."

"That is not what you said—"

"I, for one, found his jump highly impressive," Loretta-not-Emily says, scowling at me. "And I'm sure his sixth-place ribbon was lovely."

"Okay, sure, but this isn't high school track and field," I say, alarmed that this needs to be stated. "It's real life. And in real life, when people behave recklessly, there are very real consequences. Like a broken leg, or blunt force trauma to the head, or worse."

"Um, Mommy," one of the smaller Scouts asks, "what is blunt force trauma to the head?"

"Basically, it's injury by forceful impact with a dull object," I explain, patting the top of my head. "It can be severely life-threatening, especially if—"

"No thank you," the girl's mother says tightly. "I think that's quite enough scarring information for one day."

"Right," I say quietly. "Sorry. I wasn't trying to scar anyone. I merely wanted to point out that when you make dumb choices, people get hurt. That's all."

Ryder's eyes, which are a rich chocolatey brown that I would find incredibly striking if they weren't in his particular sockets, narrow at me.

"I appreciate your concern," he says. "But no one got hurt."

"Safety Code 28.5a got hurt," Terrence argues.

"I almost got hurt," says the elderly gentleman leaning on his trekking pole.

"My feelings are actually very hurt," says Loretta's husband Stan.

"Oookay," Ryder says with a shrug. "Well then, I apologize

to those of you who were hurt or offended by my actions." His gaze bores into mine when he says *offended*, and I'm pretty sure if looks could kill, we'd both be dead. "And for everyone else: surf's up, baby!"

Loretta and the Scouts and everyone on the ferry who's not me, trekking pole guy, or Terrence lets out a whoop of approval, and Ryder bows like he just delivered a masterful performance. Never mind that *surf's up* doesn't make a shred of sense, or that he wouldn't be smirking so proudly if he'd impaled his manhood on the railing.

Then again, I'd rather not think about Ryder Fleet's manhood.

"Now," he says, beaming at the gathered passengers, "if you fine folks could help me find Emily Edwards, I'd really appreciate it. Emily Edwards, anyone? Emily Edwards?"

The passengers glance around at one another curiously, whispering among themselves, and Ryder smiles widely as he waits for the lucky girl to raise her hand and come forward. I know I should speak up, but I'm too stunned by the realization that I'm about to spend six days and nights with the freewheeling showboat in front of me.

"She's gotta be here somewhere, folks!" Ryder says, his smile faltering. "Unless I jumped on the wrong boat . . . fuuuuck," he says with a groan. "Did I jump on the wrong boat?"

"No." I clear my throat, cursing Jason for dumping me and putting me in this position. "You're on the right boat."

"How do you know?" he asks. "Where's Emil—*oh*." Realization dawns across his face, and his smile disappears completely.

"Emily Edwards," I tell him, crossing my arms over my chest. "Pleased to meet you."

"Emily Edwards," he repeats, staring at me in disbelief. "Well, shit."

FOUR

EMILY

I am not, in fact, pleased to meet him. And judging by the scowl on his face, which resembles that of someone who just stepped on a LEGO, he isn't pleased to meet me, either.

"I meant 'well, shit' in a positive way," he says, looking slightly embarrassed. "Just in case you were wondering."

"Of course," I reply. "Because everyone knows you say 'well, shit' when you're happy about something. That's definitely what people say when they win the lottery and not when they get cut off in traffic."

"To be fair," Ryder counters, "I say much, much worse than that when I get cut off in traffic."

"Now, that I can easily believe."

He glances toward the railing like he's contemplating jumping again, except this time off the boat and directly into Lake Superior.

"So," he says finally, "it seems like we may have gotten off on the wrong foot."

Well, that's one thing we can agree on.

"Yes," I say. "It does."

Ryder takes a deep breath and reaches up to scratch the back of his neck, and I make a concerted effort not to notice his very noticeable triceps muscle.

"Look, I really am sorry that I offended you by jumping onto the ferry," he says.

"It's not about *offending* me," I insist. "It's about endangering yourself and others, which is not something I take lightly."

"Right, you've made that pretty clear. But what did you want me to do—miss the ferry?"

"No," I say, marveling at his audacity. "I wanted you to be on time. So that you could walk onto the ferry like a normal person."

"Well, I want a million dollars," Ryder says dryly. "But we can't always get what we want."

"How is that even remotely the same thing?" I ask, waving my hands in frustration.

Ryder sighs. "Look, ma'am, I'm sorry I—"

"Whoa," I say, raising my hands in front of me. "There is no need to call me ma'am."

He furrows his brow in confusion. "What's wrong with calling you ma'am?"

"Ma'am is what you call a Karen who's yelling at the manager. I am *not* a Karen."

Ryder raises an eyebrow, and I realize that my incensed tone is not helping my case.

"I mean, I am not a Karen," I say more warmly, trying to arrange my features into a pleasant expression. "In my opinion."

"Are you okay?" he asks, squinting at me. "Are you getting seasick? You look nauseous."

"What? No. I'm smiling." I point to my lips, which I'm straining hard to arrange into a grin. "This is my smile."

"Huh." Ryder nods. "Interesting."

I stop smiling instantly.

"Anyway, I don't think you're a Karen," he says. "But to be clear, you did yell at me."

"I did not *yell* at you," I clarify. "I merely pointed out that your stunt could have ended in severe injury, thereby traumatizing everyone aboard this ferry."

"Did you just say *thereby*?"

"I did," I say in a clipped tone. "Because that's a word that people use."

"Sure, maybe if you're Charles Dickens."

"I really don't know what that means."

"Look," Ryder says, "if you don't want me to call you ma'am, what would you like me to call you?"

I stare at him. "My *name* would be sufficient."

Ryder nods. "Okay, then. Edwards it is."

I actually meant my first name, seeing as how we're not two buddies at a frat party or wildly overzealous members of Jason's adult kickball team, but okay, fine. I guess calling me "Emily" would be too friendly.

"I really am sorry that I caused you stress," he says, running a hand through his hair. "It won't happen again."

"Thanks," I say begrudgingly. "And I'm sorry if I got a little intense with the whole 'blunt force trauma to the head' thing. It's just, I'm an ER physician, and I see the aftermath when—"

"When people make dumb choices," he finishes. "So you said."

He sounds almost hurt—which he shouldn't be, because I called his *choice* dumb, not him, even though he's not exactly coming across as witty—and I wonder if I couldn't have been a bit more tactful in my approach. Like not coming at him in front of the entire ferry, perhaps. But what's done is done, and Ryder seems to think so, too, because he looks at me for a long moment and then extends his right hand.

"How about we start over?" he suggests.

"Oh. Right. Sure." I place my hand in his, and between the tension in the air and the fact that my palm is alarmingly sweaty, it's the most awkward handshake I've ever participated in. And considering that my high school boyfriend tried to shake my hand farewell after dumping me during a family vacation to Myrtle Beach because he "kind of had a thing for my cousin Allison," that's really saying something.

"I'm Ryder Fleet," he says, still shaking my hand. "I'm an adventure tour guide from Colorado, and I like fishing and sleeping in."

This feels like we're contestants on one of those old-fashioned dating shows, but hey, I respect the fact that he's trying.

"I'm Emily Edwards," I tell him. "I'm a physician from Ohio. I don't like fishing and I can't sleep past seven a.m., but I do like reading and doing jigsaw puzzles."

I realize that to someone like Ryder, who cartwheels off glaciers and tromps through the wilderness for a living, I probably sound like the most boring person on the planet.

"Sometimes I make beaded jewelry," I add in an attempt to make myself sound more interesting. "Necklaces, mostly."

Ryder nods slowly, like I just announced that I enjoy watching paint dry.

"So, reading's cool," he says after a long beat. "Are you reading any good books right now?"

"Oh. Yes, actually. I'm reading *The Song of the Cell*. It's a nonfiction book about the evolution of human understanding of the cell." I squint at Ryder as the sun comes out from behind the clouds. "What about you? Are you reading anything interesting?"

"Sure am," he says, shrugging off his backpack and unzipping it to pull out a slim volume. He holds it up toward me, and I glance at the cover to find the illustration of a boy and a tiger flying out of a red wagon.

"*Calvin and Hobbes*," I say, reading the title aloud. "Oh, nice. I used to love cartoons."

"It's technically a comic strip," Ryder says. "It's an epic story about a boy and his stuffed tiger." He taps the cover with his free hand. "Calvin is the boy. Hobbes is the tiger."

"Hey, *Calvin and Hobbes*!" a squeaky-voiced Girl Scout says as she walks by. She has braces and a polka-dotted headband and cannot be more than nine years old, and she points at the book with adorable enthusiasm. "I used to love that when I was a kid. But I'm into more grown-up stuff now, like Magic Tree House."

And then, blissfully unaware that she just delivered a savage blow to a grown-ass man, she waves sweetly and trots off.

Ryder coughs. "It has a lot of valuable lessons for adults,

too," he mutters, his cheeks turning a bright shade of pink. "Anyway, I'm gonna put this away now."

"I'm sure it does," I say quickly, but he's already stuffing the book into his pack and zipping it shut.

"So," he says, his gaze not meeting my eyes, "should we talk about trail logistics?"

I want to say something comforting, because I know how crappy it feels to be judged for your tastes. Jason used to tease me about my Sunday night face mask and trash TV habit, and after a while, his casual needling took a little of the joy out of a once-comforting routine. But Ryder's jaw is set in a firm line, and I decide to let it go.

"Sure," I tell him. "I emailed Tara a copy of my itinerary, and I was thinking—"

"Hey, man!" One of the college-aged guys waves at Ryder from across the deck, a football in his hand. "We're gonna throw the ball around a bit. You in?"

"Throw it where?" I mutter. "It's not that big of a boat."

"No thanks," Ryder calls back. "I'm—"

But the guy launches the ball toward us without waiting for an answer, and I let out a petrified squeak as it flies toward my head. I swat it away as hard as I can and accidentally send it flying sideways, where it sails over the railing and plops into Lake Superior.

"C'mon, lady!" the guy cries in exasperation. "That was our only ball!"

"Boo, wet blanket," one of his buddies hollers, giving a rude thumbs-down in my direction.

And while I know a cheeky gesture from a rando in a

trucker hat shouldn't hurt my feelings, it actually kind of does. Because believe it or not, I don't go out of my way to ruin other people's fun.

I ruined enough for Dad, even though I didn't mean to.

"Hey, man," Ryder says, his tone surprisingly gruff for a man who said *surf's up* not more than ten minutes ago, "why don't you stick your thumb up your—"

"You know," I say quickly, "I think I'll pop down to the cabin for a bit and read."

"Right on. I'll join you."

"Oh, that's not necessary."

"Okay," Ryder says, "but don't you think we should review our trail routes and—"

I wince and place a hand on my stomach, suddenly feeling like I have to throw up.

"I think I am getting seasick after all," I explain, willing the churning in my abdomen to stop. "I'll catch up with you in a bit, okay?"

And then, before Ryder has a chance to argue or call me ma'am again, I shuffle toward the cabin as fast as the crushing weight of my backpack will let me.

I'm only half lying to Ryder as I hurry down the stairs, eager for solitude and a chance to hyperventilate in peace. Because I am nauseous and slick with sweat, but it's not because of the boat's rhythmic rocking or the overwhelming stink of fish or even the fact that instead of spreading Dad's ashes with someone who knows and loves me, I'll be doing it with someone who thinks I'm a tense Debbie Downer.

I'm nauseous because I truly believed that once I set out on this trip, I would somehow feel Dad's presence. I thought I would breathe in the fresh lake air—well, fresh with a subtle undernote of dead fish—and see a dazzling swarm of butterflies or a soaring eagle, and some of the crushing guilt inside me would disappear. But the only soaring thing I've seen is Ryder flying off the dock, and what's disappearing is any shred of hope that finishing Dad's bucket list will help me move forward.

Because I haven't even reached Isle Royale yet, and the truth I've spent eleven months trying to escape is finally catching up to me: if I had been a better daughter, Dad might be here right now, standing on the creaky deck instead of stuffed into an urn, all six feet and two hundred pounds of his goofy, dad-joke-loving self reduced to ash and powdered bone.

But I wasn't, so he isn't. And there's not a tour guide in the world who can help me with that.

The first thing I do below deck is tear off the bucket hat and stuff it as far down inside my backpack as I can reach. Then I park myself on a bench seat covered in squeaky blue vinyl, letting my eyes adjust to the dim light shining through the porthole windows. I open *The Song of the Cell* and try to focus, but the ink swims before my eyes and the strong scent of mildew worsens the churning in my stomach. When I glance up to blink the swirling print away, I'm startled to find a grim-faced man with a scraggly gray beard and a cold expression watching me. He's got a three-inch scar tracing down the left side of his face, paired with an unblinking stare that makes me think of *Bloodsport* and a documentary I watched last week

called *Killface: Evil in the Grocery Store* about a deranged serial killer who found his victims in the produce section.

I give the man a cautious half smile, thinking he might just
be seasick, but he doesn't smile back. Instead, he gazes at me
for a second longer before turning his attention to a map un-
folded on the table in front of him. A shiver runs down my
spine, and I pretend to read my book for a minute before I
glance up to find him watching me again. I know he's probably
just daydreaming, but the truth is, he looks like someone who
has at least three dismembered body parts in his hiking pack.
I'm not looking to be added to that collection, so I shut the
book and decide to haul ass upstairs. I'm not exactly popular
up there—Ryder seems to think I'm uptight and overbearing,
and I'm pretty sure Loretta-not-Emily would relish the chance
to throw me overboard—but it's better than getting eye-
murdered by Killface McGee over here. Besides, my tour guide
might be a total himbo, but he's got tree-trunk arms that could
easily bear-hug someone to death, or at least hold them down
long enough for me to zap them with bear spray.

I stand up from the bench quickly, clutching the book to
my chest in case I need to pelt it at Killface. But as I turn toward
the stairs, my left elbow collides with something solid.

"Oof," a disgruntled voice says, and I realize that I've accidentally elbowed a passenger in the stomach. A tall, auburn-
haired passenger wearing a tweed jacket and oversized
tortoiseshell frames. He looks like a professor—a *hot* professor, the kind that manages to make a cardigan look masculine
and only exists on soapy TV dramas.

And I greeted him with a sharp jab to the intestines.

"Sorry!" I say quickly, mortified. "Are you alright?"

"I think I'll live," Young Hot Glasses Professor says with a cheeky grin, his hot professor-ness underscored by an accent that I think is Irish. "You can bump into me anytime you like."

I feel my cheeks heat up, and the sensation makes me blush even more. Is YHGP *flirting* with me? It seems like a long shot, since the Lake Superior winds did no favors for my curly hair, but hey. Maybe he's got a thing for barely contained frizz tucked under a polyester neck nape. You never know.

"Well, I try not to make a practice of knocking the wind out of people," I tell him, reaching a subtle hand up to check the status of my hair. "But the constant rocking of the boat doesn't help."

"Indeed it doesn't." His gaze shifts toward my book, and his eyes flicker in recognition. "*Song of the Cell*? Brilliant. Just finished it myself."

He reaches inside the satchel slung over his shoulder and pulls out an identical copy, except his is littered with colorful sticky tabs poking out of the pages.

"Have you reached the part about the antibiotic revolution?" he asks. "I found it particularly fascinating that—well." He pauses and gives me a sheepish grin. "Forgive me. I'm sure you have better things to do than talk science with a certified nerd like me."

Shockingly, between options A) get shat on by seagulls above deck while I treat Ryder to an enthralling description of the puzzle I'm working on at home—a three-thousand-piece jigsaw of animals on safari complicated by the fact that the elephant and rhino pieces are the exact same shade of gray—or B) enjoy an invigorating discussion with a man who sounds like Colin Farrell and has hair that shines like the sun, I choose B.

"I really don't have anything better to do," I tell him, tossing a quick glance over my shoulder to see if Killface is still watching me. He is. "I mean, no, I haven't gotten to the antibiotic revolution yet. I'm halfway through the chapter on the universal cell."

"Ah, that's a good one." He nods approvingly and sits down on a bench, motioning for me to do the same. "Have you read Mukherjee's other work?"

I slide onto the bench opposite his and cast an assessing glance toward Killface, who frowns and returns his attention to his map. "Not yet. You?"

Young Hot Glasses Professor shakes his head. "Unfortunately not. I don't have much time for reading anything besides dissertations and academic research."

Aha. So he *is* a professor. "Dissertations? Do you teach?"

"Yes. I teach and I research, and very rarely I stumble into pretty brunettes on boats." He smiles, and I know if I'd been a student in his course, I would have had a hell of a time focusing on the material.

His compliment causes a warm flutter in my belly. "Can't say it happens to me all that often, either," I tell him. "But I'd take ferry rides more often if I knew it meant crossing paths with handsome professors who read for pleasure."

I can hardly believe my gumption. Not only did I say something flirty, but my voice also rose saucily in pitch when I said *pleasure.* Forget boring bucket hat Emily; there's a new harlot in town.

"I guess it's a lucky day for both of us, then." The fair-skinned researcher extends a hand toward me. "I'm Dr. Killian Sinclair, chair of Science of the Human Past at Harvard."

Harvard. Wowza. I shake his hand, hoping my palm is less of a sweaty mess than it was earlier. "Science of the Human Past? Are you a historian?"

"Archaeologist, actually," he explains. "I specialize in maritime and underwater archaeology, with a particular interest in the protection of underwater cultural heritage."

"Oh. Wow." That sounds a lot more exciting than my job, where I extract a Tic Tac from the nose of a small child at least twice a week.

"It's a fancy way of saying I study shipwrecks." He adjusts his glasses and studies me. "And you are . . . ?"

Oh. Right. I should probably introduce myself, too. "Dr. Emily Edwards," I say. "Emergency medicine physician. I'm from Ohio."

"Emergency medicine, huh?" He leans forward, his elbows resting on the table between us. "How impressive. You're a literal lifesaver."

"Sometimes," I admit. "But in between the true emergencies, it's mostly a lot of sprained ankles and worried parents freaking out because their kid took a sip out of the bubble bath."

Killian laughs. "I'm quite sure that's not true. You must be excellent under pressure."

"I'm practiced under pressure. That's what counts. We have protocols for every situation, and as long as I follow those, I have no reason to be anything but calm."

I don't tell him the full truth—that since Dad's death, I've started taking my work home. I used to be reasonably skilled at keeping the personal and professional parts of my life separate, but now I can't close my eyes at night without seeing the anguished faces of the patients I treat during the day. I can't take a shower without hearing the pained cries of the guy who lost half his leg in a motorcycle accident, or the hushed prayers of a wife begging the universe not to let her become a widow. I can't eat or read or bake without picturing the details of Dad's final moments, and I can't help but see his face in every person who comes through the doors of the Greater Columbus Medical Center. Unfortunately, this kind of bleeding-heart emotionality isn't conducive to the clear, composed thinking necessary to do my job well, and it turns out that bursting into tears in the middle of your shift kind of freaks the patients out. Or so I've been told by the department chief, who pulled me into her office to order me to pull myself together in the nicest tone possible.

"Anyway, I'd love to hear about what it's like to study shipwrecks," I tell Killian, trying not to think about how a shipwreck is an excellent metaphor for the current state of my life. "Are we talking, like, the *Titanic*?"

He shakes his head. "The *Titanic* is the most famous case, of course, but I'm more interested in smaller, less illustrious wrecks. The wrecks that few people have heard of and almost no one has explored."

"Are there many of those?"

Killian smiles. "More than you'd imagine. The *Titanic* garners so much attention because of the glitz and glamour of the ship, but I think we can learn just as much, if not more, from the humble sunken fishing boat and the capsized passenger steamer. These smaller shipwrecks are untapped artifacts of the human condition, and if we allow their secrets to become lost to the passage of time, we're losing more than just historical data and physical artifacts. We're losing a chapter in the story of humanity."

He pauses, his smile turning bashful. "My apologies. I get quite melodramatic when I talk about my work."

I'm all for melodrama if it means he'll keep going with that charming accent. "There's nothing wrong with being passionate about your job."

"It's more of a calling than a job, really. Saying that out loud makes me want to kick my own arse, but it's true." Killian laughs, and I feel a pang of nostalgia for the days when I felt that way, too.

"That's why I'm headed to Isle Royale," he continues. "To study the *Explorer*."

"Is that a ship?"

He nods, pulling a slim book from his satchel and opening it to reveal pages of black-and-white maps. "It was a package freighter that sank in 1897, just off the coast of Isle Royale. Right here." He taps a black dot on the map with his finger. "There was a terrible storm one night in early summer, and lightning struck the hull, creating a massive hole. There were thirty-five crew members and twelve passengers aboard."

"What happened to them?" I ask breathlessly. "Did they die?"

"No. All survived, actually, except for one." He flips to another page, where the black-and-white portrait of a dashingly handsome naval officer stares out at me. "Captain Sebastian Evermore, forty-two years old. He directed his crew and their passengers onto the lifeboats, waiting to board one himself until every man, woman, and dog was safe."

"There were dogs on the ship? Really?"

"The engineer had an English setter named Madeline," Killian says with a grin. "She never really took to maritime life, not that you could blame her." He turns the book toward me, and I study the captain's raised chin and stern, determined expression. "The ship rolled dangerously in the rough waters, but Evermore held it steady until everyone was accounted for. Tragically, when it was finally his turn to escape, the water rushing in became too much for the ship to bear. It capsized quickly, and Captain Evermore sank with it."

"Damn. Poor guy." It's bleak, but it's also way more interesting than listening to Jason recount the colonoscopies he oversaw in excruciating detail over dinner.

"He was a hero. A good writer, too. A previous dive team brought back letters from the wreck, beautiful love letters he wrote to his wife Katherine." Killian sighs and tucks the book away. "I'm leading an artifact recovery team to see what more historical knowledge we can gather from the ship."

"That's fascinating."

Killian gives me a cheeky grin. "It is, isn't it?"

"I mean, love letters and a shipwreck?" I say. "Sounds like something out of a movie."

"That it does," Killian agrees. "But it's not just one ship-wreck. Isle Royale's seen more than twenty. Most people visit the national park for its remoteness, or to say they lived among wolves for a while. But it's the ghosts of all those ships, and all the magnificent and ordinary lives that went down with them, that makes me so enamored with the island."

"Enamored," I repeat, my heart thumping as he adjusts his glasses. "Right."

He perks up like he has an idea. "You know, I could show you some of the shipwrecks, if you want. I have a pair of very expensive, very precise binoculars on loan from the Smithsonian, and if you promise not to drop them into Lake Superior, I'm happy to take you above deck and point out the wrecks as we go. If you're interested, of course."

An above-deck field trip with a man who talks about beautiful love letters and has the coolest job ever? Hell yeah. Don't mind if I do.

"I'm interested," I say quickly. "In the wrecks, I mean."

"Brilliant. Follow me, then."

I stand up and hoist my pack over my shoulders, marveling at the fact that not only have I found the one person on the ship besides Terrence who doesn't think I'm a serious killjoy, I get to spend even more time with him. And as I follow Killian out of the cabin, I realize that for the first time since I left Ohio yesterday morning, I feel somewhat like myself.

FIVE

RYDER

I am a jackass. I am *the* jackass. I am such a massive jackass that I make all the other jackasses in the world look like tiny jackass ants in comparison. Because in classic Ryder fashion, I managed to screw up the trip before it even started.

I swear I had good intentions. After my call with Tara, I spent the next two and a half weeks learning everything I could about backcountry camping. I rummaged through Caleb's old gear to grab the supplies I needed and watched every YouTube tutorial on fire starting and survival skills I could find. I went to the freaking *library*, for Christ's sake, and checked out an actual, physical book called *Survival Instinct: 101 Ways to Die in the Wild, and How You Can Avoid Them.* It was a petrifying read, but I slogged through it, and I even convinced my neighbor Lulu, who is eighty-three years old and the only person I hang out with on a regular basis, to let me practice my first aid skills on her. In exchange, I'll have to watch Hallmark Channel Christmas movies with her all winter, and she gave me a withering glare when I suggested applying a tourniquet to her arm, but all in all, I was getting my shit together. I was preparing to make Emily Edwards's trip as safe, fun, and comfortable as possible.

And then, last night at the motel, a cheap, rundown place that smelled of cigarettes and has certainly been the site of at least two grisly murders, I turned on the TV and stumbled upon *The Sandlot*. It was one of Caleb's favorites, and I couldn't get through a single scene without remembering how he spent an entire summer eating s'mores and vowing that Wendy Peffercorn was the only woman he would ever consider marrying. As the movie continued, I got too deep into my feels and too deep into a six-pack from the convenience store next door, and the next thing I knew, I woke up to a pounding headache and the realization that I'd slept through my alarm.

Panicked, I threw my gear into my rental car and sped to the marina, and when I got there and saw that the ferry was already pulling away from the dock, I knew I had to jump. Sure, it wasn't the safest idea in the world, but I didn't want to let my client down after promising myself that I would take care of her. And I sure as hell didn't want to miss out on the paycheck that will let Tara and me buy Caleb's boat. Of course, it just so happened that the one person on the ferry who didn't find my jump even the slightest bit spectacular turned out to be Emily, and so I've managed to convince her that I'm a foolhardy idiot before we've even reached Isle Royale.

Honestly, I don't blame her for looking at me like I'm surprise dog shit stuck to the bottom of her hiking boot. Sure, she's a little high-strung and wasted no time dressing me down in front of the entire boat, but she had good reason. As much as I don't want to admit it, she was right. I could have gotten hurt jumping onto the ferry, and judging by the sharp pain that pierces my groin every time I take a step, I think I really might have.

But it sure doesn't help that Emily is strikingly pretty, with full pink lips, dark brown hair that lands just past her shoulders in curly ringlets, and gray eyes so piercing that they'll probably see straight through my bullshit in no time. And it *really* doesn't help that while she's a successful doctor who reads Very Serious books and gets paid to save lives, I packed a children's comic strip and sometimes mix up *you're* and *your*. I could practically smell the judgment wafting off her when I showed her *Calvin and Hobbes*, and she'd probably spontaneously combust if she knew that my other most recent read was a weathered copy of *Where's Waldo?* I found in my dentist's waiting room—not to mention that it took me way longer to find Beach Waldo than I'd ever publicly admit.

It's not that I'm unintelligent so much as unable to sit still for long periods, a problem that made me come across as a slacker in most school subjects except for PE and recess. But I'm not a restless little kid anymore. I'm a grown-ass man, and I need to start acting like it, which means smoothing things over between me and Emily and making sure the rest of her trip goes off without a hitch. So I went down to the cabin to check on her shortly after she ran off, only to find her talking to a guy in a tweed jacket. I didn't know people actually wore tweed outside of old Sherlock Holmes movies, but she looked way more relaxed with him than she had with me, and I heard just enough of their conversation to see the way her eyes lit up when he said he taught at Harvard. So, feeling more than slightly dejected, I went back above deck to chill with my buds Calvin and Hobbes and try to remember what I read in *Camping Is for Everyone, Yes, Even You: A Beginner's Guide to the Great Outdoors.*

It wasn't long before I spotted them cozied up close together along the railing of the boat, the tweed guy getting right up in Emily's personal space as he looped a pair of binoculars around her neck. But she didn't seem to mind, and so I stress-ate beef jerky and tried to ignore the flicker of jealousy I felt when she laughed at something he said. She hadn't laughed at anything I'd said, but that's what I get for saying dumb shit like *surf's up* and trying to act like Rambo. Anyway, women like Emily don't go for down-on-their-luck guys who lean more *Jackass* than *Jeopardy* and occasionally work a side gig as a backyard pooper scooper. Of course she'd be interested in Harvard Tweedster, who probably never goes more than ten minutes without mentioning Harvard but at least wakes up to his alarm clock.

Finally, after I've demolished a bag of beef jerky that was supposed to last me three days, I see Emily approaching me with her new friend at her side.

"Ryder, hey," she says, the binoculars still around her neck. "This is Killian. Killian, this is Ryder."

"Well, if it isn't the ship daredevil," the annoying tall man says, placing a hand on the small of Emily's back in a way that seems entirely too familiar. "I'm Dr. Killian Sinclair, chair of Science of the Human Past at Harvard."

"Ryder Fleet," I say, shaking his hand. "Ambassador of adventure."

Sinclair smiles in a way that vaguely resembles a German shepherd baring its teeth. "Splendid. And what an adventure today is turning out to be, hm?"

"Ryder is my tour guide," Emily explains before glancing at me. "Killian is an archaeologist. He studies shipwrecks."

"An archaeologist?" I ask. "Like Indiana Jones?"

"Exactly, sport," Sinclair says. He grins. "Minus the giant boulders, of course."

Gross. The only person who ever called me *sport* was my great-grandpa Walter, and I only tolerated it because he was a million years old and sent me five bucks every Christmas.

"You know, I had a friend in prep school called Ryder," Sinclair says. "He was named after Ryder Kensington-Grant, an esteemed equestrian out of Cowden. He was quite a bit taller than you, though."

"Nice," I say flatly. "I was named after my grandpa, an esteemed plumber out of Pittsburgh."

"Sinclair, there you are!"

Our friendly conversation is interrupted by the arrival of a wiry man sporting a graying goatee and a newsboy cap who lifts a hand in greeting as he approaches. A younger red-faced man hurries after him, carrying one hiking backpack on his back and another on his front and wheezing like he might collapse at any second.

"Ah, Dr. Sharp," Sinclair says, greeting the older man with a handshake. He motions toward Emily. "Dr. Sharp, I'd like you to meet Dr. Emily Edwards. Emily, this is Dr. Benning Sharp, my mentor."

"Nice to meet you, Dr. Sharp," Emily says. "This is my tour guide, Ry—"

"I've been telling Emily all about our work on the *Explorer*," Sinclair interrupts, dismissing me entirely. "And the exciting prospect of unearthing whatever secrets it holds."

"It sounds very exciting," she agrees.

"Well, sometimes our work is exciting, and sometimes it's drudgery," Dr. Sharp replies with a shrug. "Don't get me started on our trip to Bermuda last year. We set out in search of an undiscovered vessel, but all we found was a pod of rather un-friendly sperm whales."

"The Smithsonian was not pleased about that one," Sinclair agrees, laughing dryly.

I don't have a clue in hell what they're talking about, but I don't want to be left out of the conversation, so I laugh, too. Except my laugh comes out too loudly, making me sound like a braying donkey, and the archaeologists glance at me with mild alarm.

"That's the beauty of our work, though," Sharp says, after I clear my throat and he's confident that I'm not choking to death. "Every lake and ocean has its secrets, and so does every ship. Be patient enough, and you might just discover them. Shipwrecks are like people that way." He glances at Sinclair, who's gazing starry-eyed at Emily, who's gazing back at him with the fawning equivalent of cartoon hearts in her eyes.

"Speaking of the Smithsonian," I say quickly, wanting to remind Emily that I exist, "who here enjoys *The Wizard of Oz*?"

When I'm met with blank expressions, I clarify my question. "You know, Dorothy and Toto and the gang? *There's no place like home?* Anyway, I heard you can see Dorothy's ruby slippers at the Smithsonian. So that's pretty cool."

"That is very cool," Em says, giving me the same polite smile I give my four-year-old cousin Maverick when he launches into one of his long spiels about trash trucks.

"I love *The Wizard of Oz*," says the red-faced dude wearing two massive backpacks. "The flying monkeys freak me out, though."

I watch as he struggles to maintain his balance, grimacing like he's about to buckle under the backpacks' weight.

"Hey, man, you need a hand with those bags?" I ask.

The baby-faced pack mule looks at me like I offered him a billion dollars. "Really? That would be—"

"Don't worry about Taggart," Sinclair interrupts. "He's my assistant. You don't mind a little grunt work, do you, Taggart?"

Taggart, who looks like he might keel over and die at any moment, shakes his head. "Of course not, Dr. Sinclair."

"You know, I just love this blue-collar camaraderie," Sinclair says, adjusting the small satchel he's carrying. "Assistants banding together, looking out for each oth—"

"I'm an *ambassador of adventure*," I say through gritted teeth, but Sinclair only looks more amused. I can't entirely blame him. There are some things even Dwayne "The Rock" Johnson couldn't sound tough saying, and *ambassador of adventure* is one of them.

"Right, right," Sinclair says breezily, not even looking at me and turning his attention to Emily. "Now, Emily, would you describe yourself as an art afficionado? Because back at Harvard, we have a budding collection of ancient Near Eastern art from the Mediterranean coast. I personally am working with a team of art conservators to develop new technology for restoring art found below sea level. It's an utterly fascinating science."

"Oh, yes, I like art," Emily says, looking way more intrigued by this conversation than the one we had about a fictional boy and his stuffed striped tiger.

"Fantastic. Well, perhaps when we're both back from our trips, we could—"

"I like art, too," I butt in, wanting Emily to think I'm not a total idiot. But it's a tall order, considering I kind of am.

"Do you, sport?" Sinclair asks, looking doubtful. "Well, good for you. Anyway, Emily—"

"I love it, actually," I interject again, looking straight past Sinclair to Emily.

"Do you?" she asks, smiling at me, and suddenly I feel like a million dollars. Suddenly I want to make her smile again, and again, and I want Dr. Killian Sinclair and his Harvard credentials to take a long walk off a short pier.

"Of course," I say. It's not entirely a lie. I did enjoy the performance art course I took in college, even if mostly because the professor let me do a stand-up comedy routine in lieu of writing a final paper. It wasn't a *good* stand-up routine, but it was still better than writing ten thousand words on the nuances of interpretive dance.

"Some might regard me a connoisseur of art," I continue, which is true if you consider old episodes of *Beavis and Butt-Head* to be art. "An art-oissuer, if you will."

"I don't think that's a word, sport," Sinclair says, laughing coldly.

I shrug. "I'm pretty sure it is."

"Do you have a favorite artist?" Emily asks, brushing a stray curl out of her eyes.

She sounds genuinely interested, not like she's quizzing me, and I scramble to think of a legit-sounding answer.

"Well, uh, I'm a big fan of Michelangelo," I tell her. "And uh, Leonardo. And Donatello. And of course, Raphael. He's great. So much talent."

"I'm sorry, sport, but did you just list the names of all four Teenage Mutant Ninja Turtles?" Sinclair asks, watching me incredulously.

"No," I respond without even the slightest pause. "I listed four artists so groundbreaking that the Teenage Mutant Ninja Turtles were named after them."

"Of course you did," Sinclair says evenly, raising his eyebrows toward Emily in a way that makes my skin itch.

"But my very favorite artist," I continue, wishing Sinclair would eat shit and leave me alone, "is Foxamura."

"Is he the newest member of the Turtle gang?" the archaeologist asks, his tone mocking.

"The Teenage Mutant Ninja Turtles would never refer to themselves as the Turtle gang," I tell him. "And no. He's a Canadian painter recently featured in the *New Yorker*."

"Oh, awesome," Emily says. "What's his medium?"

I pause, trying to remember anything useful Lexi the homeowner told me about her ugly paintings.

"Paint," I say after a long pause.

"No way," Sinclair butts in. "A painter whose medium is paint? You don't say."

"Finger paint, actually," I say, wishing someone would hit me over the head with a buoy and put me out of my misery.

"He *finger paints*?" Emily asks in disbelief. "There's a market for that?"

"Well, you see, he used to finger paint," I say quickly, wiping sweat off my brow. "As a child. He got his start as a finger painting prodigy, and now he specializes in watercolor."

"Fantastic," Killian says. "And what does he paint, Riley?"

"Ryder," I correct him, even though he damn well knows. I try to remember what Lexi told me, something about humans and horses and causation. Fuck if I know.

"He paints dudes on horses," I say finally. "With flags."

"Dudes on horses with flags," Sinclair repeats slowly, drawing out the words so I can fully appreciate how stupid they sound. "Wow. Sounds positively groundbreaking. Now, *Ryder*, what's your favorite piece of Donatello's?"

Well, shit. "It really is so hard to choose," I say finally, scratching my chin like I'm really thinking hard and trying not to sweat my balls off. "I guess, at the end of the day, if I had to choose from all his brilliant artworks, I'd go with . . ."

But I'm saved by the bell, or in this case, the ferry captain, who switches on the PA system to announce that we're nearing Isle Royale. I breathe a sigh of relief as we all begin to prepare to get off the boat. Within minutes, we reach a slanted coastline bordered by jagged rocks and towering white spruce trees, and the ferry docks at Washington Harbor on the southwestern side of the island.

"It was my pleasure to meet you all," the elder archaeologist, Dr. Sharp, says as we file off the boat, our shaky legs adjusting to being back on land. He shakes Emily's hand and then mine, and it's good to know that not all archaeologists are condescending jerks.

Sinclair doesn't even look at me, and he doesn't shake Emily's hand. Instead, when we reach the end of the dock, he presses a lingering kiss to her cheek. And when he leans forward to whisper into her ear, something tight and hard coils in my stomach.

"Well. Happy trails, then!" I say brightly, clapping my hands so loudly that Sinclair jumps back from Emily. "We'd better be on our way, Edwards. We have a full day of hiking ahead of us."

Sinclair looks like he wants to rip my head straight off my body, but he only flashes me a tight smile. "The wilderness can be a dangerous place, sport. Take good care of her, aye?"

"Thanks for the concern, *chief*," I say smoothly, zipping up my parka. "But I've got everything under control."

Considering I can't even remember most of the tips I learned in those YouTube tutorials, I don't actually have anything under control, but as long as I don't let anyone know that, everything will be just fine. Hopefully.

"Ready?" I ask Emily, watching disappointment flash across her face as Sinclair and his crew head in the opposite direction.

She sighs and glances at the unassuming brown cabin in front of us. The Windigo Visitor Center will be our last glimpse of civilization for the next six days, and then it'll just be me, her, and miles and miles of untamed, wolf-laden wilderness. And judging by the mournful expression on her face, she's not looking forward to one single second of it.

Her gaze shifts toward me, and she musters a weak smile. "Yep. Ready as I'll ever be."

SIX

RYDER

As it turns out, ready as she'll ever be isn't nearly ready enough. Because Emily may be smart and beautiful and probably reads more books in a year than I do in a decade, but she is not a strong hiker. This becomes very obvious when, not even ten minutes after we leave the Windigo Visitor Center with our permits, she stops, rests her hands on her knees, and lets out a miserable groan.

"Just so you know," she says, gasping for air, "I am not a strong hiker."

"You don't say," I reply, trying to make her laugh, but she only grunts in response.

I remember a passage I read in one of Caleb's camping books, one that talked about the best way to arrange items in your backpack to make it feel lighter.

"Here," I tell her, eager to help. "Give me your pack."

She shimmies her backpack off with a pained expression and whimpers as she hands it to me.

"Jesus Christ," I mutter when her pack nearly takes my arm off. "Nobody would be a strong hiker carrying this thing! How much stuff did you bring?" Her pack feels bulky even to me, and I've probably got a good four inches and sixty pounds on her, minimum.

She bristles. "A lot. I didn't want to be underprepared."

"I don't think there's any risk of that. Do you mind if I re-organize your gear? It might make things easier to carry."

Emily shrugs, and so I open her pack and begin to remove the contents of what I can only assume is an entire Super Target. She's brought all the standard camping equipment—tent, sleeping pad, headlamp—along with a bunch of stuff she wouldn't need on a spa vacation, much less a trek through the wilderness.

"Jesus, it's like a clown car of personal items," I say as I remove two books, a handheld fan, a clear toiletry bag with enough hair conditioner to last a decade, and a box of mini Jenga blocks.

"I have curly hair," she says defensively. "You wouldn't believe the amount of product it requires."

"But you won't be able to wash your hair," I point out. "There's no running water."

"I know," she says, pointing at one of the items left in her pack. "Which is why I packed the solar-heated shower." Her gaze flits toward a fuzzy blanket and a box of Little Debbie Cosmic Brownies. "I'm very attached to my creature comforts."

"Okay. But do you really need . . ." I pull out another item. "Glow-in-the-dark toilet paper?"

She nods. "The guy at the camping store said it's essential for nighttime bathroom excursions."

"The guy at the camping store was working on commission. And is this bear spray?" I ask, gripping a cylinder the length of a fire extinguisher. "There are no bears on Isle Royale."

She snatches it out of my hand. "No bears *that we know of*. Besides, we'll be glad we have it if we run into the Ripper of the Rockies."

I stare at her. "The who of the what?"

"He was a serial killer who lurked along desolate trails in Wyoming, waiting for the chance to nab innocent hikers and slice their throats," she says calmly, as if she's reading a grocery list and not recounting a horrific tale of murder. "He—or she, I guess, but let's be real, he's definitely a he—has never been caught, but he's believed to be responsible for the disappearance of more than a dozen hikers, including the 2010 disappearance of the entire McAdams family."

"All of the McAdamses?" I ask, my stomach twisting.

"Yep. Even the family dog, Skippy."

"Jesus," I say, running a hand through my hair. I tried to prepare myself for starting campfires and setting up tents, not fighting off deranged killers. "That's dark as hell."

"Yeah, well, that's why I brought the bear spray." Emily shrugs. "Skippy made it out alive, if it makes you feel any better. He turned up near a ranger station a week later."

"How would that make me feel better? Skippy lost his whole family!"

"It's super tragic," Emily admits.

Trying my best not to think of the horrors poor Skippy

witnessed, I busy myself pulling a camp chair, a French press, and a package of dryer sheets out of Emily's pack.

"Edwards," I say, adding a water filter to the pile. "I have *so many questions*."

"What? You're telling me I'm supposed to spend six days in nature without a solar-heated shower or a portable coffee maker?"

My jaw drops. "Yes."

Emily clutches a package of freeze-dried ice-cream sandwiches to her chest like she thinks I might rip them away. "I think not."

"Well," I say, holding up the purple life vest she wore on the ferry, "Terrence isn't gonna be happy when he realizes you didn't turn in your personal flotation device. And that's probably an even worse offense than violating Safety Code 36e."

"28.5a," Emily grumbles. "And that life jacket is mine. I brought it from home."

"Seriously?" I ask, puzzled. "Why? I'm sure the ferry has some on hand for emergencies."

She looks at me like I'm insane. "Right, and the passengers aboard *Titanic* were sure it had enough lifeboats."

"Stark example, but okay."

"Listen, a life vest is a must-have," she says, grabbing it out of my hands. "I mean, did you know that almost a thousand people die every year from ferry-related causes?"

I'm learning a lot of super un-fun facts that I wish I could delete from my brain forever, and I shake my head. "No, I did not."

"Well, now you do." She shakes her head, folding the life

vest into a small square. "You might think I'm paranoid, but working in the ER has taught me to be ready for anything. Hence the bear spray and the life jacket."

"And the tiny Jenga blocks, of course."

She rolls her eyes. "I'm just saying, I have a morbid story for everything. It's like a sick party trick."

"You can't possibly have a morbid story for *everything*," I counter.

Emily folds her arms over her chest. "Try me."

"Challenge accepted." I ball up a pair of thick woolen socks, remembering the pathetic dinner I microwaved at the motel last night. "Ramen noodles. I bet you don't have a morbid story about those."

"*Ramen noodles?*" she repeats, her eyes so wide you'd think I said *Roman candles.* "Those are a leading cause of burns in children! They're as dangerous as dull knives or backyard trampolines!"

"What's wrong with backyard trampolines?" I ask, and the look she gives me tells me that I'm three seconds away from sending her into convulsions. "Never mind. Look, I get why you brought one life jacket, but a backup, too?" I hold up a second deflated life vest, this one the color of an unripe banana. "Seems just a little bit excessive."

Emily shakes her head. "That's not a backup. I brought that one for you."

"Oh. Wow," I say, caught off guard. "Thanks, Edwards."

It's been such a long time since someone's gone out of their way to look out for me that the simple act of her saying, *Hey, how about you don't die in a ferry boat crash?* unearths something vulnerable and tender inside me, and I can't help but stare at the hideous yellow material like it's real gold. Not wanting to let the unwelcome rush of emotion get the best of me, I drop the life vest onto the growing pile of junk and clear my throat.

"That was, uh, really thoughtful of you."

She shrugs. "Sure. I mean, despite our rocky start, we're a team now, which means my crippling paranoia is your crippling paranoia." She raises an eyebrow. "As long as you don't make me get rid of my glow-in-the-dark toilet paper."

"Wouldn't dream of it." I rest my hands on my knees to survey the pile, then reach inside her pack to make sure I removed everything. My fingers meet something long-ish and round, but before I can retrieve the object from her backpack, Emily grabs my forearm to stop me.

"Don't!" she says suddenly, her eyes wide.

"Oh, um, sorry," I tell her, wondering what the hell is going on. "I was just making sure I got everything out, and—"

"Leave it, please," she says in a clipped tone, a warm flush creeping over her cheeks. "It's private."

She's reacting the same way I did when my mom almost stumbled upon the hidden copies of *Playboy* in my room, and I release my grasp on the object. "No problem at all. I'll just—"

"It's a vibrator," she adds quickly. "In case you were wondering. Just a standard, ordinary vibrator."

Jesus.

"Oh," I say, trying to keep my tone neutral. "Right. Good

idea. You never know when you'll need a . . . anyway," I say, sweat pouring down the back of my neck, "you weren't lying. You really are prepared for everything."

That just makes her blush more brightly, and between her flushed skin and the bomb she just dropped, I have no fucking clue how I'm supposed to sleep at night in a tent just feet from hers and not imagine her tugging down her underwear, reaching down with her vibrator to—

"So," I say with a cough, refusing to let my mind go anywhere so unprofessional, "now that we have everything out, let's rearrange it."

I return some of her gear to her pack, explaining how to position the heaviest stuff toward the center and the lightest farthest from her body. It's better, but still ridiculously heavy, and so I bite the bullet and transfer some of her weightier stuff to my backpack. After the reckless behavior I demonstrated on the ferry, the least I can do is help carry some of her load. Besides, it might help me feel less guilty about the fact that she thinks I'm much more qualified than I am.

"Better?" I ask when Emily slips her pack back on.

She rolls her shoulders back and nods. "Much."

"Good. Now we just need to get you fitted in right. Stand still, okay?"

She nods and drops her hands to her sides as I reach forward to tighten her hip belt. I whistle as I adjust her shoulder straps and load lifters, trying not to think about the fact that beneath the overpowering scent of what I can only assume is SPF 6000, she smells faintly of lavender shampoo. It's been months since I've been close enough to a woman to notice her scent—the cloud of Bengay constantly wafting off my neighbor Lulu doesn't count—and I'm so overwhelmed by the sensation that my fingers miss the sternum strap buckle and graze Em's right breast instead.

She startles, letting out a surprised *eek*, and I drop my hands immediately.

"Jesus, I'm sorry. I did *not* mean to touch your boob." Wait, is *boob* too unprofessional? I realize I haven't exactly treated her to a five-star tour guide experience so far, but I really am trying my best to do this right.

"Your breast," I correct myself, but somehow that sounds worse. "Er, I mean, your chest. Your, um, chesticle region."

Chesticle region? What the fuck is wrong with me?

"Your breast," I correct myself again, settling on the anatomical term. "I did not mean to touch your breast."

My words are the conversational equivalent of the ferry sinking to the very bottom of Lake Superior and exploding into smithereens, and I would very much like for the ground to open up and swallow me whole.

"I'm also sorry for saying 'breast' so many times," I add quietly. "And for saying it again just now."

Emily stares at me, blinking like someone who just walked out of a movie theater into blinding sunshine. And considering she just walked out of what I can only assume is a neat, organized life and into my tornado of chaos, I don't blame her one bit.

"It's okay," she says finally. "Just please, for the love of God, do not call them funbags."

"Edwards, I promise you, I would throw myself off a cliff

before I refer to your breasts as funbags." I pause to tighten my own sternum strap. "I also promise to stop talking about your breasts."

"Excellent," she says, striding down the trail at a much faster pace than she was before we stopped. "Now let's get moving."

Emily seems like the last person on earth who would want to encounter a gigantic wild animal in person, but the first item on her Isle Royale itinerary—a six-page, color-coded document that has an actual header and footer—is SEE A MOOSE AT WASHINGTON CREEK. Of course, this item is followed by a dozen bullet points describing the route to the creek, the appropriate time intervals to stop and apply more sunscreen, and whether or not we'll take a bathroom break on our way there. (Spoiler alert: we won't. Bathroom breaks are listed in dark purple, and we won't have one for another two hours.)

"So," I say, the trail narrowing as we approach a sprawling creek surrounded by high grasses and a sloping, rocky bank. "What's up with wanting to see a moose?"

"What do you mean, what's up with it?" Emily asks, her face glistening with sweat.

I glance sideways at her. "I mean, you have a personal vendetta against instant soup. Encountering a wild animal that's roughly the size of a car doesn't seem like something you'd be thrilled about. I'm just curious, is all."

"Well, you'd be wrong," she says, stumbling over a tree root. "I'll be very thrilled to see a moose. And I do not have a personal vendetta against instant soup. I have a professional one."

We stop to rest when we reach the creek, sitting down on a fallen log littered with mushrooms sprouting from its cracks. Emily pulls out a canteen of water and a sandwich wrapped in brown paper, and I close my eyes and tilt my face toward the sun, letting its rays warm my skin. Farther down the creek, the rocky bank slopes off, forming a small waterfall, and I take a deep breath and let the sound of the rushing water relax me. I might be the adult equivalent of a little kid playing cowboy, since I have no clue what the hell I'm doing out here, but I forgot how much I enjoy being outside.

"I don't understand how you do this for a living," Emily says after a minute, twisting her canteen open.

My heart skips a beat, and I open my eyes quickly. Is my incompetence really that obvious? I know I screwed up on the ferry, but I feel like I've been doing a decent acting job since then. At one point, I even licked my finger, held it in the air, and said, *Ahh, a nice northeasternly breeze*, which seems like something a real ambassador of adventure would say.

"What do you mean?" I ask, trying to keep my tone neutral.

She sips her water. "I mean, I don't know how you spend your life carrying fifty pounds of camping gear on your back and sleeping outside like an animal. Not to mention traipsing around in the middle of nowhere. I mean, don't you get tired? Don't you get cold? Don't you wish you were home in your own bed, with access to Netflix and running water?"

"No, I don't." It's the answer a real tour guide would give, but it takes me a second to realize that I actually mean it.

Home these days means the dingy apartment where I drink too much and sleep too little, where the shower only gets luke-warm and the laugh track from Lulu's nightly *Everybody Loves Raymond* marathon blasts through thin walls covered in yel-lowed, peeling wallpaper. Being outside in the crisp September air, where I'm surrounded by white spruce and paper birch trees instead of oil-stained pizza boxes and piles of dirty laun-dry, is a welcome change of pace. Sure, my groin aches from where I strained a muscle jumping onto the boat, and I might have lost the ability to father children, but I feel better here than I have in a long time.

"Well, we're a different breed, you and me," Emily says. "All I want right now is to be home in my own bed, with a pie bak-ing in the oven and a cool breeze coming in through the win-dow." She stares out at the creek, where we see plenty of turtles and dragonflies but not a single moose. "I miss Door-Dash and running water. I miss Starbucks. And I really miss my cooling eucalyptus bed sheets."

She speaks with the forlorn tone of a grizzled veteran de-scribing life before the big war, and I don't have the heart to remind her that we've only been in the wilderness for a few hours.

"If it makes you feel better," I tell her, "I miss Starbucks, too. I'm in a real Folgers Classic Roast phase of life."

Never mind that it's because I'm broke, not because the nearest gourmet coffee shop is on the other side of Lake Su-perior.

"Can I ask you something?" I say, watching a hawk circle the creek in search of its dinner. "Why are you here?"

She brushes a stray crumb off her bottom lip with her tongue. "What do you mean?"

I shrug. "I don't get why you came to Isle Royale. I know we just met, and people have layers or whatever, but this doesn't exactly seem like your cup of tea. Not that it's any of my business."

As if to prove my point, she lets out a screech and swats frantically at something on her leg.

"I think it was just a mosquito," I reassure her, but she shudders anyway.

"Saying a bug is *just* a mosquito is like saying Jeffrey Dahmer was just a man."

I stare at her. "Uh, okay. Anyway, I guess what I'm asking is, is this trip kind of a *Live, Laugh, Love* thing for you?"

"A what?" she asks, wrinkling her nose in confusion.

"You know," I say, "*Live, Laugh, Love*. That movie where Julia Roberts dumps her husband and travels the world to find herself, or whatever."

Understanding flickers across her features. "Ohhh. You mean *Eat, Pray, Love*, the memoir written by Elizabeth Gilbert. I read that one."

The only memoir I've read in the last decade was written by a dude who starred on *Jackass*, and it was literally titled *A Hard Kick in the Nuts*. I do not mention this to Emily.

"No," she says, shaking her head as she tears off a piece of her peanut butter sandwich. "This is not me living out my *Eat, Pray, Love* fantasy. I mean, I did just go through a breakup, but I was the dumpee, not the dumper. And Isle Royale is pretty, but it is not Italy, India, or Bali."

It takes my brain a second to process the fact that somebody dumped Emily. Sure, she's the walking definition of a type A personality and could probably find a way to make tissue paper seem dangerous, but she's also thoughtful enough to pack a life jacket for a total stranger and so nice to look at that it almost hurts to sit this close to her. If I'd met her in my old life, the one I lived before I got the four a.m. call telling me that Caleb was gone, I might have stood a chance of getting her number. Not just because I had a healthy bank account and an expensive haircut and a social life that involved more than sitting on my elderly neighbor's floral-printed couch while we drink Fresca and she fills me in on the latest bridge club hookup scandals. But because I was a whole person back then, the kind of person people liked. The kind who cared about things and didn't cry at *The Sandlot* and would never in a million billion years refer to a woman's breast as a chesticle.

But that seems like ages ago, because grief years, like dog years, play funny tricks with time.

"Well, I don't know the circumstances, but I'm sure your ex is an idiot," I say, meaning it. And I should know, because I'm kind of an idiot myself.

"Thanks," she says. "He was an anesthesiologist, so he wasn't an idiot, but he was kind of emotionally detached. It wasn't the worst breakup I've ever had, but it was rough. He broke up with me for a professional dog walker who goes to Burning Man and has a pixie cut." Her mouth twists like she swallowed a lemon. "I could never do that."

"What? Anyone can go to Burning Man."

She looks at me. "I haven't left the house without an umbrella since third grade. I don't think I'd thrive at a desert festival where everyone does ketamine and hangs out in an orgy dome."

"Sorry, did you say 'orgy dome'?" I ask, my brain zeroing in on that little detail, but my question goes unanswered. Because Emily stiffens suddenly, her whole body going rigid like a dog that spotted a squirrel.

"Hey, did you hear that?" she whispers, her head swiveling from left to right.

I heard nothing after *orgy dome*, but I don't tell Emily that. "Hear what?" I ask.

She presses a finger to her lips. "Footsteps, I think. Close behind us."

I listen for a moment, but all I hear is the buzz of a dragonfly circling nearby.

"It was probably just a bird," I tell her.

Emily side-eyes me. "Since when do birds have heavy footsteps?"

"Well," I say, "it could have been a large bird. Like a crane, you know. Or an ostrich."

Her eyes widen. "Do you hear yourself? There are no ostriches in—"

She freezes, because the sound repeats, and this time, I hear it, too. But it's not footsteps so much as two *thuds* followed by the sound of something being dragged across pebbled dirt, and we both spin to glance behind us.

"See?" she whispers, elbowing me. "Footsteps!"

The sound echoes through the towering balsam fir trees that surround us, and I strain to listen.

"It's not footsteps," I whisper. "It's more like a *thump, thump, drag.*"

"What the fuck?" she asks, glancing at me fearfully. "A bird doesn't make a thump, thump, drag sound, Ryder!"

"No," I agree. "It doesn't. Actually, it kind of reminds me of this scary story I heard at Boy Scouts when I was a kid. See, there's this murderer who escapes from an insane asylum, and he breaks into a random house where there's a babysitter watching some children. And he cuts off the babysitter's arms and legs, and then she has to sort of *thump, thump, draaag* herself up the stairs to warn the children—"

Emily looks at me with eyes wide as saucers, and I shut the hell up.

"And then everyone turns out perfectly fine," I lie, changing the story quickly. "The babysitter gets her limbs successfully reattached at the hospital, and—"

"Ryder," Emily says, "please stop talking."

"Right," I say quickly. "Sorry. But I'm sure whatever's making that sound is perfectly harmless. Like, a deer or a fox or a wolf dragging its prey."

"A *wolf*?" she repeats in disbelief. "Hell no. We need the bear spray."

But before she can reach inside her pack to retrieve it, another *thump, thump, drag* sounds from the other side of the small hill bordering the creek, and we turn in unison as a figure emerges at the top of the hill. It's not a wolf or a bird, but a man—a man with long gangly limbs, gray disheveled hair, and a scowl that would look right at home on a wanted poster.

"Um, Emily," I ask, gulping, "are there any insane asylums around here?"

She shushes me, and I watch, startled, as the man moves toward us, dragging some kind of tarp behind him.

"Jesus," I whisper. "He looks like Scary Gandalf."

"No, it's Killface," Emily whispers, grabbing my hand and curling her fingers around mine.

"I'm sorry, did you just say *Killface*?" I whisper back. "You know someone named Killface?!"

She shakes her head. "Yes. No. I mean, that's not his real name. That's just what I started calling him in my head when I saw him in the ferry cabin. He was staring at me right before Killian showed up."

My gut twists at the mention of the snobby archaeologist, but I have a more pressing issue on my hands. Namely, the scowling man in front of us who looks like he'd enjoy nothing more than slicing the arms off a babysitter.

Or two incompetent hikers.

"Let's get out of here before he sees us," I whisper, but it's too late.

The sound of my voice carries in the wind, and the disheveled-looking man glances up suddenly, his beady eyes meeting mine.

"What are you kids doing out here?" he asks, his tone practically a growl.

I stare at him, trying not to imagine exactly what kind of instrument he uses to chop up bodies, until Emily nudges me in the ribs.

"Oh, um, hello, Mr. Killface, sir!" I say, lifting a hand in greeting. When Emily uses her elbow to jab me in the ribs again, I grimace. "I mean, um, hello there, sir. We're just, uh, out here enjoying all the natural beauty that America's national parks have to offer. Thanks, Teddy Roosevelt!"

I beam at him, but he continues to scowl at me like his face is stuck that way.

"So, yeah," I continue, nodding way too many times. "Just, uh, enjoying the great outdoors, you know. How about you? Enjoying a little fresh air?" I crane my neck to peer at the tarp he drags behind him. "What do you have in that, uh, scary-looking tarp there? Camping supplies? Firewood?"

"A mutilated body?" Emily whispers, her hand gripping mine so tightly I can barely feel my fingers.

Killface narrows his eyes at me. "What's in my tarp is none of your damn business."

"Oh," I say, my tone still overly peppy. "Well. Okay, then. Happy trails, sir!"

His scowl deepens. "There's nothing happy about this trail. You kids shouldn't be out here."

"Oh? Why's that?" I ask, wincing as Emily practically crushes my pointer finger.

He sniffs the air and wrinkles his nose. "There's a storm brewing. A bad one. I can smell it. You should find shelter now, if you know what's good for you."

I have no clue what's good for me—the fact that I'm on this

trip, not to mention my pitiful credit score, proves that—but I sniff the air just in case. All I smell, though, is fresh mud from the creek and a slightly stale odor that may or may not be coming from the decaying body hidden in his tarp. I glance up at the sky, which is the kind of bright, perfect blue you dream about all winter. There's not a single storm cloud in sight, and as if to prove how crazy Killface is, a robin flits from branch to branch on a nearby birch tree, trilling happily.

"Thanks for the heads-up!" I tell Killface, giving him the same glassy look I give my great-uncle Randy whenever he starts ranting about the deep state in the middle of Thanksgiving dinner. "I think we're good, though."

"Suit yourselves," he grumbles, shaking his head like we're a real pair of idiots. Then he ambles down the hill and past the trail, his tarp making a high-pitched scraping sound as he drags it along behind him.

"Well, that was terrifying," Emily says, watching until he disappears into the woods.

"Nah, don't worry about him," I say, ignoring the shiver that runs down my spine. "He seems harmless enough."

He actually seems like the kind of person who would kidnap an entire family of hikers, including their droopy-eared dog, but I keep that thought to myself. I can't afford to let Emily get so rattled that she decides to cut her trip short. I need every dollar I'll earn from this gig if I want to pay for Caleb's boat. Besides, I meant what I told her earlier: I don't wish I were at home, at least not in the sense of what home is now. My true home was my old life, the one with Caleb in it. The lonely studio apartment where I spend my nights drinking alone now, hoping that one more sip will numb the pain, well, that isn't home. And I'm sure as hell not ready to go back there yet.

"If you say so," Emily says uneasily, tearing her gaze away from the woods to look at me. Her gray eyes are wide, uncertain, with tiny flecks of white forming a ring around her pupil. "Do you think he's right about the storm?"

I glance up at the postcard-pretty sky again.

"No," I say, shaking my head and returning to my spot on the log. "I think he's full of shit. Because what we've got here is a perfect Isle Royale day."

"Fine." Emily sighs and sits down beside me, but she's clearly still shaken, because she sits so close to me that her knee brushes mine. "I hope we see a freaking moose soon."

I watch as she pulls a bottle of sunscreen out of her bag and begins applying it vigorously, careful not to miss a single inch of exposed skin. She whips out bug spray next, spraying enough of it onto her skin to repel every insect within a three-mile radius. I can't help but wonder why someone so obviously uncomfortable in nature has decided to spend an entire week in it, and I realize that both questions I asked her earlier— *What's up with wanting to see a moose?* and *Why are you here?*—have gone largely unanswered.

But before I can bring them up again, the single cloud above us darkens suddenly, swelling from a fluffy bundle of white to a menacing gray shadow faster than I can snap my fingers.

"Hey, Ryder," Emily says, looking toward the sky uncertainly, "are you sure it's not going to storm?"

I don't answer her, and she couldn't hear me if I did. Because with no warning other than the foreboding words of an old man much less idiotic than me, the skies open, unleashing a sudden torrential downpour that soaks my clothes—and hopes—in seconds.

Well, shit.

SEVEN

EMILY

My dad, Roger Edwards Jr., was born a daredevil. At least that's what my grandma Nora used to say, and she had it on good authority, considering she was there when it happened. She went into labor three weeks early, while she was watching an episode of *Gunsmoke* in her living room, and he was born before she could even make it to the phone to call my grandpa for help. By age six, he was legendary in their small town for being the only kid brave enough to climb all the way to the top of the sycamore tree that overlooked the park, a feat that earned him bragging rights on the playground and more than a few expensive trips to the emergency room.

By eight, he had perfected the art of backflipping off the tire swing and onto his skateboard, a nailbiter of a trick that wowed his peers but resulted in a broken arm. And by high school, when other kids his age were still deciding who to ask to homecoming, he'd figured out his entire life plan: he was going to become a journalist, the kind that traveled every inch of the globe in search of a good story and traipsed through tropical jungles to report on the vanishing habitats of endangered tree frogs. When he fell in love with my mom, a raven-haired schoolteacher with matching dimples and a great laugh who wanted to settle down and get married, they reached a happy compromise: Dad could live out his globetrotting dreams, as long as he was home for three-fourths of the year, and he could never be gone for more than three weeks at a time.

It worked well for a while, even when Brooke came along and I soon followed. Dad worked as a global correspondent for a regional press syndicate, and I remember him walking in our front door after short trips, his suitcase heavy with trinkets and treasures from the places he traveled. He would tell us exciting stories from his adventures, like how he was chased by a wild monkey in Ecuador and how he met a shaman in Vietnam who used mushrooms to navigate between the spirit world and this one. In the evenings, I would cuddle up in bed with a Junie B. Jones book and a flashlight, feeling snug and safe as the sound of my parents' laughter floated down the hallway.

And then, like all stories worth telling, there was a plot twist. Mom got sick, fast, and the laughter stopped, replaced by the relentless beeping of an IV pump and the hushed voices of my grandparents whispering in the living room. And when she died, leaving behind a husband and two little girls and a beagle named Rascal who still wagged his tail and waited by the door every night at the time Mom would usually get home from work, Dad knew his adventures were over. He quit his job and got a new one as editor of *The Lakewood Gazette*, the small-town paper that covered hot topics like the fiercely competitive school board election and the annual Halloween pumpkin drop. He devoted himself to raising Brooke and me, trading transatlantic flights for bike rides around the block, and interviews with global leaders for painfully detailed explanations of why Brian Stiller was the sexiest boy Lakewood Intermediate School had ever seen. He learned about periods and Sillybandz and fishtail braids, and he fulfilled his need for adrenaline with *Indiana Jones* rewatches and navigating the treacherous minefield of being a girl dad. He'd have his chance at adventure later, when Mom's medical bills were paid off and Brooke and I were grown and he found someone to take the reins at the paper.

Except, of course, his chance never came. Which is why, instead of taking the father-daughter hiking trip Dad dreamed of, I'm shuffling miserably along behind Ryder, thick mud squelching underneath my boots as we trudge through the dense forest. And while Dad would have found Ryder downright hilarious, I'm growing increasingly concerned about the navigational abilities of the man I hired. For one thing, he seemed completely shocked by the sudden thunderstorm that rattled my teeth and soaked me to the bone. Granted, it surprised me, too, despite Killface's warning—after all, the sky *was* clear—but I'm not an expert outdoorsman who makes her living on the trail. I can't be expected to know these things, which is why I hired a guide.

But a surprise storm is small potatoes compared to the fact

that we've been searching for our campsite for almost two hours, and my patience is running thin.

"Are you sure we're going the right way?" I ask, watching as Ryder glances from the map in his left hand to the compass in his right like he's never used them before in his life.

"Of course we're going the right way," he says, frowning at the map and then scanning the stretch of trail behind us. "I think."

"You *think*?" I ask, my voice reaching a pitch so high it squeaks. "What do you mean, you think? This is your area of expertise, right?"

"Well, it's not *not* my area of expertise," he says, which does absolutely nothing to help the panic creeping into my chest. He scratches the back of his head and shakes the compass like it's a Magic 8 Ball. "I think there's something wrong with this compass. Oh wait, never mind. I was holding it upside down."

It takes all my restraint not to scream. Not only am I exhausted from a long day of travel and hiking, I'm also wet, cold, and paranoid that Killface is going to pop out from behind a tree and murder us. I haven't seen a single thing I could interpret as some kind of meaningful sign from Dad, and to add to the fun, I'm growing increasingly worried that the tour guide I shelled out a decent chunk of money for—the one whose agency promised to bring me *all the adventure with none of the hassle*—had last-minute availability for a reason. Because I'm feeling very, very hassled.

"No, there's definitely something wrong with the compass,"

Ryder says, shaking it again. "I can't get the pointy thing to move."

"The *pointy thing*?!" I repeat. "Do you mean the orienteering arrow?"

"Um, I think so?" he says, his voice bearing not a single hint of confidence. He holds the compass up toward me. "Do you know how to use it?"

"Do you not?" I ask, my frustration bubbling over. "Ryder, answer me yes or no: are we lost?"

He stares at the map again, which is a soupy, illegible mess of wet ink.

"I mean," he says slowly, "'lost' is a relative term, you know? 'Cause if you think about it, you can know exactly where you are and still feel lost, and you can be lost but still feel good about where you are. Kind of like how you can feel all alone in a crowded room, or how you can be alone but not lonely, or—"

"Ryder," I say, closing my eyes and praying for patience, "please stop rambling."

He sighs and runs a hand through his hair, and it's deeply unfair that someone can be so infuriating and also so completely jacked. "Look, the good news is that we aren't lost. I figured out exactly where we are."

"Okay," I say warily, wondering why he still looks uneasy. "And is there bad news?"

"Uh, yeah. Sort of." He grimaces. "The bad news is that where we are is five miles away from where we want to be."

I can practically feel smoke coming out of my ears.

"How is that *sort of* bad news?" I ask. "That's terrible news, Ryder! How in the hell are we five miles from the campsite? It was only supposed to be a three-mile hike from Washington Creek!"

"Right, and it would have been," he mumbles, looking everywhere but at me. "Except we accidentally went a little too easty-east and not enough northy-north."

"*We* didn't do anything," I hiss, my normal levels of patience severely deflated by the fact that I've gone more than twelve hours without access to WiFi and caffeine. "*You* went the wrong way. I just followed you!"

"I know." Ryder's voice is quiet. "I'm sorry. I'm just . . . very off my game right now."

"Okay, well," I say, forcing myself to speak at a normal volume, "how do you plan to get back on your game? And why are you relying on that wet map and a compass? Why aren't you navigating with one of those fancy satellite GPS things?"

His answer is so hushed I have to strain to hear it. "Because I don't have one."

"Huh?" I ask, puzzled. "But it's listed on your agency's website as a provided amenity. Why are you not providing that amenity, Ryder?"

He winces. "The thing is, I did have one. And I made sure to store it safely in my day pack. I was super careful! Unfortunately, I forgot my day pack in the motel room, which is about forty miles that way." He points left, then frowns and points right instead. "Or maybe that way. Anyway, I'm not exactly sure which way the GPS is, but I know it's not here."

"Unfortunately, you forgot your day pack," I repeat, stunned. That sounds to me like the exact opposite of being super careful. "How, pray tell, does that happen?"

He shakes his head. "It's a long story involving *The Sandlot* and a case of beer."

"*The Sandlot*?" I ask, trying extremely hard to follow. "The children's baseball movie with the scary dog?"

"Oh, Hercules isn't actually scary," Ryder says breezily. "He's actually a very good boy who—" He pauses. "Never mind. That's not super important right now."

I take a deep breath to collect my thoughts. "Okay, so, to recap: we're five miles from the correct route, we don't have the one thing that could help us in the event of a true emergency, and Hercules is a very good boy. Did I miss anything?"

"Uh, yeah," Ryder says, looking like he wishes a tree would blow over and put him out of his misery. "The personal locator beacon was also in my day pack. So I forgot the *two* things that could help us in the event of a true emergency. To be, you know, precise."

I want to rip his head off verbally, but instead I take a long inhale and remind myself that he didn't *mean* to forget the pricey, life-saving equipment our contract promised he would bring. Yelling at him won't help anything.

"Okay," I say, tugging on the straps of my backpack. "So we need a new plan. We don't have much daylight left, so maybe we should just set up camp somewhere around here." I glance toward the surrounding forest, frightened that a wolf or a Killface is lurking in the shadows. "Tomorrow, we'll get back to our planned route. We don't have the GPS, and our map is pretty ruined, but none of this is a huge deal, right? I'm sure you've guided tons of trips where things go a little haywire."

"Well," Ryder says, avoiding my gaze in a way that does not inspire confidence, "not exactly."

"Well, I'm sure you can find your way using the stars, right?" I ask, my desperation growing. "I'm sure you figure out directions all the time by looking at the Big Dipper or Cassiopeia or whatever, right? Or you lick your finger and hold it up to the wind like people do in movies? Just like you did earlier?"

"Sorry, what's Cassiopeia?" Ryder asks, massaging the back of his neck. "Is it an app? Because there's no cell service here, so we can't—"

"Oh my God, Fleet, I *know* there's no cell service here!" I seethe, finally losing my patience. "What I *don't* know is why my tour guide, who is supposed to be an expert in all things outdoorsy, isn't familiar with basic constellations! Or why you showed up so late to the marina that you almost missed the boat. Or why you didn't know that a storm was coming, or that glow-in-the-dark toilet paper is a must-have on the trail—"

"Nobody needs glow-in-the-dark toilet paper, Edwards!"

"I do, too, need it! And I need an explanation for all the stuff I just mentioned." I pause to catch my breath, watching as Ryder's jaw tightens. "What's going on?"

He exhales, letting out a *pfft* of air that can't mean anything good. "I have an explanation, but you're not going to like it. The thing is . . ." He pauses, really amping up the suspense as well as my cortisol levels. "I'm not what some might call an 'experienced' tour guide."

I gape at him. "Why are you making air quotes around 'experienced'? Exactly how many tours have you led?"

"Uh, one," he says in a whisper, his gaze fixed on the ground in front of him. "Including this one."

I swear I can actually hear the record scratch that happens inside my brain.

"One tour?" I ask, keeping a cool head be damned. "*This* tour? Are you telling me that I am your first and only client?"

"In a technical sense, yes, that would be correct. And also in every other sense."

"How?" I ask, my mind imploding. "There are pictures of you on your agency's website! Pictures of you hiking and leading some kind of stargazing class and looking at a compass like it's not an alien object. This doesn't make any sense." My breath catches. "Oh my God, this is just like the beginning of *Bloodsport*."

"What's *Bloodsport*?"

"It's the podcast about—never mind, it doesn't matter! What matters is that I'm stuck in the wilderness with no map and no clue who the man in front of me is." I put one hand on my pack, ready to grab my bear spray. "You need to make this make sense."

He puts his hands up as if my desire to bear-spray him in the eyeballs is written all over my face.

"Okay, let me explain," Ryder says. "I do work for Fleet Outdoor Adventures. I mean, I did. I guess I still do, technically, but the agency kind of fell apart a while back."

"Fell apart?" I repeat, my head swimming.

"It's a long story. But to make it simple, I was the marketing and outreach guy. I wasn't out in the field."

"But the pictures," I say, my heart pounding.

"The pictures are photo ops," he explains. "I was at the stargazing class, but I was in charge of s'more supplies. The picture of me looking at the compass was for our Instagram page. And I have hiked before, but it was always with a group, and I was never in charge. I thought that would be enough experience to get me through this gig, but clearly it isn't."

It takes me a full five seconds to process what he's saying before I speak.

"So you're telling me," I say quietly, "that I'm lost in the wilderness, on a remote island with no Wi-Fi and no way to call for help, with the camping equivalent of a *water boy*?"

Ryder flinches. "I mean, that's kind of a hurtful way to put it, but yes. That's correct."

I bury my face in my hands. "But why? I don't understand. Fleet Outdoor Adventures has excellent reviews. Why would they send somebody with no on-the-ground experience? Were all the other tour guides booked?"

"Uh, well, as I mentioned, the agency kind of fell apart," he says. "As in, the other tour guides all left about a year ago. The ones who were still alive, anyway."

My blood curdles. "The ones who were still *alive*? Did you, like, *murder* some of them?"

"What? No. Of course not." Ryder looks genuinely hurt by my question, and I almost feel bad for asking it before I remember that that's exactly what a real murderer would want.

"Look," he says, shoving the map into his pocket. "The agency was started and run by my brother, Caleb. He brought me along for the ride, but the business was his baby. He was in charge of the tour guides. He knew the ins and outs of every trail and probably could have led you across Isle Royale with his eyes closed."

"Okay," I say, not understanding what any of this information has to do with our current predicament. "So why isn't he here with me?"

Ryder flinches as if I've struck him. "Because he's dead, Emily. He died almost two years ago."

His words are like a bucket of ice water dumped over my simmering anger. "Ryder," I say, "I—"

"I tried to keep the agency running without him, but it crumbled last year," Ryder explains. "Because it can't exist without him, and frankly, I don't know how to, either." His voice is rough, and his eyes shine bright with the threat of tears, and something about watching this devil-may-care man care so deeply about something makes me want to cry, too.

"I took this gig because I needed the money," Ryder adds. He clears his throat and looks at me straight on. "I know it doesn't matter, but I really thought I could manage this. I'm sorry I wasn't up-front about my lack of qualifications. I'm sorry for jumping onto the boat, and for deceiving you. I'll figure out how to get you safely back to Windigo, and then I'll give you a full refund. And I will never, ever, do something like this again."

I watch as he wipes his eyes quickly with his sleeve, trying to pass it off as a cough. I don't know what to say to everything he just dumped on me, so I say the first thing that comes to mind.

"I'm so sorry, Ryder," I say quietly, releasing my grip on my pack. "I'm so sorry for the loss of your brother."

He glances at me in surprise, as if he'd been expecting me to tear him a new one. "Thank you, Emily."

And as he squints at the map again, then holds the compass up to his mouth and blows on it like it's a malfunctioning Nintendo cartridge, I know exactly what I should do. I should find a way to get back to Windigo ASAP and hop on the first ferry back to Grand Portage, then blast Fleet Outdoor Adventures' Yelp page with the most scathing review ever written. I should accept the fact that I have no business trying to finish Dad's bucket list, because he might have been born a daredevil, but I was born an overly anxious scaredy-cat who considers going grocery shopping without a list to be a grand adventure.

I should, but I won't. Because there's a brokenness in Ryder that I recognize, a desperate longing for someone who isn't here that mirrors the anguish I feel every time I think about Dad. And even though I'm furious that a completely unqualified guy from the *marketing department* had such an inflated sense of his own abilities that he led both of us astray in the dangerous wilderness, I can't just give up. I made a promise to Dad, and I intend to keep it.

"You were wrong to lie to me, but we can't just go back to Windigo," I tell him. "It's not that easy. Because I have a secret, too."

EIGHT

RYDER

Emily Edwards is merciful. I could tell that she was about three seconds away from blasting me in the face with bear spray, and frankly, I would have deserved every drop. But instead, she's standing in front of me with her hands at her sides, wearing a somber expression.

"A secret?" I ask, confused. "What secret?"

"I don't have a vibrator in my backpack," she says, biting her bottom lip. "I lied."

"Okaaay," I say slowly. "I mean, I forgive you for lying, because who the hell am I to judge, but that's kind of a strange thing to bring up—"

"No," she interrupts, tapping her foot impatiently. "That's not the secret. I lied about having a vibrator in the bottom of my pack because I didn't want to tell you what's actually in there."

"Alright, well," I ask, "what's actually in there?"

She takes a deep, shaky breath, and I wonder what she

could possibly have in her pack that necessitates such secrecy. She's acting like she has something really damning in there— illicit drugs, a severed head, a bloodstained murder weapon— but those all seem like pretty unlikely possibilities for a woman who packed three different kinds of hand sanitizer.

"It's an urn," she says, her words rushed and quiet. "A travel urn."

"A *travel* urn?"

"Yes. It's like a regular urn, except it's nonmetallic and TSA approved—anyway, that doesn't matter. What matters is that I have an urn in my backpack, and inside that urn is my dad. My dad's ashes, I mean."

My heart sinks for her. "I'm sorry."

"Thanks." She nods, and she blinks the way Lulu does when she's trying not to tear up at the part in the Hallmark Channel Christmas movie when the big-city architect with a bloodlust for profit and the small-town carpenter with a heart of gold realize they're perfect for each other.

"I, um, well," Emily says, touching a hand to her neck. "He had a heart attack last year. Eleven months ago. In a book-store. It happened next to a giant cutout of Clifford the Big Red Dog, which is kind of funny in a dark way, if you really think about it, because you don't think of Clifford as being deeply tragic, or anything—anyway. Before he died, he was planning this whole bucket list retirement thing where he was going to visit every national park. I was supposed to come to Isle Royale with him, but it didn't work out. Obviously. Since, you know, he died."

"I gathered that," I say gently.

"Right. Well, after he passed, I promised myself—and him—that I would finish his bucket list. That I would sprinkle a little bit of his ashes in the parks he was most excited to visit, starting here. At Isle Royale." She wrinkles her nose. "'Sprinkle' is a terrible word choice, but you know what I mean."

I nod. "I do."

"So," she says, "as much as I would love nothing more than to go home and forget this trip ever happened, I can't. I won't. I mustn't."

I'm pretty sure I've never heard someone say *mustn't* before, outside of an old black-and-white movie, but I'm just relieved that she isn't chucking mini Jenga blocks at my head.

"My dad was the best dad who ever existed," Emily adds, "and I can't let him down again."

I wonder what she means by letting him down *again*, because it's hard to imagine her ever letting anybody down in the first place. But it's not my place to ask, and besides, I sure as hell know how painful it is to walk around carrying that kind of regret. I don't want to make it worse for her by asking too many personal questions.

"He sounds like an incredible guy," I say instead.

"Yeah. He was." She sniffles and clears her throat. "Anyway, I'd like to keep going. If you're still up for it, that is."

I don't even have to think about my answer. Without a doubt, I'd rather be out here, deep in the woods with no phone or beer or Totino's Pizza Rolls than at home in my bed, staring at the ceiling and trying to keep the dark thoughts at bay.

I'd rather be with Emily—with whom, it seems, I have a lot

more in common than our initial meeting on the boat would have me believe.

"Of course I'm up for it," I tell her.

She nods. "Good. Then the job is still yours, on one condition: we're honest with each other at all times. You don't know which trail we should be on? You tell me. You aren't sure about something? You tell me, and we'll figure it out together. Or at least, we'll try to. Deal?"

She extends her hand, and I look at her for a long moment before I reach out to shake it. I've spent most of the last two years completely alone, and figuring something out together sounds like a damn good change of pace.

"Deal," I say, gripping her hand in mine.

"Okay," she says, giving me a small smile as we shake on it. "Well then, adventure awa—"

But she doesn't finish her sentence. Instead, a look of pure horror crossing her features, she points at something behind me and lets out a terrified, hair-raising scream.

"Ryder!" Emily hisses in a frantic whisper. "Stop screaming."

I close my mouth, realizing that her sudden terror frightened me so much that I let out a shriek of my own.

"I screamed because you screamed," I whisper back, my heart pounding in my chest. "Why did you scream?"

"Turn around," she says, still staring in alarm at something behind me. "Slowly. Don't make any sudden movements."

But the best way to get me to make a sudden movement is

to tell me not to, and I whip around to see what the hell she's pointing at.

"Jesus Christ," Emily mutters, but my heart is beating so loudly that I barely hear her. Because there, not twenty feet in front of me, is a giant fucking moose. And it does *not* look happy.

"Okay," I whisper, motioning for Emily to stay back. "Step one: everybody stay calm."

"What's step two?" she asks, huddling so close to me that her warm breath tickles the back of my neck and sends a tingle down my spine. You'd think it was physically impossible for me to get turned on with a car-sized animal staring me down, but apparently, it is not.

"Step two," I repeat, racking my brain for solutions. "Step two . . . shit, I don't know. Let me think."

The moose, who seems highly uninterested in letting me think, opens its mouth and lets out a bellowing moan so loud it makes my hair stand on end.

"Do you know anything about moose?" Emily asks, grabbing my hand and gripping it so hard that I have to bite my tongue to stop myself from crying out in pain.

"Just what I've seen on *Rocky and Bullwinkle*, and I really don't think that applies to this particular situation."

"Fuck," she whispers, her voice frantic. "Fuckety-fuck-fuck."

"Don't worry," I tell her. "I have a plan. On the count of three, we're gonna stop, drop, and roll."

"That's what you do in a fire, Ryder, not when you're cornered by a wild animal!"

"Well, the idea was that we roll *away*," I grumble.

Emily whimpers as the moose raises its front leg and slams it down hard, snapping a log in half like it's a tiny twig.

"Okay, plan B," I tell her. "We get something red and toss it in the other direction. Do you have a red T-shirt in your pack? A handkerchief, maybe?"

"It's a *moose*, not a fucking cartoon bull," she seethes. "And no, I don't. I look awful in red."

I very much doubt that, but it doesn't matter anyway, because the moose lets out an earth-shattering grunt and takes a step toward us, its massive body so close I could almost reach out and pet it. I close my eyes, trembling as the animal lets out a moan so loud I swear it rattles the trees.

"Oh my God," Emily whispers, "we're going to die here. I'm going to get stomped to death by a moose, and whoever cleans out my apartment is gonna find my entire vibrator collection, and—"

"You have really gotta stop talking about vibrators," I say, forcing myself to open my eyes. "I'm not going to let you die, okay? So on the count of three, you run. Run as far and fast as you can, and don't look back no matter what."

"What about you?" she asks, grabbing a fistful of my T-shirt.

I curl my hands into fists and raise them toward the moose like I'm ready for a schoolyard fight. "I'll stay here and fend him off."

"He'll squash you like a bug!"

"I'll take my chances," I say, adrenaline coursing through me as the moose rears its head back. We wouldn't be face-to-face with a pissed-off animal right now if it weren't for my inability to read a map, and I'm not about to let Emily pay for my mistakes.

"One," I whisper, circling my fists. "Two . . ."

"Ryder!"

"Three!" I yell. "Run!"

But Emily does not run. Instead, she grabs hold of my pack and yanks, dragging me backward. Caught off balance, I slip on the wet leaves and we go tumbling down, down, down, my elbows and knees and chin colliding with the earth and sending shock waves of pain through my body. I'm barrel-rolling down a hill, my skin scraping against jagged rocks, and the world is a blur of pain and motion until I land on wet grass with a dramatic *thump*.

"Ow," Emily moans, and it takes my rattled brain a second to realize that her voice sounds muffled because her face is pressed into my neck. She somehow landed on top of me, her chest against my chest and the top of her head butting up against my chin, and the sensation of her warm body pressed against mine is a welcome distraction from the throbbing, stinging pain racking my limbs.

"I *hate* the outdoors," she says, her lips moving against my skin, and I know I should force myself to sit up, but the feeling of her on top of me is the best thing I've felt in a long time, and so I can't. I won't. I mustn't.

"You were supposed to run," I grumble, wincing as she jams an elbow into my rib.

"I did run. I just brought you with me." She pulls a clump of soggy leaves out of her hair and tosses it aside in disgust. "You can't seriously be annoyed at me for saving your life."

"Excuse me, *I* was saving *your* life," I protest, wiggling my fingers and toes to make sure I'm not paralyzed. "I had everything under control."

She snorts. "Seriously, why are men like this? You all think you can fight off a moose and land a plane with no training and that you would have thrived during the Roman empire. Guess what? You're wrong!"

"Okay, I never claimed that I would thrive during the Roman empire," I correct her. "I have eczema and can't see without my contact lenses."

"But do you think you could land a plane with no training?" she says, using her elbows to push herself up so that she's basically straddling me.

"That depends. Do I have my contacts in? Is there turbulence? Do I have a functional line of communication with air traffic control?"

"Oh my God, you're ridiculous," she says, flinching as she brushes grass and gravel off her arm.

"What's *ridiculous* is presenting a life-or-death scenario with absolutely no context," I argue. "You can't just—"

But I shut up quick, because a sound even more terrifying than the moose's deafening bellow echoes through the forest. It's a prolonged, guttural howl coming from the cluster of mountain ash trees in front of us, and Emily and I both scramble to our feet.

"What was that?" she whispers, her voice tinged with fear. "Was that a wolf?"

"Doesn't sound like a wolf," I say, remembering the haunting howls Caleb and I heard the time he dragged me on a nighttime hike through Yellowstone. The sound we just heard was too mournful, too pained to be a wolf.

"Well, what does it sound like?" she asks, gripping the back of my shirt.

Another tormented cry sounds from the forest, piercing the quiet night with its eerie woe.

"The Blair Witch," I say plainly, whipping off my pack to grab my flashlight.

"Oh my God, what is wrong with you? Don't talk about the Blair Witch when we're lost in the middle of the woods!" Emily hisses.

"I said it *sounded* like the Blair Witch, not that it was," I remind her. "It's probably just the wind."

The sound rings through the forest again, but this time it's more of a harrowing screech than a howl.

"That is not the fucking wind," she whispers, grabbing hold of my arm.

"No," I realize, feeling her fingers tremble against my skin. "It sounds . . . human. Like somebody's hurt, badly."

Emily's humanitarian instinct seems to override her fear, and she grabs my hand and tugs me toward the woods.

"Hurry!" she says, twigs snapping under our boots as I rush to get in front of her. "I might be able to help."

"Wait!" I say when we reach a small stream, a slow trickle of water separating us from the woods on the other side. "Stop. Look."

I point toward a clearing in the distance, a steep bluff just past the trees where a rocky ledge juts out over Lake Superior below. Two men are fighting on the bluff, peppering each other with jabs and kicks and elbows to the stomach as they get closer and closer to the ledge with each swift attack. They're both limping, one gaining the upper hand for a moment and relinquishing it the next, and I strain to make out details, but it's too dark to see much besides a blur of flying fists and tangled limbs.

"What do we do?" Emily asks as one of the men, clearly injured, lets out a cry of pain and wrestles away from the other.

But we don't have a chance to do much of anything. Because the men grapple toward the edge of the cliff, shouting and grunting as each tries to best the other, and we watch in horror as one lets out an animalistic cry and shoves the other with all his might. His victim delivers a chilling, desperate scream and flails his arms for something to cling onto, but it's too late. He sails backward, flying off the edge of the cliff and disappearing into the dark night.

"Ohhhhhmigod," Emily cries, and I reach behind me to cover her mouth with my hand.

"Shhhh!"

"Sorry," she whispers, wrenching my hand away. "But holy shit, did we just witness a *murder*?"

My heart pounds as the remaining figure whips his head toward us, and I freeze, not even breathing until he limps away into the forest.

"Wait here," I tell Emily. "Don't move!"

I sprint toward the cliff, my heart pounding and my arms and legs pumping. When I reach the edge, I glance down toward Lake Superior and my head swims. I've never been good with heights, and I close my eyes for an instant before I force myself to open them and peer down at the waves lapping against the shoreline. All I can see are rocks and gritty sand and—wait. There! A flash of yellow and a bobbing head, someone gasping for air and fighting to keep his head above water. I scan my surroundings for a way down to the lake that doesn't involve jumping off a steep cliff, and I spot a path farther down the bluff with a more gradual incline. I scurry down it on my ass, crab-walking downhill as fast as I can with a sixty-pound pack strapped to my back. Every second matters, and I barely feel the sharp rocks scraping my palms as I hustle toward even ground.

When I reach the shore, rolling my ankle as I take the last few meters too quickly, I sprint across the sand and wade into the lake, gasping as the cold water shocks my system. I reach the struggling man in a few quick strides and groan as I haul him out of the lake, my limbs burning with exertion.

"Here!" Emily cries, ushering us onto the sand, and I scowl at her as I lower the man onto the ground.

"I told you not to move!"

She shrugs. "I didn't listen."

She helps me flip the guy from his stomach to his back, and we gasp when Emily shines my flashlight onto his face. Because the shivering man in front of us is none other than Dr. Killian Sinclair.

NINE

EMILY

"Oh my God," I cry for what must be the twentieth time tonight. "Killian!"

He sputters, hacking up a lungful of Lake Superior, and Ryder scrambles to elevate his head as I look on in shock.

"Killian, are you okay?" I ask, reaching for his wrist so I can check his pulse. "Do you know where you are? Do you know what happened to you?"

He coughs again and opens his eyes, wincing at the brightness of my flashlight.

"Emily?" he asks, blinking up at me in a daze. "Emily, is that you?"

"Yes, I'm here." Satisfied that his pulse is normal, I give him a quick once-over for blood or signs of gross injury. "Can you move your fingers and toes?"

He winces as he wiggles his fingers and nods, pushing himself up to a sitting position with Ryder's help.

"Emily," Killian says again, his accent making my name sound downright musical. "You saved my life."

"Uh, *I* saved your life, actually," my tour guide says. "Emily helped." He clears his throat. "Anyway, minor detail. Glad you're not dead, Sinclair."

"Thanks, sport," Killian says, grimacing as he presses a hand to his rib. "I'm glad I'm not dead, too."

"What the hell happened, man?" Ryder asks, watching as I fish my first aid kit out of my backpack and start bandaging a cut on Killian's leg. "Who was that dude who shoved you off the cliff?"

"Was it Killface?" I ask, glancing over my shoulder warily. "You know, scraggly hair, deep scowl, creepy killer murder eyes?"

"Who's Killface? No." The archaeologist shakes his head, his brown eyes haunted as they look into mine. "It was Sharp."

"Dr. Sharp?" I ask with a gasp. "Your mentor? The super nice guy we met on the ferry?"

Killian clenches his jaw. "Turns out that 'nice guy' is a thieving, cold-blooded psychopath who will stop at nothing to get what he wants. Not even murder."

"I don't understand." Ryder studies Killian in confusion. "Why would a friendly old man in a newsboy cap want to kick your ass and murder you?"

Killian's nostrils flare. "To be clear, he did not kick my arse. We kicked each other's arses." He winces as I apply a compress to a gash on his cheek. "And he did it because I tried to stop him from stealing a precious piece of history and selling it for his own selfish gains."

"What are you talking about?" I ask, wondering if Killian

somehow hit his head when he landed. "What precious piece of history?"

"A jewel," Killian says, his tone reverent. "A rare and precious diamond worth more money than you or I could ever dream of."

"Uh, hold up," Ryder says, lifting a hand for quiet. "Sinclair, are you okay, dude? Because you're telling me that your boss, who, let me repeat, wears a *newsboy cap*, shoved you off a cliff so he could get his hands on some kind of diamond?" He squints at Killian. "Do you have some sort of concussion, maybe? Because this is all sounding very *National Treasure*."

"I assure you that it's very real," Killian says, gritting his teeth as he clambers to his feet and tries to limp toward the woods.

"Where are you going?" I ask, grabbing my bandage roll. "Your body just suffered a major trauma. You need to rest and warm up, and then we need to take you to a ranger station to get help from the authorities."

I tug at my hood, my teeth chattering. The rain has stopped, but the shock of what I just witnessed sends chills through me.

"There's no time to rest!" Killian's gaze darts around the beach as he shivers from the wet cold. "Sharp and his underlings are probably already halfway here on their speedboats to make sure I'm dead and finish me off if I'm not. I need to get out of here, now."

"His *underlings*?" Ryder says, but I shake my head at my tour guide. If Killian's life is really in danger—and seeing as how we just watched Sharp shove him off a cliff, it clearly is—we need to help him first and ask questions later.

"We'll help you," I assure Killian, switching off my flashlight. "We were looking to set up camp for the night anyway. You can camp with us, and we'll help you figure out a plan for the morning."

"We will?" Ryder asks, but Killian ignores him.

"Thank you, Emily," he says, taking my hands in his. "You're saving not only my life, but also the future of maritime archaeology as we know it."

"Tad dramatic," Ryder whispers, but he jogs to catch up to us and slings the archaeologist's arm over his shoulder to help him along.

I loop my arm through Killian's on his other side, and as we shuffle toward higher ground together, step by careful step, I realize that maybe the sign from Dad I was looking for was never going to come in the form of a bird or a butterfly or a sudden, gorgeous rainbow. Maybe it could come in the form of another person, in the form of a bright, brilliant archaeologist who desperately needs my help. Maybe everything that's happened tonight is a sign from my dad that there's still a way to honor him, to feel close to him.

All I have to do is be up for the adventure.

"It all started," Killian says, staring into the fire, "in 1897."

We hiked for an hour before pausing to set up camp for the night, stopping only when Killian was satisfied that we were well out of sight of the coastline. I dressed his wounds while Ryder got the campfire going—an arduous process that involved a stunning amount of curse words and at least one anguished cry of *Why, God, why!*—and cooked a simple dinner of freeze-dried chicken teriyaki over his camp stove. Killian also changed out of his soaking wet clothes and into dry ones he borrowed from Ryder, which is why the Harvard PhD is currently sporting camo hiking pants and an oversized sweatshirt that says 70% OF PEOPLE ARE STUPID, I'M OBVIOUSLY WITH THE OTHER 40% in ugly block letters.

The fire snaps and crackles, and I curl up in my camp chair with my fuzzy blanket over my shoulders and a bowl of steaming chicken on my lap. Ryder, who insisted on setting up his tent and mine so I could rest and eat, sticks a tent pole into the ground and glances at Killian.

"What started in 1897?" he asks.

"The saga of the Evermore diamond," Killian says dramatically, like he's introducing a stage play.

Ryder nods. "Cool. You know, this is very *Are You Afraid of the Dark?*-y."

"Sorry, am I afraid of the what?" Killian asks, sipping from a mug of hot coffee.

"The dark," I explain. "It was a children's show that was on in the nineties. A bunch of kids told scary stories around a campfire."

"Okay, it wasn't just any children's show," Ryder says, using a rubber mallet to hammer a tent stake into the ground. "It was an entire generation's first introduction to horror, and it was a true masterp—"

He's not wrong, but now is hardly the time for a stroll down memory lane.

"I think we should really focus on hearing what Killian has

to say," I interrupt politely. "Since, you know, someone just tried to murder him and all?"

Ryder rolls his eyes but nods at Killian. "Continue."

"It all started in 1897," the archaeologist repeats, "when the SS *Explorer* wrecked just off the coast of Isle Royale."

He'd already told me about the wreck on the ferry, but he recounts some of the details now for Ryder—how the ship was struck by lightning and how the courageous Captain Sebastian Evermore perished in his efforts to save everyone else onboard. How he left behind beautiful, evocative letters to his wife Katherine, who, despite not being the seafaring sort, chartered a ship of her own to look for the *Explorer* after it disappeared.

"Sharp and I led the dive team that found those letters," Killian says, raising his hands toward the fire to warm them. "When we got back to our offices at Harvard, I combed through every passage and was stunned to find references to a jewel. The letters made numerous mentions of a rare blue diamond that Evermore procured for Katherine during his travels, a gemstone the likes of which the modern world had never seen."

"Shiiiiit," Ryder says. "It must be quite the rock."

"Shit indeed, old chap." Killian nods and takes another sip of coffee. "I took the knowledge I gained from the letters to Sharp and the Smithsonian, and they dispatched us and our dive team to return to Isle Royale and search the ship for the stone. When we found it, we were to hand it over to the museum for historical preservation and public display. But as you saw when you stumbled upon us in the woods, Sharp had other plans. He intended to abscond with the diamond and sell it to a private merchant for his own profit."

"Bastard," Ryder whispers.

"Indeed," Killian says. "I'd had suspicions about Sharp's true intentions for months, but I didn't want to believe that my mentor—a man I saw as a father figure, really—could throw away the principles we hold so dear for something as trivial as money."

The hurt evident in Killian's voice breaks my heart, and I can't even begin to imagine the depths of Sharp's betrayal.

"Of course you didn't," I tell him. "How crushing."

Ryder thrusts another tent stake into the ground. "So, how much money are we talking, exactly? What's Evermore's diamond worth?"

"Well, it's not technically Evermore's diamond anymore, is it?" Killian asks. "Since he's perished, you know, God rest his soul."

He bows his head for a moment, holding his own private tribute for the fallen sea captain, and I do the same. After a minute, he takes another sip of his coffee and answers Ryder's question.

"Millions," he says, looking into the fire and watching the flames dance. "Millions upon millions."

"Well then, I get why Sharp wanted it so badly," Ryder says with a shrug. "Principles are cool, but money buys Ferraris."

"Ryder!" I scold, tempted to toss my fork at him.

"What?" he asks. "I didn't say *I'd* shove Sinclair off a cliff to get my hands on millions of dollars. But I can see why someone would. Besides," he adds, swinging the mallet again and coming dangerously close to smashing his thumb with it, "money isn't trivial. Only someone who's never been broke would say that."

"The point is," Killian says, giving my tour guide a rather frustrated look, "that when I confronted Sharp with my suspicions, he turned on me. He attacked me with a trowel, we exchanged blows, and as you saw, he shoved me off the cliff to what he hoped would be my death. What would have been my death had you not saved me, Emily." He extends an arm out to take my hand and presses a kiss to my fingers.

"No biggie," I say, blushing as his lips touch my skin.

"Emily *and Ryder*, you mean," Ryder says, watching Killian press his lips to my hand with a look of pure distaste.

"Sure thing, sport." Killian adjusts his glasses, wincing at the cut near his temple. "Anyway, I need to get back to the *Explorer* first thing tomorrow. If I leave before dawn, I should get there in time—"

"You want to go back to the *Explorer*?" I ask, stunned. "Where Sharp is? No. You need to get to a ranger station and call for help. That man tried to kill you! He's incredibly dangerous!"

Killian shakes his head. "If the authorities get involved, they'll interfere with the dive, and the Evermore diamond could be lost forever. That's assuming, of course, that Sharp hasn't already paid them off, which is not a risk I'm willing to take." He reaches into the pocket of the tweed coat he laid out to dry and removes a square of paper, unfolding it to reveal a map of Isle Royale.

I lean forward to look at it, the fire warming my face.

"We're here," Killian says, pointing to a spot on the north-western side of the island, "but I need to be here." He slides his finger eastward, tapping a marked X just off the northern coast. "It's a day's travel on foot. If you're willing to spare me some food and water for the journey, Emily, you'll be helping me save the Evermore."

"Emily *and Ryder*," Ryder says again, looking like he'd very much relish the chance to smack Killian with the rubber mallet.

But I'm too busy staring at the map, butterflies swirling in my stomach as I realize that Killian's ship is only a short distance from the route Dad had planned to take across the island. This can't just be pure coincidence, can it? I mean, I'm as science-minded as anyone, but the fact that Ryder and I are headed—or were headed, before we got lost—in the same direction where Killian needs to go is downright uncanny. Besides, we're in the perfect position to help each other out. Killian has a legible map, which we desperately need, and we can offer him food, water, and company as he races to the *Explorer* to stop Sharp from stealing the diamond.

"We'll go with you," I volunteer, my heart thumping. "We'll help get you to the ship. We're going that way anyway."

Ryder peeks at the map. "How is this not ruined from falling into the lake?"

Killian laughs like the question is a joke. "It's waterproof, sport. Only a fool goes to an island without a waterproof map."

I grab the mallet from Ryder's hand wordlessly, tucking it under my camp chair lest he get any violent ideas.

"Hey, Emily," Ryder says, not taking his eyes off Killian, "can you help me with something for a second? In there?"

He points to my tent, which is upright and tethered but clearly set up on uneven ground. Oh well. He did a pretty decent job, all things considered.

"I need help, uh, organizing all our weapons," he says in a ridiculous stage whisper. "You know, the guns and the knives and extra-large canisters of bear spray."

Trying not to roll my eyes at his complete lack of subtlety, I give Killian a reassuring smile and follow Ryder to the tent.

"What is this about?" I ask once we're inside. "We don't have any weapons."

"Shhh," he says, putting a finger to his lips. "We don't need Sinclair to know that."

To my surprise, it's actually pretty cozy inside the tent. Ryder's set up my sleeping pad and bag and placed my battery-operated lantern next to it, along with my toiletry kit and the roll of glow-in-the-dark toilet paper.

"Anyway, what do you think this secret meeting is about?" he asks, motioning wildly toward the campfire. I don't bother pointing out that there's nothing secretive about it. "Other than the fact that you just volunteered us to escort a total stranger to the site of a high-stakes jewel dispute!"

I'm trying to focus on what he's saying, because his concerns are perfectly legitimate, but it's made difficult by the fact that we're enclosed in a space so tiny that he can barely sit up without his head brushing against the top of the tent. The lantern casts a warm glow on Ryder's face, and he smells of pine needles and campfire, and honestly, sitting in this tent with him is the coziest I've been in a long, long time. It's even cozier than my Monday night routine of lighting floating tea candles in the bathtub, turning on some Norah Jones, and soaking all my troubles away until my skin wrinkles. In fact, the only way the Monday night routine could hold a candle to this—no pun intended—is if I wasn't in the bathtub alone.

"Edwards?" Ryder asks. "Are you listening?"

"Yes," I say, working hard not to remember how warm and sturdy his body felt underneath mine when I landed on him after our downhill crash. After all, the fact that my body, given the choice, would have melded itself to Ryder's strong frame when I laid on top of him probably has little to do with him and everything to do with the dry spell Jason and I went through before our eventual breakup. Of course I responded to the feel of his touch; the last time a man touched me was two months ago, and it was an elderly patient in the ER who threw up in my hair.

"I'm all ears," I tell Ryder, pushing thoughts of his warm chest out of my mind. "What were you saying, again?"

He rolls his eyes. "I'm *saying* that I don't think it's a good idea for us to partner up with Sinclair. I mean, he's a stranger who you've known for all of one day."

"*You're* a stranger I've known for all of one day," I tell him. "And I partnered up with you."

"Exactly my point!" Ryder says. "Did you forget that we were almost just impaled by a moose?"

I more distinctly remember the sight of his back in front of me, guarding me from danger, and the immensely stupid but also hotly heroic way he tried to sacrifice himself to the moose.

"Anyway," he continues, "don't you think Sinclair is a little bit, I don't know, off?"

I shrug. It's true that Killian's mannerisms are different than Ryder's—he, I imagine, has never said *surf's up* in his life, but then again, neither have I. Besides, Killian made me feel comfortable and admired on the ferry, and I appreciate his steadfast devotion to doing the right thing even in the face of danger.

"I don't know," I tell Ryder. "I mean, wouldn't you feel a little off if your mentor shoved you off a cliff? Besides, Killian's an academic. Academics are a little quirky, you know?"

Ryder shakes his head. "It's not that. It's . . . the guy wears a tweed coat, Edwards! Willingly. That's super shady in my book. And he says he's an archaeologist, but I don't think that's even a real job. It's a job people have in movies, like pumpkin farmer or professional Christmas tree stylist."

"Where exactly do you think pumpkins come from?" I ask, puzzled. "And of course archaeology is a real job. It's the noble science of preserving history!"

"If you say so," he grumbles. "But can we talk about the fact he has the name of a Bond villain?"

I roll my eyes. "Killian Sinclair is a perfectly nice name, *Ryder Fleet*."

He raises an eyebrow at me. "What's that supposed to mean?"

"It means," I explain, "that your name sounds like the big-man-on-campus character in any nineties teen drama."

He smiles like I've paid him a huge compliment. "Thank you."

"Listen," I tell him, my exhaustion mounting, "we have to help Killian. *I* have to help Killian."

Ryder frowns. "Because of the diamond?"

"No." I shake my head, trying to figure out a way to explain my thoughts to Ryder without sounding completely unhinged. "Because of my dad."

I tug the sleeves of my sweatshirt over my hands and wrap my arms around myself. "Look, my dad loved adventure. And he gave up a whole life of it to take care of me and my sister. Not just because he was a single dad after my mom died, but because he was *my* dad." I blink at the lantern, remembering the journals I'd found in his office after he died, how I'd opened them hoping to find something to comfort me and found a different truth instead.

"My dad wanted to travel and climb mountains and see the world, but all I wanted to do was stay home. He was brave, but I was terrified of everything. I still am." I look everywhere but at Ryder, embarrassed to admit to a man fearless enough to jump onto a moving boat that I'm afraid of the whole damn world.

"I don't ride roller coasters or drive over the speed limit or jaywalk even when the street looks empty," I explain. "Because I know how quickly bad things can happen. One second you're a happily married teacher with two little girls, and the next you're sitting in a sterile doctor's office getting diagnosed with invasive breast cancer. One second you're a newspaper editor nearing retirement, finally free to chase adventure, and the next you're coding on the floor of a secondhand bookstore."

I swallow, wishing away the tears burning my eyes.

"One second you think you have all the time in the world to go backpacking with the guy who raised you," I tell him, "and the next you're tucking his urn inside your suitcase."

"Emily," Ryder says, but I shake my head. This is too important.

"My dad asked me to go to Isle Royale with him three times, and the first two times I said no. Because I was scared of the idea of going to a remote island where there's no hospital and no 911. The third time he asked, I finally agreed because I knew it was important to him. But then he died. I didn't go with him because I was scared of bad things happening, but then the worst thing happened anyway. I missed the chance to go on this trip with him because I was too much of a coward to take it, and since he died, I've been looking for a way to make things right."

I sniffle and point toward where Killian sits by the campfire. "That's my way to make things right. Dad would have jumped at the chance to do something as exciting as help save a priceless diamond from falling into the wrong hands. I have to do this for him." I brush my eyes with the back of my sleeve. "Maybe this is the sign I've been waiting for. A chance to be part of a great adventure, to show my dad that I really am his daughter through and through."

I don't speak the other thought that's burrowed its way into my head and heart: that if I can help Killian save the Evermore, I'll be able to let go of some of the guilt I carry around inside me. I'll be able to make meaning out of my bad choices, make my initial rejections of Dad's invitation seem less like an act of cowardice and more like clear evidence that some things happen for a reason. I'll be able to believe that Dad sent me this chance as a sign that he loves and forgives me, that he's still out there somewhere having an endless grand adventure.

"You don't have to help me," I tell Ryder, still avoiding his gaze. "I know you didn't sign up for this."

"Emily." His voice is soft, tender, bearing none of the bluntness you'd expect from a man who probably owns at least one garment of clothing with the words PAIN IS WEAKNESS LEAVING THE BODY on it.

"Emily," Ryder says, "look at me."

He reaches forward to take my hand, and so I do look at him—at this man with impossibly strong hands and ridiculous cheekbones and a reckless streak a mile wide but also, I suspect, a heart that's bigger than he knows what to do with.

"I'm not going anywhere without you," he says. "We're in this together, like it or not." He leans closer to me, so close that I could count the lines on his forehead and reach out and touch them if I wanted. "But Edwards?"

"Yes?" I say, a shiver running through me.

"Don't ask me to trust a man who doesn't carry his own pack."

TEN

RYDER

Killian Sinclair will not shut the fuck up. From the moment we packed up our campsite well before dawn and hit the trail, he's tried to impress Emily with infinite mentions of Harvard this and Harvard that and hey, did she know that if she were to visit him at Harvard, he could show her around the Harvard campus and buy her a Harvard scarf and give her a tour of the Harvard faculty offices? It's all I can do not to roll my eyes every time he mentions the Ivy League, because if I did, I'd probably go cross-eyed.

"I did like the Harvard episode of *Gilmore Girls*," Emily says politely, which gives him the burst of energy he needs to launch into a mind-numbingly boring description of the history of the school's mascot, which is apparently a pilgrim, but also sort of a color.

"And that's how the Crimson came to be," he says, concluding his tedious story. When he runs out of Harvard topics, he launches into a long monologue about the fascinating flora and fauna one can find on Isle Royale—*fascinating flora and fauna* being his words, not mine.

As we pass a small section of shoreline covered in black rocks, I glance at the map Sinclair lent me to double-check that we're headed the right way. Emily follows along behind me with the compass—which apparently does work, if you're holding it right side up, and I slow my pace until she's even with me.

"Hey," I say, falling into step beside her. "How are you? Did you sleep okay?"

I did not sleep okay, considering that I shared my tent with Sinclair, who snores like a freaking bulldozer, but I don't mention that. I also don't mention that I slept with practically one eye open, ready to defend her from another moose or, God forbid, Killface.

"I tossed and turned a lot, actually," Emily says, tucking a loose curl behind her ear. "Kept having nightmares of—"

"Now, take lichen, for example," Sinclair says, practically elbowing me out of the way to walk next to Emily again. "It can appear green, so people mistake it for moss. But actually, lichen has leaves and a more leatherlike texture."

I let out a disgruntled noise and fight the urge to flick him in the back of the head.

Sinclair raises an eyebrow at me. "You alright back there, sport?"

"Sure thing, *chief*," I say tightly. "I was just remembering all the times I saw lichen and thought, hey, that's moss! So embarrassing."

Emily shoots me a look, and I roll my eyes as Sinclair

launches into a long-winded explanation of the life cycle of the American horsefly. I would rather sit through an entire weekend of old *Touched by an Angel* episodes with Lulu than spend another second listening to this guy try to flirt with Emily.

"When you come visit me in Boston," he says, pressing a hand to the small of her back, "I'll take you to this great Turkish restaurant in Back Bay. I know the chef personally, and—"

Nope. I get that I don't have a chance in hell with Emily, since she dates anesthesiologists and made a disgusted expression when she said her ex was dating a professional dog walker—something I take real issue with, as a paid dog sitter myself—but I don't have to listen to their budding romance with a smile plastered on my face. Instead, I fish a portable Discman CD player out of my pack, slip headphones over my ears, and press play, letting the sweet, sweet, tones of early 2000s pop drown out Sinclair's endless bullshit.

To anyone else, the Discman probably seems as useless in the wilderness as Emily's glow-in-the-dark toilet paper. And to be fair, it is. But I didn't bring the clunky vintage device to Isle Royale for practical reasons. I packed it because Caleb never hiked without it, and bringing it on the trail with me felt like bringing along a small piece of my brother. He saved up from his paper route to buy it when he was a kid and then spent an entire summer listening to a *Now That's What I Call Music!* album on repeat. Wherever he went, the Discman and Shakira's non-lying hips went with him, and even as an adult, he considered it an essential piece of backpacking gear. For one thing, he explained, the Discman ran on batteries and didn't require charging, and for another, there was something satisfying about bringing a piece of his childhood on the trail with him.

When Caleb died, Tara wanted me to have it, and so I tucked the Discman safely inside the bottom drawer of my nightstand. I was scared to use it, certain that I would some-how rob it of its specialness—its Caleb-ness—by putting my dirty little paws on it. But a year after he died, on what would have been his thirty-fifth birthday, I got into an argument with Hannah and missed my brother so much I thought it might kill me. Desperate for a way to feel closer to him, I drank too much vodka, slipped on his old headphones, and cried my eyes out while I jammed to a compilation album of 2003's top hits. That night taught me three things: 1) I should never buy vodka again, 2) listening to Caleb's Discman succeeded in making me feel less alone, and 3) Black Eyed Peas' "Where Is the Love?" still slaps. Hard.

We stop for a pee break, each of us finding a private spot to handle our business, and when I return to the trail to wait for Sinclair and Emily—actually, just for Emily, because I'm seriously hoping Sinclair gets picked off by a wolf—I suddenly feel the harsh tug of someone ripping the headphones off my ears. Startled, I turn around to find Sinclair watching me with an amused expression, Emily's Hydro Flask in one hand and my headphones in the other.

"What the fuck, man," I seethe, resisting the instinct to kick him in the nuts. "What are you doing?"

"Sorry, old chap," he says, giving me a cold smile. "I called your name a few times, but you didn't hear me."

"What do you want?" I hit pause on the Discman, my blood pressure rising. If he calls me an old chap one more time, I'm going to lose my shit. I am not his chap, and I am not old. I'm a strapping young man who doesn't need an assistant named Taggart to lug my gear around, and my patience is running out fast.

"Just wanted a quick look at your ancient relic there." He points at the Discman, then reaches forward and yanks it from my hands before I can stop him.

He holds the CD player at eye level, marveling at it like it's the freaking Evermore diamond.

"Forget the artifact collection we've got at Harvard, because *this* is a true fossil," he says, letting out a whistle as he opens the Discman and peeks at the CD inside.

"Careful," I warn him, gritting my teeth.

"You don't mind if I have a listen, do you?" Not bothering to wait for an answer, Sinclair plugs the headphones back into the player and slips them over his ears. He presses a button on the Discman, listens for a moment, and bursts into laughter.

"I'm sure you're full of surprises, Fleet, but I never pegged you for a Christina Aguilera fan," he says, grinning.

"It's a mix CD," I say tightly. "It was my . . . you know what? Forget it. It's none of your damn business. Just give it back."

"I didn't mean to cause any offense, sport," Sinclair says, raising his hands innocently.

"Don't call me sport."

His eyes narrow into thin slits. "What would you prefer, then? Dude? Man? Buddy?"

"Silence," I say dryly. "I would prefer silence."

He lets out a humorless laugh. "Look, I get that you're a bit peeved. It's sweet, your little crush on Emily, and I'm sorry if I'm stepping on any toes here—"

"You're not stepping on any toes," I interrupt, hating that he's noticed my affection for Emily. "You are, however, touching my personal property, and I'd like you to give it back now."

"Aw, come on. I see the way you look at her, sport," Sinclair says, bobbing his head along to the music. "And I'm sorry to tell you, I don't think you're her type. She told me herself on the ferry. A *himbo*, I believe she called you."

I do my best not to let his words sting, but they do, and so I try not to let my hurt show on my face. I know I'm not Emily's usual type, and I know I'm not a Harvard archaeologist with a hard-on for truth and academic integrity, but it doesn't feel great to have that thrown in my face. And it really doesn't feel great to know that the intelligent, beautiful woman I'm traveling with thinks I'm the male version of a brainless bimbo.

Sinclair presses a button on the Discman, and his smile widens after a moment. "Nickelback? Really, Fleet?" He shakes his head. "I must say, your taste in women is vastly superior to your taste in music."

"Give it back," I tell him, my blood boiling.

"Oh, I wasn't trying to hurt your feelings," Sinclair says, his tone unnervingly pleasant. "I just think it's helpful, in matters such as these, to face reality before you let your imagination get carried away. She's never going to see you the way you see her. This song's a banger, by the way."

He points to the headphones, grinning, and something about watching this smarmy jackass mocking Caleb's music makes me want to burn the whole world down. It's one thing to know in my head that Emily doesn't go for ex–long jumpers who never qualified for an honors class in their life, but it's another thing to hear Sinclair say it out loud. The idea of the two of them laughing about me together makes my skin itch, and worse than that, it hurts. I don't give a shit what Sinclair thinks, but the thought of Emily seeing me as a himbo, as nothing more than a stupid doofus in a Fleet Adventures T-shirt, makes my heart sink.

And the worst part is that she's right.

"I don't look at Emily any way," I lie, my tone even. "I look at her the way I look at you, or that tree over there." I point to one of the countless balsam fir trees crowding the trail, wishing I'd never answered Tara's phone call. "Now give me back my goddamn Discman."

I reach for the headphones as Sinclair darts sideways, and my stomach drops at the thought of something happening to the Discman. Of it falling out of Sinclair's hands and breaking, costing me yet another piece of my brother.

"Give it back, please," I say tightly, "or I swear to God, I'll—"

"Ryder," Emily says, and I look behind me to see her watching us with her arms crossed over her chest. "What's going on?"

Sinclair gives her a broad smile. "I was just checking out Fleet's ancient music player here. Thanks for the listen, sport." He removes the headphones and hands them and the

Discman back to me, then extends a hand toward Emily. "Shall we?"

She watches as I loop the headphone cord around the back of my neck, and I wonder how much of our conversation she heard. The expression on her face is closed, unreadable, and I don't get the chance to say anything to her because she turns away from me and toward Sinclair, placing her hand in his.

"Let's go."

We near the sunken remnants of the SS *Explorer* just after nightfall, turning off our flashlights when the Smithsonian base camp comes into view. Tents and string lights dot the shoreline, and the tilted railing of Captain Evermore's ship peeks out of the water. Pale moonlight shines overhead, giving the scene a haunting glow, and I shiver at the chilly night air. The sooner Emily and I get away from this aquatic graveyard and back onto her planned route, the better.

"Hide," Sinclair instructs when we reach the wreck, and we duck behind a row of trees at the edge of the woods, Emily and I watching as he whips out his binoculars and inhales hard.

"Sharp, you thieving bastard!" he whispers, adjusting the lens as I peer through the darkness to try to see what's happening. The lights strung up around the base camp provide just enough visibility for me to make out people in wet suits gathered near the shoreline.

"Well, we made it in time," Sinclair says, lowering his binoculars. "Sharp's still here, which means the Evermore must be, too." He nods at me and Emily. "Thank you again for saving me. The world of maritime archaeology will forever be in your debt."

"It was our pleasure," Emily says, blushing, and as much as Sinclair annoys me, I find myself pretty pleased at the thought that we played a part in stopping a jewel thief. After all, it'll make a good story to tell my grandkids someday, and Caleb would have loved it.

"You gonna be okay from here?" I ask Sinclair.

I can't stand the guy, but he is about to face his murderous mentor, and thinking he's a gigantic asshat doesn't mean I want him to get hurt.

"I will be," he assures me. "Thank you, Ryder Fleet."

The use of my full name seems a tad dramatic, but then again, so is this entire situation, and I clasp him on the back when he shakes my hand.

"Good luck, man," I tell him. And good riddance.

"Emily," Sinclair says, turning toward her, "my dearest Emily. Meeting you has been like finding a jewel even more precious than the Evermore."

It's such a hokey statement that I can't help but snort, and I clear my throat when both Emily and Sinclair glance at me.

"Sorry," I whisper. "Swallowed a bug."

"I'll write to you," he promises Emily, taking both her hands in his. "And I look forward to the bright, beautiful day when I get to see you again." He releases her hands and presses his lips to hers, sighing dramatically, and I grimace and look away. It's one thing to know she's never going to fall for me, but it's another thing entirely to watch her fall for someone else in real time.

"You should both leave now," Sinclair says once he releases her. "This is a highly dangerous situation, and I don't know what Sharp might do if he sees you. Farewell, friends!" he calls, blowing Emily a kiss as he hops out from behind the tree and runs toward the base camp. "Godspeed!"

"Okay, well, that was a fun little adventure," I tell Emily once Sinclair runs off. "Now let's get the hell out of here."

She shakes her head and pulls her own set of binoculars from her pack. "No way. We can't leave until we know he's safe."

"He told us to head out, Edwards," I argue. "He said it was highly dangerous!"

"Well, he's not my boss, and neither are you," she says, holding her binoculars up to her face. "I'm staying."

Sighing, I shrug off my pack and retrieve my own set of binoculars, watching through them as Sinclair runs toward the ship like a bat out of hell.

"Guess I won't be getting my sweatshirt back, then," I mutter.

Emily pokes me in the arm and shushes me, and I get goose bumps at her touch. How ridiculous am I that I'm practically melting when she pokes me like we're two feuding children at recess, and Sinclair got to freaking *kiss* her—

"There's Dr. Sharp," she says, narrating the events like she's a color commentator on ESPN. "He sees Killian, and ooooh, he looks *angry*."

I peek through my binoculars, watching as an incensed-looking Dr. Sharp points at Sinclair and yells to his colleagues for help.

"What a jerk," Emily says as we watch the scene unfold. "I bet Killian's going to give him a real firm talking-to about the importance of professional integrity."

But Sinclair, who's sprinting toward his mentor like he wants to throttle him dead, does not give the older man a talking-to. Instead, he reaches into his satchel and pulls out a pistol, brandishing it like a gun-slinging cowboy.

"Uh, what the fuck," Emily says, staring at the scene with her mouth agape. "Did you know Killian had a gun?!"

"No, Edwards," I say tightly, not tearing my gaze away from the action. "I was not aware that the strange man you invited to join our little tour group had a fucking gun."

"Give me the Evermore, Sharp!" Sinclair cries, waving his weapon at his colleague. "Don't make me shoot you!"

"Um, do you think this is some kind of hidden camera show?" I whisper, my heart pounding. "Like *What Would You Do?* or that *Jury Duty* show where everyone was an actor except the one guy Ronald?"

Emily doesn't respond, and we watch as Dr. Sharp raises his hands and takes a step back from Sinclair.

"You don't frighten me," the mentor says, but his trembling voice betrays him.

"Good," says Sinclair. "Because I don't want you to be frightened. I want you to give me the diamond."

The older man reaches into the pocket of his jacket and removes a small bag, holding it up in front of him.

"Yes, good," Sinclair says, motioning for Sharp to hand him the bag. "Give it to me."

Sharp holds the bag out toward Sinclair, and I hold my

breath as he reaches for it. But Dr. Sharp pulls the bag away at the last second, eliciting a cry of fury from the Irishman.

"Never!" Sharp says, emptying the contents of the bag into the palm of his hand. He casts the empty bag aside and holds up a shimmering object, closing his fingers around it.

"I'll die before I let the Evermore fall into your treasonous hands, Sinclair!" Sharp declares.

"That can be arranged," Sinclair says calmly. He lunges at Sharp, who turns and hurls the jewel into Lake Superior.

"Wait, *Killian's* treasonous hands?" Emily asks, gripping her binoculars so tightly her knuckles turn white. "Oh my God, Ryder, is Killian the bad guy?"

As if to answer, Sinclair raises his gun and fires two shots into the older man's back.

Emily collapses onto her knees, letting out an anguished cry, and I'm frozen in place as I watch Dr. Sharp fall to the ground. My ears ring with the echo of the gunshot and Emily's scream, and I clench my jaw to stop myself from retching.

When she cries out again, I reach out to grab her and pull her toward me, my chest muffling the sound.

"Shh," I whisper, my hands trembling as I wrap my arms tighter around her.

"Shit, fuck, mother*fucker*," Emily whispers, her voice shaking. "Killian's the bad guy. We helped the *bad guy,* Ryder!"

I try to respond, but my mouth goes dry and my throat burns with the threat of bile. I couldn't stand Sinclair, but I'd pegged him as a pompous jerk, not an unhinged murderer, and the realization leaves me sickened.

Emily pushes against me and scrambles to scoop her

binoculars off the ground, her chest heaving as she peers into them. "Why is no one helping Sharp?" she whispers. "He's going to bleed out!"

I watch in silent horror as not one of the men who witnessed the shooting makes a move to aid Sharp. Instead, Sinclair's colleagues rush toward Lake Superior, frantically searching for the gemstone.

"Find the diamond!" Sinclair shouts at the men furiously. "Hurry!"

I've never claimed to be the brightest crayon in the box, but it's clear to me that the rest of the dive team pays no attention to poor Dr. Sharp because they're part of Sinclair's twisted scheme.

"They're in on it," I tell Emily, my hands so slippery with sweat that my binoculars slide right out of them. "They're all in on it. Oh my God, it's a conspiracy!"

"Even *Taggart*?" she asks, clutching my arm. "Holy shit, this is bad. This is so bad! We helped Killian so that he could turn around and kill Sharp!" Gasping, she clasps a hand over her mouth. "Do you realize what this means? I've been kissed by a murderer!"

"I really don't see how that's a priority right now," I mutter, gripping my binoculars so tightly my fingers ache. "We need to get out of here. Quickly."

But Emily, still reeling from the shock of what we just saw, doesn't seem to hear me.

"I've aided and abetted in a homicide," she whispers, her voice bearing the strained note of someone who's toeing the line of a nervous breakdown. "I'm an unwitting accomplice to a crime. I'm—"

"Emily!" I interrupt, placing my hands on her shoulders to snap her out of her spiral. "The only thing you aided and abetted was Sinclair's smug attitude. And hey, maybe Sharp will pull through somehow, okay? But we gotta get out of here—"

Her head snaps up. "You're right."

"Now let's make a break for the woods—"

She shakes her head as she tears through her pack and pulls out her first aid kit. "No, I mean, you're right about Sharp pulling through. He might have a chance if we help him."

But I've seen enough action movies to know that getting shot twice at point blank range doesn't end well, and I grip her hand as she starts to get up.

"Wait!" I insist. "There's an armed, crazy man up there, and I bet all his buddies are armed and crazy, too. I know you want to help, but—"

"There's no but," she says, shrugging me off. "I'm going. I won't ask you to come with me."

"For fuck's sake," I mutter as she jumps out from behind the trees and rushes toward the fallen archaeologist. "Emily, stop!"

But she doesn't stop. Instead, she picks up speed, and I curse the surge of protectiveness that washes over me as she nears the beach. If I had a lick of sense or self-preservation, I'd haul ass in the opposite direction and leave her to her fate. But I could never bring myself to do that. Because if a woman who's frightened of *jaywalking* can set aside her own fear to try to help a wounded man, the least I can do is shove mine aside to guard her.

My limbs leaden with terror, I grunt as I clamber to my feet and run after Emily. I catch up to her just as she kneels beside Dr. Sharp, her jaw clenched as she slips on gloves and places three fingers on his wrist in search of a pulse. There's blood everywhere, turning the rocky sand under our feet scarlet, and my head swims as I watch Emily press her hands to the wound on his back.

"He's bleeding out," she mutters, gritting her teeth as she presses harder.

Sharp makes a pained, muffled sound, murmuring something unintelligible.

I have to do something to help, but I have none of Emily's skill, and so I just do my best to comfort the injured archaeologist.

"You're gonna be okay," I tell Sharp, even though the hollow look on Emily's face tells me differently. "You're in excellent hands. Emily's a doctor, see, and she's going to save—"

"Jacket," Sharp mutters, the words coming out wheezy and strained. "Pocket. Jacket."

"Huh?" I ask, watching as Emily reaches for more compresses.

"Jacket," he repeats, the word slurred.

"Jacket. Your jacket," I repeat, finally understanding. "Your jacket pocket. Okay." My hands shaking, I ease him gently off the ground, just enough to reach inside his jacket. My fingers search for a pocket and find one on his left side, and I pull out a leather notebook and—holy shit, a fucking diamond. There's a fucking *diamond* in my hand.

"Protect it," Sharp grunts, wheezing. "At all costs."

"Emily," I realize, "he pretended to throw it! He pretended to throw the Evermore, but it's here, in my hand—"

"Shit," she hisses, her gloves soaked with blood as she checks Sharp's pulse again.

"What can we do?" I ask frantically. "What do I do?"

She shakes her head, making it clear that there's nothing left to do, and I stare at Sharp's body in disbelief.

"Emily!" an accented voice calls, and I glance up to see Sinclair striding toward us. He looks from her to me to the glittering gem in my palm, and I slip the notebook into my pocket and close my fist around the diamond.

"Emily, come here, darling," Sinclair calls, beckoning to her like he didn't just murder someone in cold blood. "Everything's alright, there's just been a slight misunderstanding—"

"Misunderstand this, asshole!" she cries, flinging her binoculars at his head and missing by a mile.

I admire her courage, if not so much her hand-eye coordination, and I rise to my feet as Sinclair approaches.

"Emily," he says, not breaking his stride, "come on, there's no need for that. We were getting along so well." His gaze shifts toward me. "You're a blathering idiot, but that's no reason for anyone else to get hurt. Hand me the diamond, Fleet, and you'll both be free to go."

"He doesn't have it," Emily lies. "Sharp threw it into the lake."

Sinclair shakes his head and makes a *tsk-tsk* sound like he's the villain from one of Lulu's melodramatic Lifetime movies. "You're not a good liar, darling."

His use of *darling* makes my skin crawl, and I place a protective arm in front of Emily.

"Yeah, well, you're not a very good person!" she retorts, jutting her chin out like she really told him off. "You're actually a very bad one!"

Sinclair grabs his chest. "Ouch. That hurt my feelings. How ever will I recover?" He laughs and raises his gun to point it at us, and something wild and animalistic washes over me when I see the look of pure terror that crosses Emily's features.

I glance around desperately for anything I can use as a weapon, but there's nothing around us but sand and blood and—wait. The Discman. Caleb's Discman is clipped to my waistband, and while the thought of using my brother's beloved CD player as a weapon makes my stomach twist, I'm running out of options, fast.

"Come on now, darling," Sinclair says, squinting at Emily. "Don't do anything rash. You're too intelligent for that."

"Yeah, well, I'm not!" I yell, hurling the Discman at Sinclair's head with all my might. My aim is much better than Emily's, and he lets out a yelp of pain when it smacks him right in the forehead.

"Run!" I tell Emily, grabbing her hand and pulling her to her feet. "Run!"

This time, she listens. She sprints toward the woods with me close behind her, both of us covering our heads as bullets whiz past.

"Into the woods! Run!" I tell her, my voice trembling as we sprint with everything we have. I can hear Sinclair screaming for his men to follow us, and I can hear my own ragged breathing and Emily's frightened whimper as the madman fires again. But I hear something else, too: Caleb from a memory, the tinny sound of his voice as he helped me train for the hundred-meter dash championships in high school. "Just run, Ry," he'd yell, holding his stopwatch up as I hurtled down the track. "Don't look back, don't think, just run!"

So I don't look back, and I don't think. I just run.

ELEVEN

EMILY

I should have done more cardio. I also should have never left Ohio, but as Ryder and I sprint through the woods, leaping over rocks and bushes in a desperate attempt to escape Killian's men, the burning ache in my chest and thighs makes me regret every single day I ever skipped the gym.

So, just ninety percent of my adult life.

"Zigzag formation, Edwards!" Ryder shouts, weaving a nonlinear path through the trees that leaves me dizzy and struggling to keep up. "ZIGZAG!"

I'm pretty sure no one has ever screamed the word *zigzag* with such intensity in all of human history, but it's not like I have a better tactic, and so I duck and weave through the trees, too, doing my best to keep pace with my tour guide.

"East! They're headed east!" one of Killian's guys calls out behind us, the sound of his voice growing fainter as we get deeper and deeper into the woods.

"Are we?" I ask Ryder, gasping for air as we scramble over a car-sized rock. "Going east?"

"Hell if I know," he grunts, gripping my hand to pull me along behind him. "Just run!"

So run we do. We run and we run and we zig and we zag, and just when I think my legs are going to call it a day and melt off my body, Ryder stops suddenly, sending me crashing into his back with a dramatic thud.

"Oof," I sputter, feeling like I just collided with a cement wall. "Can I get a warning next time?"

"Shh," he whispers, crouching to his feet and motioning for me to do the same. It's a difficult feat, considering that my calves are on fire, but I hurry to mimic him.

Under there, Ryder mouths, pointing to a fallen tree just in front of him. Its cigar-brown bark is splintered and charred, and whatever lightning bolt struck it left the trunk just high enough off the ground to let a desperate someone—or two desperate someones—seek shelter underneath its rotting branches.

It looks like a poison ivy paradise, but beggars can't be choosers, and so I duck underneath the tree quickly, crouching beneath its boughs. Ryder squeezes in after me, cursing when he hits his head on the trunk, and we lie there for a moment, both trying to catch our breath and make sense of what the hell just happened.

"Good call with running in a zigzag formation," I whisper finally, my breathing still ragged. "Where'd you learn to do that?"

"*Grand Theft Auto*," he says simply, wiping sweat off his brow. "And elementary school dodgeball."

It says a lot about my distaste for sports that even now, when I just witnessed a murder and had to run for my life, the mere thought of gym class still manages to fill me with dread.

"Huh," I say. "I hated dodgeball. I was slow and uncoordinated, and nobody ever wanted me on their team."

Ryder pokes the trunk above us gingerly, testing its sturdiness. "Yeah, well, it's your lucky day, Edwards. I was always picked first."

Confident that the tree isn't going to collapse with us underneath it, he quickly reties a lace on his boot and studies me like he's waiting for something.

"So," he whispers, "what's your plan?"

"My plan?" I ask, my eyes widening in disbelief. "I don't have a plan. I thought you did. You were the one telling me where to go and screaming about zigzags."

"That wasn't a plan, that was a Hail Mary," he whispers tightly.

"Well, we need a plan, Ryder!" I whisper-screech, the shock of Sharp's death robbing me of the ability to think of one myself. "We can't escape Killian's henchmen and get off this island without a plan!"

"I know we need a plan! But I'm struggling to come up with one, considering I had no idea that *henchmen* existed outside of *Indiana Jones* movies!"

I don't have an argument for that, and so I close my eyes and try to come up with a strategy of my own. Unfortunately, my mind is overrun with the memory of Sharp's desperate, wheezy gaps, and I find myself wishing, now more than ever before, that Dad was here with me. He'd know what to do. And if he didn't, well, he'd help me believe that we could figure it out together.

"Hey," Ryder whispers, drawing me out of my reverie. "Are you okay? Are you cold?" He motions toward my hands, which are trembling so badly they couldn't hold a scalpel.

"No," I say, realizing that I'm still wearing the bloodstained gloves I used for Dr. Sharp. I stare at the crimson-splattered latex, trying not to remember the sight of him falling to the ground. "I mean, yes. I mean . . ."

I will my fingers to stop shaking, to become useful again, but it's no use.

"I should take these gloves off," I say, uncertain if I'm talking to Ryder or myself. "We should save them as evidence."

My voice sounds hollow, distant, and I'm trying to tell myself that they're just gloves, it's just blood, when Ryder reaches into my pack, puts on a fresh pair himself, and uses them to peel the gloves off my hands. Then, after storing them in a zippered compartment of his own pack, he slides his gloves off and wraps his hands around mine. The warmth and pressure of his touch relax my clenched fingers, and I take a deep breath as the trembling eases.

"Thank you," I whisper.

Ryder nods, and if he thinks it's weird that I'm clutching his hands like my life depends on it, he doesn't show it.

"Sorry for snapping about the henchmen thing," he says, his voice low. "I think I'm still in shock from seeing a man's insides on his outsides."

I see people's insides on their outsides more often than I'd like to in my line of work, but I've never watched someone get shot before, so I can certainly understand his shock.

"You're not the only one," I whisper. "I still can't believe Killian tried to shoot us. And I can't believe I kissed a *murderer*."

My voice catches on the last note, and Ryder grips my hands a little tighter.

"It could have happened to anyone."

"Uh, really?" I ask dryly. "To anyone? Have *you* ever kissed someone who turned out to be a bloodthirsty psychopath hell-bent on stealing a diamond for his own selfish profit?"

Ryder blinks at me. "No. But I did date a woman who dunked her Oreos in water."

I don't know whether to laugh or cry, and so I settle for both, clasping a hand over my mouth to muffle the sound.

"What the hell are we supposed to do?" I ask, dropping my hands into my lap. "Killian has guns and a whole team of minions at his disposal. We've got no guns, no sense of direction, and no wilderness skills."

"I wouldn't say I have *no* wilderness skills," Ryder counters. "I read, like, three books on outdoor survival for this trip. And one of them had an acronym for the steps you should take if you get lost or stranded during a hike."

"Great," I say with newfound optimism. "What's the acronym?"

The blank look that crosses his face does not inspire confidence. "Um, SURVIVE, I think. Or was it SURVIVAL? Or maybe—"

"Seriously?" I grumble, my hope evaporating. "If you can't even remember the acronym, how are you going to remember what it stands for?"

"I'll remember," he insists, rubbing his temples like he can massage the answer out. "There was definitely an S. Which was for 'shelter,' I think. Or maybe 'stop.' And the U was for, oh! Undue waste makes haste." He smiles proudly before frowning. "Or maybe it was undue haste makes waste . . ."

"Oh my God," I mutter. "We're gonna die out here."

"We are not going to die out here," Ryder insists. "I might not be Bear Grylls, but I'll be damned if I let that asshole Sinclair harm a single hair on your head. Or mine."

It's dark out, but I can practically see his eyes blazing, and he leans closer to whisper into my ear.

"Believe it or not, I'm going to protect you, Emily Edwards," he promises, his voice unwavering. "If it's the very last thing I do."

And in that moment, with Ryder's body so near and smelling of sweat and pine and what I can only assume is raw testosterone, I believe him. Because he might not be the adventure expert I was promised, but he cared enough to join me when I ran to help Dr. Sharp. I didn't ask him to follow me into danger, but he did anyway, and without him and his inexplicably vintage CD player, I might be dead, too.

"Besides," he adds, leaning back to reach into his pocket, "we have one thing Sinclair doesn't."

I watch as he opens his hand to reveal the most stunning jewel I've ever seen, and I can't help but gasp in awe as the Evermore diamond shimmers in the moonlight. The round, golf-ball-sized stone is hypnotizing in its beauty, so deep blue and sparkling that I couldn't look away if I tried.

"You're right," I tell Ryder, blinking at the gem. "Killian will at least want us alive long enough to get the diamond back. So as long as we've got it, we've got a chance."

"Exactly," he says, his voice full of wonder as he cradles the gemstone in his hand. "The Evermore diamond is our ticket off this island alive."

And then he drops it into the puddle at our feet.

"Fuck," Ryder says as we each plunge a hand into the puddle at lightning speed. My pulse racing, I feel around with trembling fingers, desperately closing my fist around a couple of large pebbles and then, finally, the diamond.

"Holy shit," I say, ready to collapse with relief when I pull the Evermore out of the puddle.

Our hands, which brushed against one another as we both searched for the gem, are still touching, and I'm pretty sure I should pull away, but I'm not so certain I want to. Because it feels good to have a physical connection to Ryder, a visceral reminder that I'm not in this alone. And because even though I overheard the unflattering comment he made to Killian about me—*I don't look at Emily any way,* he'd told the archaeologist, *I look at her the way I look at that tree over there*—I can't help but admit that I'm starting to see *him* in a very un-treelike manner. After all, a tree doesn't have touchable biceps and hair silky enough to run my fingers through. A tree didn't fling a Discman at my attacker to help me escape. A tree isn't brushing my fingertips with a rough, calloused hand, the same hand he used to peel off the bloody gloves I could barely look at.

A tree didn't vow to protect me in a voice low and rumbly enough to sound like thunder.

"So," I say suddenly, forcing myself to pull my hand away from Ryder's. "How about I hang on to this from now on?"

"Sure, right," he agrees after a beat, nodding. "You safeguard the diamond, and I'll safeguard you."

"Exactly," I say, hoping he'll guard me a tad more carefully than he did the jewel. "I know the perfect spot to hide it."

I unzip my pack and reach to the bottom, past my toiletry bag and mini Jenga blocks until my hands, not quite steady yet but not shaking anymore either, find Dad's urn.

"You sure you want to do that?" Ryder asks when I remove the urn from my pack.

I nod and uncap the bamboo canister, drop the Evermore inside, and close it quickly.

"If there was one thing Roger Edwards Jr. always dreamed of, it was adventure," I say, gripping the urn in my hands. "So here we go. Adventure awaits."

"Adventure awaits," Ryder agrees, watching as I carefully return the urn to my pack.

"So," I whisper, almost jumping out of my skin when an acorn falls from a nearby tree and lands on the ground with a *plop*. "What now?"

He shrugs. "The guidebooks didn't exactly cover what to do if you get caught in the crosshairs of a diamond heist, but I say we keep moving. The farther away we can get from the *Explorer*, the better. And it makes sense to move under the cover of darkness."

He gives me a small smile, looking pleased with himself.

"Never thought I'd get to say something that cool. You know, if somebody makes a movie about this someday, that's what they should call it—*Cover of Darkness*."

I stifle a laugh. "More like *Two Idiots Walk into a National Park*."

"Don't quit your day job, Edwards," Ryder says. "That sounds like a box office bomb."

He peeks out cautiously from the tree, then stands up and scans the area for any signs of danger.

"All clear," he says in the authoritative tone of a member of SEAL Team Six. "Ready to move out?"

I reach up and tighten my ponytail, taking a deep breath. I am absolutely not ready and I'm certain Ryder isn't either, but at least we have each other. And, for now, the cover of darkness.

"Ready," I tell him.

He pulls me to my feet, my head nearly grazing his chin when I'm fully upright.

"Alright," he says, rolling his sleeves up to reveal several inches of well-muscled forearms. "Let's roll."

TWELVE

RYDER

Hiking under the cover of darkness sounds cool in theory. But in reality, it's a total fucking shitshow. For one thing, without the warmth of the sun, it's cold as balls out. For another, the darkness makes it impossible for Emily and me to see where we're going. It wouldn't be so bad if we could use our flashlights, but I'm paranoid about inadvertently alerting Sinclair's men to our whereabouts, and so we hike and hike and hike through inky darkness until our legs threaten to give out.

Finally, when I ask Emily how she's doing and she only groans in response, I know it's time to call it a night. We need to rest at some point, and while I'm in better shape than my partner in battle, I'm pretty sure my legs won't last another mile.

"Look," I say, pointing to a cavern-like opening in one of the sloping rock formations bordering the forest. "We could ride out the night here."

Emily blinks at me. "You want me to spend the night in a cave? Are you aware that *bears* live in caves?"

"It's not a cave," I insist, shining my flashlight into the wide opening between the rocks. "See? It's just a hollow groove where the rock layers formed together."

She peers into the opening—which, granted, looks very much like a cave—and raises an eyebrow.

"Can't we just set up our tents?"

"Sure, but tents might draw attention, and I'd very much like it if Sinclair *didn't* find us."

She peers into the cavern again, biting her lip uncertainly, but whatever reservations she has are clearly trumped by exhaustion and hunger.

"Fine," she says, relenting. "But if a bear eats me, I will haunt you from beyond the grave for all of eternity."

"Frankly, I'd expect nothing less."

Tossing my pack into the cavern, I clamber over several loose rocks and step inside, surveying my new surroundings. The rock walls are gray and streaked red with mineral, and I can't stand upright without bumping my head against one, but other than the unsettling darkness and a dartboard-sized spiderweb that I will definitely not point out to Emily, it seems like a safe enough place to ride out the night.

"You coming?" I ask as I extend a hand toward her. "Or should I book you a room at the Ritz-Carlton?"

She rolls her eyes but weaves her fingers through mine, allowing me to help her into the not-a-cave cave.

"Charming," she says as she glances around warily. "This

does not at all look like the haunted home of an ancient demon."

She's right; this place is creepy, but so is the whole island at night. I'm doing my best to project an air of confidence and not startle every time I hear the hoot of an owl or the cry of a loon, but it's hard to stay calm when an armed assailant could jump out and grab us at any moment.

"Better a demon than a deranged archaeologist," I tell her.

She coughs as I unzip my pack to pull out a handful of protein bars, passing some to her. "Ugh. This whole forest smells like a freaking Yankee Candle."

"I think you mean a Yankee Candle smells like this forest," I correct her, scarfing down a protein bar in a few swift bites.

"Yeah, well, after this whole ordeal is over, I'm never buying a nature-scented candle again," she says. "No more Amber Leaves or Balsam Forest or Crisp Campfire Apple for me. From here on out, it'll only be Clean Cotton and Chocolate Chip Cannoli."

I shake my head as I unfurl our sleeping bags. "I understand none of what you just said."

She raises an eyebrow. "What else is new?"

In retaliation, I toss her camping pillow at her, and she laughs and flings it back at me. Emily has a great laugh—it's throatier than you'd expect, and she wrinkles her nose when she does it—and something inside me buzzes at the sound of it. It feels like a reward, and I find myself wanting more.

Then again, laughter is hard to come by when you're hiking across an island with henchmen in hot pursuit.

After we dig into a mouthwatering dinner of protein bars and unsalted almonds and wash it down with cold coffee, Emily switches on her lantern and opens the leather notebook I took from Dr. Sharp's pocket.

"A little late-night reading?" I ask, watching as she removes her ponytail elastic. Her hair falls over her shoulders, giving her a softer, less composed look, and I can't help but wonder what her curls would feel like underneath my fingertips.

She shrugs. "Beats replaying a mental reel of Sharp's death as I try to fall asleep."

Her words conjure up flashbacks of bloodstained sand beneath my feet and the high-pitched whine of bullets flying past me, and I shake my head as if I can somehow dislodge the memory.

"Touché," I tell her.

She glances up from the notebook, watching as I return the leftover protein bars to my pack.

"Come here," she says, patting the rocky ground next to her. "Come read with me."

I rezip the pack, considering. There's really no need for both of us to peruse Sharp's journal—I'm an embarrassingly slow reader and would inevitably just slow her down—but I also don't think it's a great idea for me to sit any closer to Emily than absolutely necessary. My initial physical attraction to her morphed into a full-on crush the second I watched her sprint toward Sharp with all the courage and badassery—if not the natural athleticism—of Wonder Woman crossing No Man's Land, and the last thing I need is to develop real feelings for someone who thinks I'm a himbo. I'm already in grave danger of losing my life on this trip; I don't need to risk a bruised ego and a broken heart, too.

"You know," she says, studying me, "there's growing evidence that playing Tetris after witnessing a traumatic event might help prevent PTSD. That's no help to us now, considering we're trapped on a Tetris-less island, but who says reading a dead archaeologist's notes isn't the next best thing?"

"Sure, of course," I say dryly, leaning in to glance at Sharp's notebook. "Who needs therapy when you've got a hundred pages of barely legible chicken scratch?"

Emily rolls her eyes but smiles as she flips through the notebook. "Let's see."

She flips her hair over her shoulder, and I swear that beneath the strong scent of mud and bug spray, I catch the faintest hint of her lavender-scented shampoo.

Dammit. Now I have no choice but to join her.

"Here," she says as I settle next to her, her knee brushing mine as she tilts the notebook toward me. "Let me know when you're done reading this page."

I stare at Sharp's terrible handwriting, trying to decipher his words, and Emily waits approximately ten seconds before asking, "Done yet?"

I'm only on the first paragraph, a boring passage in which Dr. Sharp speculates on the best time of year to explore a shipwreck in Key West, and I raise my gaze to meet hers.

"No, Hermione Granger. I am not. Some of us are slow readers. We can't all be valedictorian, you know."

She wrinkles her nose. "How'd you know I was valedictorian?"

"You give off very valedictorian vibes," I say, squinting at Sharp's scribbles. "I know you got straight As in school, just like I know you've never gotten a speeding ticket or been sent to detention."

"For your information, I did sit through detention once."

I look at her in surprise. "Oh yeah? For what?"

She blushes. "Well, technically, I sent myself there. I was doing an undercover report for the school paper on student disciplinary protocol."

"Now, that," I say, crossing my arms over my chest, "is the most valedictorian thing I've ever heard."

"Whatever, prom king," she says with a huff.

"Who said I was prom king?" I ask, amused.

"Oh, I don't know. Maybe all of this?" Emily waves a hand around, as if to encompass my face and hair and body, then drops her hand suddenly, her cheeks pink. "Anyway. We should focus."

"We should," I agree. "Please stop distracting me."

I return my attention to the page, but it's hard to concentrate when I can practically feel her eyes boring into me as I read.

"Here," I say, passing her the notebook so that she doesn't spontaneously combust from impatience. "Read your little valedictorian heart out."

"Thank God," she says, snatching the notebook from me and turning to the next page. "And just so you know, I'm normally very patient."

"Sure. And I'm normally a member of Mensa."

She side-eyes me but doesn't reply, and I set about searching my pack for a dry pair of socks.

"So, to summarize," Emily says after a minute, flipping through the pages at warp speed, "Sharp had suspicions about Killian for months. He considered taking his concerns to the Smithsonian, but he convinced himself that he was being too paranoid. He saw Killian as a son, basically. Didn't want to believe he had it in him to steal the diamond."

"Oh, he had it in him, alright," I say, marveling at the nerve Sinclair had to give me a hard time about the Teenage Mutant Ninja Turtles while he was planning a multimillion-dollar robbery.

"Oh, this is interesting," Emily says, running a finger down the notebook's spine. "Dr. Sharp copied some of the letters Captain Evermore wrote for his wife, Katherine."

She glances up from the pages as I dump out half the contents of my pack and rummage through it. "What are you doing?"

"Searching my pack for anything we can use in self-defense," I tell her.

"Any luck?"

"Well, we've got your mini Jenga game," I say dryly, holding up the tiny wooden blocks. "So I think it's safe to say we're saved."

She lets out an indignant huff, then raises an eyebrow at me as I dig a pair of boxers out of my pack and set about removing the elastic from the waistband.

"Do I want to know?"

"I'm going to make a slingshot," I explain, "with this elastic and a stick."

"Will that work?"

I shrug. "I used to watch a reality survival show where they'd dump a bunch of losers in the jungle with nothing but a knapsack and the clothes on their backs and make them fend for themselves. The contestants made slingshots for hunting rabbits and sharpened sticks into daggers, and it seemed to work pretty well."

"A bunch of losers in the jungle?" she repeats. "That's not very nice. What was the show called?"

I smirk at her. "*Losers in the Jungle.*"

Her eyes widen with the confusion of someone who probably only watches prestige dramas and fancy French cinema.

"I didn't say it was a *good* reality survival show."

She laughs, then pauses as something in the notebook catches her eye. "Hm. Looks like Captain Evermore ended most of his letters with poems. *Love* poems."

She waggles her eyebrows at me playfully, but the mere mention of poetry brings me back to a harrowing lit seminar in college where I had to write a ten-thousand-word paper on the works of T.S. Eliot. I hadn't been able to make sense of poetry then, and I'm sure as hell not in a place to make sense of it now.

"Ugh," I say with a shudder. "I never understood that."

"Which one?" Emily asks, her tone playful. "Love or poetry?"

"Poetry, Edwards. Believe it or not, I know plenty about love."

I'm not sure that I do, actually, considering that I thought Hannah was The One and she ended up hating my guts, but I don't admit that out loud.

"Poetry just never made sense to me," I explain, uncapping my water bottle and taking a sip. "I mean, why use fancy words or get all *roses are red, violets are blue* to tell someone you love them when you could just show it through your actions instead? Violets aren't even blue! They're purple."

"To be fair, purple's a lot harder to rhyme with. But poetry isn't that complicated, when you really think about it. It's just a way of using words to make something seem more beautiful." She shrugs. "Besides, it gives you license to be footloose and fancy-free with punctuation."

I've never needed a license to be footloose and fancy-free with punctuation—just ask every English teacher I've ever had—but I only nod at her.

"If you say so."

"There's got to be some poetry out there you'd like," she says, the lantern casting a warm glow on her face. "You just haven't found it yet."

"There was one poet I liked, actually," I say, rezipping my pack. "When I was a kid, Caleb got this book of funny poems from our grandma, and he would walk around reciting them. They're stuck in my head to this day."

I blink, remembering the sound of young Caleb's laughter, how he'd let out an uncontrollable snort when he found something especially hilarious.

"The poet's name was Shelly, I think," I tell Emily. "Shelly Silverstein, maybe? I'm not sure. But she wrote silly stuff about sidewalks ending."

I go quiet, realizing I've pretty much admitted that I'm a man child who thinks poems written for small children are the height of comedy, but Emily doesn't give me a chance to feel embarrassed.

"Shel Silverstein," she says. "Oh my gosh. I loved his books! My dad used to read them to me at bedtime, and sometimes we'd try to come up with silly poems of our own." She smiles. "I haven't thought about that in a long time."

She's quiet for a moment, her expression wistful, and then she clears her throat and taps the notebook.

"Well, Captain Evermore was no Shel Silverstein, but he wasn't a total slouch, either. Listen to this poem he wrote for Katherine. It's one that mentions the diamond."

"*As I sailed from sea to sea,*" Emily reads, raising the book toward the lantern, "*I sought the perfect gift for thee.*

> *More constant than the sun and moon*
> *is my ardent want for you.*
> *Your laugh, your voice, your raven plait,*
> *you are my love, my sweet, my fate.*
> *And if death takes me while I sleep,*
> *do not tremble. Do not weep.*
> *For you I shall wait in the silver mist,*
> *dreaming of your touch, your kiss.*
> *For you will never be alone,*
> *as long as you still wear my stone.*
> *Diamond bright, diamond strong,*
> *forever you and I belong.*
> *My soul, my lust are yours alone,*
> *you, my Katherine, are my home.*"

The wind howls outside our cave. Leaves rustle, and somewhere in the distance, a loon cries. But as Emily reads the captain's words aloud, the outside world falls away, and all that exists is me and her and the burning passion that survived a tragic shipwreck even when its owner didn't.

I know if I were reading the words on paper, I'd be too distracted by the loopy handwriting and lofty language to really grasp their meaning. But with Emily bringing them to life, the light from the lantern flickering across her face as she reads, I can actually appreciate the beauty and intensity of Captain Evermore's message.

"See, it's just a pretty way of saying that love can overcome anything," Emily says, glancing up from the notebook. "Time. Distance. Even death."

"Even death," I repeat, thinking of Caleb walking around the house with a black-and-white book full of silly doodles, reading me ridiculous poems about pancakes and snowballs. The memory makes my chest ache and my eyes burn, and I must not be able to keep my emotion off my face, because Emily reaches across the distance between us to place her hand over mine.

"I know," she says, as if she can see the memory playing in my brain. As if her own mind is playing a near-identical one, except hers features a little girl and a doting dad instead of two goofy brothers. "Me too."

Her hand is soft on mine, warm, and when I raise my gaze to meet hers, the ache in my chest and the burn in my eyes turn into a different kind of sensation altogether. A burn of desire, of want, of wishing I could show her who I used to be so she might want me, too.

"Well," I say, clearing my throat and pulling my hand back before I let myself get any ideas, "we really should try to sleep."

"Right, sleep. Of course." She nods, as if to snap herself out of a spell. "We've got a long day of running for our lives tomorrow."

We huddle into our sleeping bags, and she switches off the lantern, sending us into complete darkness. I close my eyes and try to sleep, the world quiet except for the sound of Emily's soft breathing. I try not to think about the shiver that ran through me when she reached for my hand, or about how it felt to have her body pressed against mine after we tumbled down the cliff.

I try not to think about how it would feel to have her pressed against me for real, with no bulky backpacks or inhibitions or fear of getting killed off by crazy people.

And I try not to wonder if Emily's wondering that, too.

THIRTEEN

EMILY

My dreams are filled with the sounds of violence. I toss and turn for hours, waking up in a cold sweat in between nightmares of Dr. Sharp crying out in pain or Killian firing his gun. In my current dream, a haunting howl rings through the air, and then another, until I open my eyes to find that I've somehow become the little spoon. Whether Ryder moved toward me during the night or I moved toward him, I don't know, but I wake up to find his arm slung over me, my back pressed against his torso, and his hand resting dangerously close to my chest. Deliciously close, actually. So close that if I just shifted slightly, wiggling sideways an inch, his fingertips would brush against my nipple, and maybe he'd wake up and respond with his hands and his mouth and—

Howl.

The sound sends a jolt through me, and I wonder how the creepy noise from my dream crossed over into reality. And then I realize that the sound isn't coming from inside my head; it's coming from outside.

"Ryder!" I whisper-shout, panicked.

When he doesn't respond immediately, I reach over to smack his chest.

"Ow," he mutters, not opening his eyes. "Rude. I was having a dream that we had electricity."

Hooooooowl.

Fully alert now, Ryder sits up so quickly that he knocks over the lantern, and I shiver at the sudden absence of his warm body pressed against mine.

"What the hell was that?" he asks.

"I don't know!" I say, my heart pounding. "You tell me."

"It sounds like a goddamn werewolf," he mutters as another howl pierces the air.

He really needs to stop saying stuff like that, because I'm freaked out enough already.

"Werewolves aren't real, Ryder!"

"Yeah, well," he says, reaching past me to grab a flashlight, "neither are archaeologists."

I'm about to point out that now is not the time for snarky commentary, but I don't get the chance. He scrambles out of his sleeping bag, and I can't help but notice that his sweatpants aren't quite thick enough to conceal the rigid outline of his—

Hooooowl.

"Oh my God," I cry, goose bumps sprouting up on my skin.

"Get back," Ryder orders, striding past me with flashlight in hand.

I scramble out of my sleeping bag and take a step backward, almost tripping over my canteen. Regaining my balance, I suck in my breath as he reaches the opening of the cave and raises his flashlight, transforming the darkness to light. And then, unable to control myself, I scream.

Because there, lurking just outside our shelter with glowing yellow eyes and sharp, snapping teeth, are wolves. Five, to be exact. Their heads lowered and their ears perked, they howl in near unison, the sound so haunting I have to press my hands over my ears.

"Fuuuuck me," Ryder says, backing up quickly. "It's wolves."

"I noticed," I say tightly, every muscle in my body shaking as I press my back against the rock wall.

"Don't wolves avoid people?" he asks, his voice tinged with fear. "The guidebook said they were skittish!"

"I think they generally do avoid people," I hiss. "Except the ones stupid enough to set up camp in their den!"

"Oh, shit," Ryder says, realization hitting him. "Yeah, this is really bad."

He swings the flashlight back and forth like it's a light-saber, trying to scare the wolf pack away. But the blinding light only serves to piss them off, and the biggest animal snaps and growls.

"Okay," he says quickly, lowering the light. "What do you know about fighting off wolves?"

"Uh, very little!" I screech, my terrified voice almost as piercing as the wolves' howls. "What do *you* know about it?"

Ryder pauses, thinking. "Well, do you remember the scene from *Beauty and the Beast* where the beast saves Belle from the wolves by flinging them off her and into the snow?"

My heart pounds. "Vaguely."

"Well, that's it," he concludes. "That's what I know about fighting off wolves."

"Fuck," I whisper, my blood curdling as I realize that our entire combined library of wolf attack knowledge comes from an animated Disney movie.

"I have an idea," Ryder says as I swallow down the bile rising in my throat. "Hand me some food, quick. I'll throw it as far as I can, and maybe they'll chase after it."

My teeth chatter. "Seriously? They're wolves, Ryder, not Australian shepherds!"

"You have a better idea?"

I don't, and so I grab some protein bars with shaking hands and fling them toward Ryder.

"Here you go, guys," he says, his voice trembling as he launches one bar and then another into the forest. "Birthday cake flavored! Go get 'em!"

But the wolves do not go get 'em. Instead, the largest one bares his teeth, and it's all I can do not to pee my pants in terror.

"Ryder," I say, tugging on the back of his shirt, "this isn't working!"

"I can see that it's not working!" He holds the flashlight up as one of the wolves takes a step toward the den. "Quick, hit me with the bear spray!"

Of course, the bear spray. I *knew* it would come in handy. I hurry to dig through my pack, rifling through my belongings frantically.

"The bear spray!" Ryder repeats, adopting a wide defensive stance. "Now!"

"I can't find it," I say through gritted teeth.

"Well, find something, Edwards! Otherwise I'm gonna have to *Beauty and the Beast* it!"

Feeling so dizzy that I'm convinced the rock walls are spinning, I reach past a water bottle and the stupid glow-in-the-dark toilet paper until my hand lands, finally, on the bear spray.

"Got it!" I yell, grabbing the canister and swiftly removing the safety clip. "Here!"

"Yippee-ki-yay, motherfuckers," Ryder grumbles. "Here we go."

I intend to hand him the canister, but I don't get the chance. Because the lead wolf lets out an ear-piercing howl and lunges toward the den, and I know I have to act. Letting out the same terrified screech I did the time my sister Brooke convinced me to go on a Ferris wheel, I close my eyes and pull the trigger. There's a split second of deafening silence, and the next thing I know, Ryder lets out an anguished wail that muffles the howls of the wolves, who flatten their ears and turn away to run off into the dawn.

"Hoooooly fucking fuck," he hisses, writhing on the ground like I blasted *him* with bear spray.

Because . . . oh my God.

Because I blasted him with bear spray.

"To be clear," Ryder says an hour later, his breathing ragged as we trudge up a rocky hill, "when I told you to hit me with the bear spray, that is not what I meant."

Terrified that his pained scream had drawn the attention of the henchmen, we grabbed our gear and sprinted away from the den as fast as my tour guide's burning eyes permitted. Now, my quads aching as we hightail it to safety, I'm relieved that Ryder is at least feeling well enough to speak.

"Once again," I say, biting my lip, "I am very, very sorry. But in a way, if you think about it, everything kind of turned out for the best, right?"

I'm working hard to stay positive here, but when Ryder looks at me with eyes so red and swollen that I can't help but gasp, I realize that's a fruitless effort.

"Oh really, Edwards? It all worked out for the best?"

"Scratch that," I say, grunting as the trail steepens. "I just meant that we got away without being eaten, and the wolves got away unharmed. Who knew that all you had to do to scare them off was scream bloody murder?"

Ryder blinks.

"I really am very sorry," I repeat, cringing when I look at his alarmingly puffy eyes. "And just so you know, I plan to add a bonus onto your service fees to cover any therapy you might need after this trip is said and done. Which, at least in my case, is a lot."

He only grunts in response, and I can't say that I blame him. After all, getting pelted in the face with a blast of capsaicin isn't known for boosting one's mood.

"Maybe it would help to think of something that makes you happy," I suggest, trying to ease his discomfort. "Happiness can help reduce pain, you know."

"Like what?"

"I don't know." I pause, remembering the comic strip he showed me on the boat. "Maybe you can think about Hobbes and his little tiger friend."

"For the love of God, Edwards, *Hobbes is the tiger*," Ryder says in a clipped tone. "*Calvin is the boy*. It's like a crime against literature that you don't know that."

I'm not convinced that he's qualified to determine what counts as a crime against literature, but this isn't the time or place for that discussion, so I steer the conversation toward logistics instead.

"So," I say, pausing to catch my breath and examine my compass once we reach the top of the hill, "if we read the map right—which, let's be honest, is a big if—we'll want to head southeast from here. And then we'll . . ."

I trail off as Ryder, with absolutely no warning, shrugs off his pack and lets it land on the ground with a thud.

"What are you doing?" I ask, watching as he unties his muddy hiking boots and peels off his socks.

He grunts as he yanks his T-shirt over his head in one smooth motion, revealing a bare torso so taut and sweaty that I drop my compass in response.

"Going for a swim," he says, nodding to something behind me.

I turn around to see that our steep uphill climb landed us at the base of a serene pond, the waning rays of the sunrise streaking the water pink.

"There's no time for swimming!" I protest, trying to avert my gaze from Ryder's broad chest. It's difficult, considering that he's positively glistening with sweat, and my cheeks burn when he runs a hand through his tousled hair.

"It's not for fun. My eyeballs are melting, in case you forgot, and I'm covered in two days' worth of dirt and grime."

My eyeballs are melting, too, but not because of the bear spray. I swallow audibly as Ryder strides toward me, bending down to grab my compass off the ground.

"You dropped this," he says, placing it in my hand and closing my fingers around it. And then, a playful smirk crossing his face, he actually *winks* at me.

"You dropped your jaw, too," he adds, his smirk widening. "But I can't help you with that one."

I huff as he struts past me, his broad back and toned triceps on full, uninhibited display.

"My jaw is perfectly intact, thank you very much!" I protest, but he only laughs.

"I'm going in *au naturel*, so unless you want to be further scandalized, I suggest you close your eyes."

"I'm a doctor, Ryder," I say, blushing. "I'm perfectly comfortable with the naked human form."

"You're a *doctor*?" he teases, unzipping his tan hiking pants. "I had no idea. Why didn't you say so earlier?"

I roll my eyes and force myself to look away from him, paying extremely close attention to a duck waddling farther down the bank. Against my better judgment, though, I can't help but open one eye as Ryder slips off his pants and then a pair of dark gray boxers. My heart thumps as he steps into the pond, his firm ass visible until he slips under the water.

"You can look now, Edwards," he calls to me, wading in up to his chest. "I'm decent."

My skin flushes at his teasing. "You are the opposite of decent."

I watch as he takes a deep breath and disappears underwater, and then I nervously scan the area for any sign of Killian or his men. The only visible danger is a bee buzzing unnervingly close to my head, but still. It would be just my luck to run into the baddies while my tour guide floats around like a mermaid.

I suck in my breath when Ryder's head pops above the surface.

"God, this feels good," he moans, which does not at all help the fierce battle I'm fighting with my hormones. "I can finally see again."

He rubs his eyes, apparently relishing the fact that they're no longer on fire, and nods at me.

"You coming in?"

I shake my head. "I don't swim in nonchlorinated water."

"Too much fun?"

"Quite the opposite, actually," I say, studying the mallard duck like it's the most fascinating thing I've ever seen. "Too many bacteria, too many amoebas, too much risk of drowning thanks to uncertain depths. I'll hold out for the pool at the Ritz."

"We were nearly mauled by wolves today, and you're worried about amoebas?" he asks, shifting to float on his back. "Seriously?"

"They cause encephalitis," I say tightly. "It's a very serious issue."

Ryder shrugs and pushes his wet hair out of his eyes. "Sounds like it."

"Anyway," I say, tightening my ponytail and trying very hard not to think about Ryder's bare ass, "don't come crying to me if you get swimmer's itch."

"You know, I don't mean this in a rude way, but you're being very valedictorian right now. Which is fine. We can't all live on the edge." He shrugs, the sun glinting off his broad shoulders. "The world needs dare people, but it needs truth people, too."

He's egging me on, I know it, and yet I can't help but take the bait. Maybe because all the adrenaline coursing through my veins over the last few days has altered my brain chemistry. Or maybe because I don't want Ryder to see me as the cautious, boring Emily who works too much and feels exceedingly naughty whenever she drinks a diet soda.

Maybe I don't want to see myself that way anymore, either.

"I've picked 'dare' in truth or dare before," I tell him, jutting my chin out. "Sixth grade, for example. Becky Cartwright knew I had a huge crush on Tony Teeman, so she dared me to call him on the phone. I did it."

"How'd it go?"

"It didn't," I admit glumly. "Tony's mom answered. He wasn't home. He'd gone to see an *Air Bud* sequel with his dad."

Ryder laughs, and the sound of it makes my stomach flip-flop. "His loss, then."

His gaze meets mine, and something tightly wound uncoils in my chest. "Come swim with me. Just for a minute. I dare you."

I start to shake my head, to remind him about bacteria and encephalitis and the fact that Killian could be lurking anywhere, but I stop myself. Because as scary as all those risks are, the way he's looking at me right now tempts me to throw caution to the wind. Besides, I, too, am covered in several days' worth of sweat and grime, and the prospect of washing it off sounds amazing.

"I triple dog dare you," Ryder says, water dripping down his chest. "C'mon, Edwards. The water's fine."

"You skipped double dare," I tell him, my heart thumping.

His gaze doesn't waver. "Like I said, I live on the edge."

I suck in my breath, knowing I have a million good reasons to reject his silly dare. But there's one compelling reason not to, and that reason is watching me from the water, waiting to see if I'll accept the challenge.

And despite my better judgment, I do.

I shrug off my pack, savoring the absence of its heavy weight, and then I remove my gross boots and socks. Ryder watches me as I unbutton my long-sleeved hiking shirt, my skin flushing as I drop it to the ground. I slide my pants off, too, my heart pounding in my chest, and then I walk toward the pond, shivering in the cool morning air.

"Turn around," I tell him when I reach the rocky bank.

I might be living on the edge today, but that doesn't mean I'm prepared to do a total striptease for my tour guide. When Ryder nods and turns his back toward me, I peel off my bra and underwear and step into the water.

"Ahh!" I cry, the cold shocking me as I sink into the pond. "Ryder! You said the water was fine!"

"Well, it is! Once you get used to it."

I gasp as the cold envelops me, but I force myself to wade

in up to my neck. After a minute, my body adjusts, and I relish the sensation of weightlessness.

"You can turn around now," I tell Ryder, tilting my head back to get my hair wet.

He does, and my heart flutters when he swims toward me, his body a blur of muscles in motion.

"See, I did it," I say, pressing my toes into the sandy pond floor.

"You sure did." Ryder's gaze sends a *whoosh* through my belly, and I shiver despite the water's now-tolerable temperature.

We look at each other for a moment, and the knowledge that nothing separates our naked bodies except for a couple feet of water makes me blush. Eager for a distraction, I focus on scrubbing the dirt off my arms, and then I dip my head underwater to clean my face. Ryder does the same, wiping a spot of mud off his forehead, and he shakes water out of his hair and studies me.

"All good?"

"You missed a spot, actually. You have dirt on your cheek. Right there." I touch my own face to show him where, and he wipes his cheek with the back of his hand.

"No, a little bit lower," I tell him when he misses the spot. "Now you're too low. No, it's more to the right—"

"Show me." Ryder cuts me off, moving closer to me in one smooth motion.

"Huh?" I ask, dizzy at the closeness of our bodies. I'm no shy ingenue, but I've never felt so *naked* before, and the nearness of his bare form feels wildly intimate.

He reaches out to take my hand and presses it to his face, grazing my skin with his fingertips.

"Show me," he repeats. His eyes flicker as he guides my hand downward from his left temple, tracing a slow path to his cheek and then down along his stubbled jaw.

My heart blazes, because the way he's looking at me—like my touch is something he's been wanting, craving, even—is not how a man looks at someone he sees the way he sees a tree. He's looking at me like his heart is racing the same way mine is. Like he, too, feels the tension that's been mounting since I landed on him after we rolled down the hill, the warmth of his body against mine assuring me that I was okay.

He's looking at me like we're lovers.

"Here," I say, rubbing my thumb on the spot he missed. His jaw tenses beneath my touch, and I swear that for the briefest of seconds, he closes his eyes like the sensation of my hand on his cheek is something to be savored.

"It's my turn," I say suddenly, jerking my hand back before I let my imagination run away any further. I sink lower into the water to cover up my blushing skin. "You gave me a dare, so I get to ask you a truth."

Ryder nods, his expression unreadable. "Okay."

"Why did you follow me when I tried to help Dr. Sharp?" I ask, voicing the question I've been turning over in my mind since yesterday. "I didn't ask you to come with me, but you did anyway. Why?"

He doesn't blink or pause to think.

"I wanted to protect you."

I move toward him, my body taking on a mind of its own as I halve the distance between us. "Why?"

He swallows, and I see a flicker of something like vulnerability cross his face. It's the same expression he wore when he told me that he wasn't a real tour guide; the same one he wore last night in the cave when I read Captain Evermore's letter aloud. It feels like a glimpse into the real Ryder, not the swashbuckling guy who jumped on the boat or dared me into the water but someone softer, someone deeper. Someone whose heart has known breaking, and who tried to conceal the shattered pieces with a devil-may-care swagger and an easy smile.

He swims toward me, just slightly, as if he were going to embrace me but thought better of it.

"I promised myself that I wouldn't fail to show up for someone when it counted," he says. "Not again."

I don't know what the *again* means, but I don't get a chance to ask, because Ryder, reaching forward to wipe a stray droplet off my forehead, keeps going.

"When I saw how brave you were," he says, his thumb brushing my temple, "I knew I had to be brave, too."

I shake my head. "I'm not brave, Ryder. I'm terrified."

I'm not just talking about the fear of diseases and injuries and accidents that's plagued me since my mom passed, or the terror I felt when Killian pointed his gun at us. I also mean that I'm frightened of whatever it is that's happening between us, of falling head over heels for someone so different from everything I'm used to.

"You are brave," he says, his hand grazing a wet curl. "I

don't know how long you've been telling yourself that you're not, but it's long past time to stop."

I swallow, wanting to believe that it's true. That he's right, and that somewhere deep inside me, I am my father's daughter after all.

"Thank you," I say. "And thank you for coming with me."

"You're welcome." Ryder shrugs. "My only regret is that I didn't have something slightly more deadly than Caleb's Discman."

I freeze. "The Discman you threw at Killian was your brother's?" I ask, stunned.

He nods. "He always carried it on the trail. Didn't feel right to make this trip without it."

"I . . ." I'm silent, thinking of everything I have that once belonged to Dad, and how precious all of it is to me now. The well-loved Cleveland Guardians ball cap I keep on my dresser. The dog-eared copy of *On the Road* he left on his living room coffee table. The half-finished grocery list I found in the pocket of his khakis when Brooke and I sorted his clothes for donation, the hastily scribbled words *milk* and *frozen waffles* reducing me to tears.

I think of how I would feel if I lost one of those items, if I had to fling it at Killian in order to survive.

"That must have been so difficult," I tell Ryder. "To make the choice to sacrifice something of Caleb's like that."

Ryder gazes down at the water for a moment, and when he looks up at me, his expression is firm. Certain.

"You were in danger, Emily," he says, his hand tracing the

ridge of my ear and then settling on my cheek. "There was only one choice to make."

His words are a balm to something pained and aching deep inside me, and I'm not sure which of us moves first. Maybe he lowers his head toward mine and I move toward him in response, or maybe it's the opposite. Either way, the coldness of the water and the cramping in my muscles and the fear that's been plaguing me since I boarded the ferry fade away as Ryder's lips meet mine. There is only us, our mouths meeting and parting and meeting again, his arms snaking around the small of my back and pulling me into him.

I wrap my arms around his neck, deepening the kiss, not thinking or questioning but simply allowing myself to feel. I savor the rough pressure of his stubbled jaw against my skin and rest one hand against his chest, his heart pounding so fast that I can feel it.

"Look at me," Ryder says, his voice like velvet, and I pull my lips away from his to glance up at him.

He studies me, cupping my face between his palms, and I swear that the world pauses in that moment.

"Emily," he says, and then he scoops me up into his arms.

I wrap my legs around his waist, letting out a soft moan at the dizzying sensation of my bare breasts against his chest as his mouth finds mine again.

"Wait," I say suddenly, a distant buzzing sound breaking the spell. "Do you hear that?"

Ryder blinks at me, confused. "Hear what?"

"That," I say, as the hum of a motor ruins the quiet serenity of the pond.

I glance up at the sky, where hazy clouds streak across a blanket of blue.

"What the fuck is that?" Ryder asks, peering at the clouds, and then he lets out another curse.

Because he sees it at the same time I do: a white-and-blue striped seaplane, its front propeller spinning so fast it makes me dizzy.

"Run," he says, grabbing my hand and rushing me toward the bank.

Because the plane is headed right toward us.

FOURTEEN

RYDER

I was so focused on kissing Emily that I wouldn't have heard that plane coming until it was right over my head. Hell, I probably wouldn't have noticed unless it landed *on* my head.

Luckily for me, she's still got her wits about her, and we rush to hide, terrified that the plane holds Sinclair or his morally inept goons.

"Wait!" she says when we near the edge of the pond, water splashing everywhere as we haul ass toward dry land. "What if that's someone who could help us? Like a ranger or a tourist plane?"

I glance from the seaplane back to her. "What if it's not?"

She bites her lip, seemingly trying to decide how much of a risk she wants to take, and then she swears and sprints out of the pond. We grab our clothes and our packs, my teeth chattering as we hurry for the woods and duck behind a pine tree. I throw my clothes back on hurriedly, holding my breath as the seaplane zooms overhead and disappears into the distance.

"If that was the Girl Scouts and we missed our one chance at rescue," Emily says, panting as she yanks her socks on, "I will never forgive either of us."

"Hey, we're gonna make it off this island," I assure her, reaching for her hand, but she pulls away quickly.

"Let's just get moving."

"Uh, yeah. Sure." I watch as she sweeps her curls into a bun, all the softness she showed me in the pond gone from her face. "Hey, are we okay?"

She sighs in exasperation. "No, Ryder, we are not okay! As we both clearly forgot for a moment back there, this is not some spring break adventure in Miami. We need to focus on getting to safety, not . . ." she trails off, not looking at me. "Whatever that was."

Whatever that was was the hottest, most intense kiss of my life, and to hear Emily speak of it so dismissively hurts my feelings even more than it bruises my ego.

"Fine," I say, trying to keep my face neutral. "Let's go."

She frowns at her compass and points into the woods. "The ranger station is this way. I think."

She takes off without waiting for me to reply, and I jog to catch up with her.

"Do you want to talk about it?" I ask, falling into step beside her. "Because, you know, I didn't plan for that to—"

"I know you didn't plan for that to happen, Ryder. We don't need to have a big discussion about it."

The abruptness of her tone catches me off guard. "Okay, well, I just wanted to make sure you were okay."

"I'm fine," she says, adjusting her shoulder straps. "I just don't want to end up maimed or murdered because I was too distracted to pay attention to my surroundings."

She tucks a curl behind her ear, and I can't help but remember the feeling that came over me when I took her hand in mine and pressed it to my face. I felt cared for, connected, like I could fight off a hundred growling wolves and a whole army of Sinclairs screaming about Harvard if she would just keep touching me. Like I was more than a down-on-his-luck has-been with more bad jokes than brain cells.

Like I was a guy she might consider worthy of her. Like I was *the* guy. But apparently that feeling, like her affection, was fleeting.

"Okay," I say, tensing my jaw. "I'll do my best not to be a distraction."

She opens her mouth like she's going to respond, but instead, she winces.

"What's going on?" I ask.

"Huh? Nothing."

"I just saw you wince," I tell her. "Which typically indicates that someone is in pain."

"I'm fine," she insists, waving me off.

"Sure. And I'm a Fulbright Scholar."

She rolls her eyes, but we only make it another few steps before she flinches and reaches down to grab her right boot.

"Emily?" I ask, my stomach twisting at the grimace on her face. "What's going on?"

"It's my ankle." She lets out a frustrated groan. "I rolled it when we got out of the pond. It's probably just a sprain. I'm sure I can walk it off."

"I'm not," I say when she takes another step, the pain evident on her face. "Here, let me see."

I crouch to examine her ankle before she can protest.

"You're bleeding," I say, studying a shallow wound just below her calf.

"I ran through some thorns. It's fine."

She bites her lip in a way that indicates she is very not fine, and I motion for her pack. "Give me one of your bandages and I'll wrap it, at least."

"We don't have any bandages. I left them on the beach with Sharp."

"Well then, there's only one solution." I stand up and take off my shirt wordlessly, then bend down to tie it around her calf.

"Ryder!" she says as if she's positively scandalized. "*That's* your one solution?"

"Emily!" I echo, doing my best imitation of her. "What seems to be the problem?"

She shoots me a dark look. "You can't just go around whipping your shirt off to use as a makeshift bandage!"

I raise an eyebrow at her as I complete my work. "Why not? It's jersey knit. That's, like, the softest of the T-shirt fabrics."

"Because it's *indecent*." She blushes, and I don't miss the glance she sneaks at my torso.

"And you can't just kneel there in front of me like that, like . . ."

"Like what?" I ask innocently, though I know exactly what she means. The thought crossed my mind, too, that this is the position I'd assume if I were to press my mouth to her most sensitive part. I'd start slowly, of course, with soft kisses to her inner thigh, and then I'd take my time as I grazed her with the stubble of my beard, relishing the feel of her as I worked my way up to—

"Stand up, please," Emily says, yanking me to my feet. The exertion throws her off balance, and she grabs my arm to catch herself.

"That better?" I ask, gripping her hips to steady her.

"No." Her gaze scales up my chest and lingers on my mouth. "Frankly, it's actually much worse."

I raise an eyebrow. "I was talking about your ankle, Edwards."

She shakes her head as if pulling herself out of a trance. "Right. Sure. I guess the T-shirt does help it sting less."

"See?" I say brightly. "Jersey knit. Now hop on." Turning away from her, I pat the back of my shoulder twice.

"Hop on?" she repeats, incredulous. "What are you talking about?"

I roll my eyes, because the answer is obvious. "I'm giving you a piggyback ride."

"Thanks, but you most certainly are not." She crosses her arms over her chest. "I'm a grown woman, not a tuckered-out child."

I turn around to face her again. "Might I remind you that we're fleeing a bunch of bad guys on foot? So as much as I admire your independence, I can't afford to let you move at the pace of a dying snail. Hop on." I tap my back again.

She rolls her eyes. "Please stop trying to make me mount you. I can walk just fine."

"*Mount* me?" I can't help but smirk at her. "Well, well, well, look who's being indecent now."

A look of pure determination on her face, she ignores me and proceeds to hobble along the rocky trail, wincing.

"Look, why are you so mad at me?" I ask when she flinches with every step. "Why won't you let me help?"

Emily sucks in her breath, annoyed. "I'm not mad at you, Ryder. I'm mad at myself."

"Mad at yourself for what, exactly?"

"For what we did back there!" she says, gesturing wildly toward the pond. "For letting my guard down long enough that we could have gotten killed. For getting mixed up—figuratively and as of ten minutes ago, literally—with someone who makes absolutely no sense for me."

Her words strike a tender nerve. "Sure seemed like we made sense together in the pond."

"Ryder," she says, "come on."

I shake my head. "I get it. You think we don't make sense because I'm not like the guys you normally date. Well, you're right. I'm not an anesthesiologist or a snobby professor. I didn't go to Harvard or Stanford or one of the other Ivies. But that doesn't mean there isn't something here."

I point to her and back to me, and she looks at me for a moment before returning her gaze to the trail in front of us.

"Stanford isn't an Ivy League school."

I shrug. "I thought it was."

"It's not," she says, wincing as the trail gets steeper. "There are eight Ivies, and Stanford isn't one of them. Neither is Northwestern, which is also commonly mistaken for—"

"Oh my God, who cares?" I cut in, my hurt and frustration bubbling over. "Look, it's fine. We both know what the issue is. You don't have to admit it out loud."

"Admit what out loud?"

"That you think I'm a brainless, unsophisticated idiot, and that's why we don't make sense together."

She stops hobbling and puts her hands on her hips, her chest heaving from exertion.

"What?"

I hold up my hands. "I'm just saying, I get it, okay? You're better than me. You're smart, I'm dumb. You're right, I'm wrong. I'm big, you're little. I get it. It's gotten. Message received."

She wrinkles her forehead in confusion as she resumes limping along. "What the . . . were you misquoting *Matilda*, the book by Roald Dahl?"

"No," I say, my tone indignant. "I'm quoting *Matilda* the movie by Danny DeVito. Which, might I add, is far superior to the book."

I can practically see her brain imploding.

"Come again?"

"I said the movie is better than the book, Edwards! And I know you think I'm not qualified to judge, since I happen to like Shel Silverstein poems instead of whatever fancy-nancy shit they read at Harvard, but oh well."

"For your information," she says in a tone that can only be

described as seething, "Fancy Nancy is a children's series about an exuberant young girl who loves all things fancy."

It's got to be the first time in human history that someone's snarled while saying the word *fancy*, but Emily's not done.

"And I can assure you," she continues, "that they don't read it at Harvard. Regardless, I would never judge you for liking Shel Silverstein poems. I loved *Where the Sidewalk Ends*."

"It doesn't change the fact that women like you don't go for guys like me."

"Women like me? What is that supposed to mean?" she asks, tripping over a loose rock and waving me away when I try to assist her.

I gesture at her as I duck to avoid smacking my head on a low-hanging branch.

"You know, ambitious, accomplished, so type A that you separate your whites and colors and actually have a favorite documentary."

"Uh, separating your whites and colors isn't a type A thing to do," she says. "That's just being civilized. And everybody has a favorite documentary!"

"No, they don't!" I insist, ready to rip my hair out in frustration. "Everybody *pretends* to have a favorite documentary, and then they go home and watch Monday Night Football like a normal person!"

"So you're saying I'm not a normal person?" she asks, looking like she'd relish the chance to bear-spray me in the face again.

"Of course you're not a normal person, Emily!" I groan,

running a hand through my hair. "You're not even close to being normal. You're way beyond normal. You're . . ." I pause, trying to figure out how to put my impression of her into words. "Exceptional."

I cough, pounding my chest as if I can dislodge the ball of emotion swelling there. Because she is exceptional, and Caleb was, too, and I never deserved either one of them. At least Emily is smart enough to know it.

"I . . . you think I'm exceptional?" she asks, her face softening.

"Obviously!" I smack a mosquito that landed on my arm in frustration. "You're a gorgeous doctor who saves lives. You charged toward danger to try to save a dying man, not to mention you traveled to this absolute hellhole of an island to honor your dad. So of course I think you're exceptional!"

Emily watches me, her mouth half-open.

"Thank you," she says finally, her tone warmer than it's been since we left the pond. "I think. I mean, you were giving me a compliment, but you were also kind of yelling, so it was a little bit confusing, but—"

"*I* wasn't yelling," I say, lowering my voice. "*You* were yelling."

"I was not yelling, Ryder! I was merely speaking loudly, with emotion, as one does when someone has the nerve to say that *Matilda* was better as a movie than a book."

I knew she wouldn't let that comment go unchecked, and it burns me up that *that's* what she took away from everything I said.

"Believe it or not, some people like movies better!" I say

tersely. "Okay? Some people like comic strips and mispronounce words and haven't saved ten lives every day by noon, and that's okay. And if that makes me a himbo in your eyes, so be it. I don't care."

My voice cracks on the last word, betraying the fact that I actually care a hell of a lot, and I grab a clean shirt out of my pack and yank it over my head.

Emily freezes mid-step. "Hang on. Who said anything about being a himbo?"

I stop, too, locking gazes with her. "You did. On the ferry, remember?"

"You heard that?"

My heart sinks at her words, because a part of me was hoping that she would deny it. That what Sinclair told me when he grabbed the Discman was just a big fat lie.

"No," I say, the truth settling in my stomach like a rock. "Your dreamy Harvard archaeologist told me."

Sighing, she runs a hand over her face. "Ugh. Ryder, I'm so sorry. I said that to Killian shortly after you jumped on the ship, and I was feeling totally out of sorts. I didn't mean it." She frowns. "I mean, I half did at the time, but that was before I knew you. And it had a lot more to do with how I was feeling about this trip than anything you did."

I listen but don't respond, because I don't know what to say. Her insult tapped into a long-held insecurity about my intellectual prowess—or lack thereof—and it stings despite my attempts to shrug it off.

"Besides," Emily adds after a moment, "it was kind of a compliment, if you think about it. People love himbos! Himbos are fun and sexy and kind. They're like the golden retrievers of men. And people adore golden retrievers! There's a reason they're one of the most popular dogs in America."

"Shockingly, being compared to a dog doesn't make me feel that much better."

"I don't mean that you're like a dog." She motions toward me, shaking her head. "I mean that it's impossible for me not to like you."

That does sound a bit better, and I perk up at the compliment.

"You really think I'm sexy?"

She rolls her eyes so hard it's a wonder she doesn't strain them. "Shut up. We both know you look like Thor and kiss like it's the last thing you'll ever do."

My ego's bouncing back pretty quickly now, thanks to her praise of my kissing skills, and I raise an eyebrow at her.

"Why do you say that like it's a bad thing?"

"Because!" Her voice is strained. "Because I know that you don't see me the same way."

I blink at her, trying to make sense of her words. I know I haven't crafted her any dazzling love poems, but you'd think kissing her and calling her exceptional might give Emily a clue that I'm seriously into her.

"What the hell are you talking about?" I ask.

"I heard what you said to Killian on the trail." She fiddles with the shirt tied around her ankle, not looking at me. "You said you don't look at me any way. You look at me like you look at a tree, right? That's what you told him."

She kicks a pebble, sending it flying, and I hate the hurt

written in her warm gray eyes. I try to recall the dumb shit I said to Sinclair in the heat of the moment, and I wish I could hop in a time machine and snatch the words back.

Actually, I wish I could hop in a time machine and kick Killian Sinclair's ass.

"You weren't supposed to hear that," I say, taking a step toward her.

She nods. "Obviously."

"No, I mean, you weren't supposed to hear that because I never should have said it. I didn't mean it. At all."

"Then why did you say it?" she asks, and the tinge of hurt she's trying to hide from her voice makes me want to punch myself right in the jaw.

"Because I was embarrassed," I admit, hating myself for what I said and Sinclair for egging me on to say it. "Sinclair was giving me shit about how you'd only ever see me as a himbo, and I wanted to get him off my back. Besides, the guy's a menace to society, but he wasn't wrong. He's much more your type than I am."

She gawks at me. "You think a lying, deceitful coward who besmirches the good name of archaeology is my type?"

"Obviously I don't think he's your type *now*, but it sure seemed that way for a while. I mean, you guys spent the whole ferry ride together. And you kissed."

"*He* kissed *me*," Emily says, shaking her head. "Look, if I'm being completely honest, did I initially find him charming? Yes. Impressive? Yes. And did I find you somewhat reckless and think to myself, *Now here's a guy who has never used a coaster of his own volition*? Also yes."

I could do with hearing a little less about Sinclair's charm.

"I use coasters," I say defensively. "On occasion."

"The point is, I was wrong about Killian. And I was wrong about you. I don't see you as a himbo, Ryder." She looks down at her ankle and then up at me, blushing shyly. "I see you as my protector."

Her words are a salve to the wound in my heart that I've been trying to heal with booze and isolation and too many old episodes of *Dexter's Laboratory*, and I want nothing more than to live up to that role. To protect her. To be there for someone I care about instead of letting them down the way I did Caleb.

"For what it's worth," I tell her, "I mean it with every single fiber of my being when I say that I don't look at you the way I look at a tree." I pause, hearing myself out loud. "And yes, I do realize that's the stupidest sentence ever constructed."

I meant the last part in jest, but Emily doesn't laugh or even smile.

"Then how do you look at me?" she asks instead.

I study her, trying to figure out how to answer. I've always been a man of action more than words, and I wish I could show her instead of tell her—wish I could lift her up and carry her into my bedroom to demonstrate exactly how I look at her. I wish I could take a steaming hot shower with her, help her wash off all the layers of worry and dirt and exhaustion, and then bend down to nudge her legs open and show her with my tongue.

I wish.

"Do you really want to know?" I ask, taking another step toward Emily as she tilts her head up toward me. Her eyes are searching, wanting, and it's all I can do not to take her into my arms and kiss her.

"Yes," she says. "I do."

But I don't get the chance to tell her. Because just as I open my mouth to tell her the truth, a man so gigantic he makes me look petite pops out from behind a spruce tree.

"Hey, lovebirds," he says, grinning at us. "I've been looking for you."

And then he pulls out a gun.

FIFTEEN

EMILY

"Oh my God, Ryder, henchman!" I cry, pointing at the terrifying man who just jumped out from behind a tree. "Henchman!"

The henchman looks at me in confusion. "No. Malcolm."

"The henchman's name is Malcolm!" I tell Ryder, who's standing right next to me and therefore doesn't actually require a play-by-play of the situation. "Malcolm has a gun!"

I curse myself for getting so distracted by Ryder's abs— again—and listening so intently to what he was about to say that I didn't notice an armed man creeping amongst the trees.

"Oh, this?" Malcolm, whose blocky head, muscular neck, and wide mouth give him the look of a human pit bull, points at the gun with his free hand. "This is nothing for you to worry about, as long as you do what I say."

He uses the gun to beckon us toward him. "Come on. I'll take you back to the ship, we'll give Dr. Sinclair his diamond, and you'll be free to enjoy the rest of your vacation. Pretty good deal, right?"

"Wrong," Ryder says flatly. "That sounds like a terrible deal. Besides, the diamond isn't Sinclair's. And this is not a vacation! This is actually the worst trip I've ever been on."

"To be honest, it's not my favorite, either," Malcolm the henchman says. "Too many insects." He swats at a mosquito, then waves his gun at us. "Come on then, lovebirds. Let's get a move on."

"Thanks, but no thanks," Ryder says. "Oprah taught me never to let myself get taken to the second location."

"And just to be clear, we're not actually lovebirds," I tell Malcolm, gesturing to Ryder and me. "It's kind of a complicated situation."

I'm pretty sure the surly giant in front of us couldn't care less about whatever romantic entanglement we have going on, but I figure that the longer we stand here talking, the better chance Ryder and I have of coming up with an escape plan.

"I'm just his client," I add. "And he's just my tour guide."

"Come on, do you have to say it like that?" Ryder asks, crossing his arms over his chest.

"Like what?"

"Like the idea of us being together is so crazy." He gives me a meaningful look, and it takes me a second to realize that for once, Ryder and I are on the same page: keep up the banter. Distract Malcolm. Survive.

"It *is* crazy," I insist, giving him a look right back. "Because how could I ever be with a man who doesn't read memoirs?"

"Great question, Edwards. Here's another: how could *I* ever be with a woman who irons her bedsheets?"

"Why do you say that like it's weird?" I ask, my response

genuine. "That's a thing that people do! It makes sheets crisp and wrinkle free!"

"Who cares about wrinkle-free sheets?" Ryder says. "It's what happens between them that matters."

"You two are something else," Malcolm says, shaking his head at us. "You remind me of me and my wife, Miriam. We couldn't be more different, her and I. It's funny how opposites attract, isn't it? She's a real stickler for the rules, and I'm . . . not."

"You don't say," Ryder says dryly, his gaze shifting toward Malcolm's gun, and I scramble to keep the chaos going.

"You know what, Fleet?" I ask, putting my hands on my hips. "I bet Malcolm here would never call Miriam ma'am. Or call her breast a chesticle. And I bet he would never in a million years imply that he doesn't find her any more attractive than a tree. Right, Malcolm?"

"Well, obviously," Malcolm says. "I'm not a total idiot."

"Listen," Ryder argues, "I already told you, I didn't mean what you heard me say. I do find you attractive. I find you *very* attractive. Even when you're correcting my speech and blasting me with bear spray and getting us tangled up with the Sinclairs and Malcolms of the world."

"*I'm* getting us tangled up?" I ask in disbelief. "*You're* the one who initially got us lost. Besides, you can say you find me attractive all day long, but everyone knows that actions speak louder than words."

"Oh, I see. You want action, huh?" Ryder says. "Like what went down in the pond?"

Malcolm glances from Ryder to me warily. "What went down in the pond?"

"Do you want me to kiss you again?" Ryder asks. He takes a step closer to me, and I swear my heart, already racing from having a gun in my face, speeds up even further at his nearness.

"Because I'll kiss you right here, right now," he continues. "Right in front of our buddy Malcolm. Would you like that?"

"Uh, not so much," Malcolm chimes in. "That kinda seems like something you should save for later."

Ryder nods.

"Malcolm's right. Our kisses should be private," he agrees, his gaze lingering on to my lips. "Intimate, if you will."

All seven trillion nerves in my body tingle at his use of *intimate*, at how he says it slowly, carefully, like his tongue is savoring every syllable.

"Besides," Ryder adds, his body mere inches from me, "I wouldn't want to start something I couldn't finish."

"No," I agree, my heart thumping. "You wouldn't."

"Yeah so, this is all making me pretty uncomfortable," Malcolm says, tapping his gun against his palm. "Let's go. My canoe's that way."

"Just let me check her leg first, okay?" Ryder says, bending down to examine my ankle. "She's injured."

I don't point out that we have more pressing matters than my sprained ankle. Instead, I watch as Ryder, quick as a flash, grabs a rock off the ground and curls his fist around it.

"She looks fine to me," Malcolm says, nudging Ryder in the back and pointing toward the stretch of Lake Superior that's barely visible through the trees. "Chop, chop."

Ryder finally breaks his heated gaze away from me and

looks at Malcolm, the show clearly over. "Fine," he says. "But I call dibs on seat one."

He takes my hand and leads me toward Malcolm, and I dig my fingernails into his palm.

"What are you doing?" I hiss, barely moving my lips to get the words out.

He squeezes my hand in response. "I've got this. Just follow my lead."

But his lead seems to be taking us straight to Malcolm, who is probably in for a hefty payday the second he hands us over to Killian. And once Killian finds the Evermore diamond hidden in my pack—well, that's a path too dark to let my mind wander down.

"Now, just so you know," Malcolm says, removing actual *zip ties* from his pocket, "none of this is personal. You two seem like nice enough folks. But orders are orders, you know?" He motions for Ryder and me to turn around. "I'll cut the ties as soon as Dr. Sinclair's got the diamond. I promise."

"How reassuring," I say dryly, waiting for Ryder to reveal his brilliant plan.

"Hey, do you guys want to hear a knock-knock joke?" my tour guide asks, grinning at the henchman and me.

"No," Malcolm and I say in unison.

Ryder scoffs at us. "Rude. Well, I'm going to tell you anyway. Knock, knock, Malcolm," he says, looking cool as a cucumber as the henchman strides toward him, gun and zip ties ready.

Malcolm, who seems to be a pretty good sport for an armed criminal, rolls his eyes. "Fine. Who's there?"

"SLINGSHOT!" Ryder cries, whipping the homemade contraption out of his pocket just before Malcolm reaches him. He loads a rock onto the slingshot, pulls it back, and releases as Malcolm lunges at him.

It would have been a decent plan if we were in a fourth-grade recess brawl, or if he had an actual functioning slingshot and not one fashioned out of sticks and underwear elastic. But we aren't, and he doesn't, and I watch, stunned, as the elastic breaks, sending the rock flying directly into the side of my head.

"What the fuck, Ryder!" I cry, my head throbbing with pain.

Malcolm, his vibe much less amicable now, curses under his breath. Then he reaches into his jacket with his free hand and pulls out a second gun, aiming one at Ryder and one at me. "I was trying to be nice about this, but no more fucking around."

"Great job, Ryder," I say sarcastically. "Way to go. Now he's double fisting guns."

"It worked on *Losers in the Jungle*," he grumbles.

"Move it," Malcolm instructs with a scowl, raising his guns an inch. "Head east."

A dejected-looking Ryder nods and begins to hike, and I take a shaky breath and walk along after him.

"That's west," Malcolm says, shaking his head at Ryder.

"I knew that," my tour guide says, turning swiftly on his heel and hiking in the opposite direction.

"Hopeless," Malcolm mutters.

"You know, you're right," Ryder says. He turns around to face Malcolm, whose gun is mere inches from his face. "I am hopeless. This whole situation is hopeless. Because we all know that once Sinclair gets the diamond, he'll have you shoot us dead."

Malcolm blanches. "Well, not me, exactly. He'll probably have Butcher handle it."

"Oh my God," I exclaim. "There's a guy on your team named *Butcher*?"

"No, no," Malcolm says, shaking his head like that's the most ridiculous thing he's ever heard. "Butcher's a lady."

My head swims, and it'll be a miracle if I don't pass out before we reach the canoe.

"Anyway, Dr. Sinclair likes you," Malcolm tells me. "He might let you live." He glances at Ryder. "You're probably a goner, though."

"If that's the case, then I accept my fate," Ryder says. He looks at me, his brown eyes flickering with defiance. "But I won't go to my grave without kissing you one more time, Emily Edwards. I need to remember how your mouth tastes, how the softness of your lips drives me wild. I need you to be mine, for real, if only just for a moment."

His chest heaves as he takes a step toward me, and I don't know if this is genuine or part of another harebrained scheme to escape Malcolm's clutches, but I honestly don't even care. All I know is that I want to remember how his mouth tastes, too. I want to feel his lips on mine again, too.

I want to feel what I felt when he kissed me in the pond, when he said my name with an ardent, heated reverence.

"You know, now is really not the time," Malcolm says, but Ryder struts past him as if he doesn't have a gun pointed in each of our faces. As if we're not in imminent danger of being killed just like Dr. Sharp. As if he doesn't care even if we are.

"Be mine," Ryder says, his voice gruff and wanting. "Please, Emily, be mine."

"I'm yours," I say, and I don't know if he means it, but I do, and my lips part instinctually as he leans his face down toward mine and grabs me by the waist, pulling me toward him. He lowers his forehead to mine, his eyelashes tickling my skin. I close my eyes and wait for the delicious sensation of his lips on mine, for one fleeting moment of pleasure in the midst of a hellish ordeal.

But his kiss never comes. Instead, Ryder snakes an arm over my shoulder, reaching past me. Then he grabs the bear spray holstered to the straps of my pack, spins around, and unleashes it on Malcolm.

"My eyes!" a stunned Malcolm cries, falling to his knees as he fires his gun blindly. Ryder torches him with another blast as I cover my head, and then he reaches back to grab my hand.

"Run!" he shouts, coughing, and he grips my wrist and leads me east.

"Run faster!" Ryder cries when I can't keep up. My injured ankle throbs with every step, making it impossible for me to pick up speed.

I grit my teeth and push through the pain, adrenaline coursing through me, until suddenly Ryder scoops me up into his arms like I'm a giant baby. Terrified, I squeeze my eyes shut as Malcolm shoots at our backs. Luckily, being temporarily blinded does no favors for his aim, and Ryder grunts as he sprints toward Lake Superior.

I have no idea how he's managing to carry me and my heavy pack, but I bury my face in the nook between his chest and neck and hold on for dear life. And though I've never been in a more dangerous circumstance than this one, the realization strikes me that somehow, in defiance of reason and logic and the bullets whizzing around us, I've never felt more protected.

"There," Ryder says finally, gasping for air. "The canoe!"

He sprints another fifty meters and sets me down unceremoniously, rushing to move the canoe off the rocky shore where Malcolm beached it.

"Hurry!" he instructs. "Get in."

I grit my teeth and clamber to my feet. "Where are we gonna go?"

"I don't know, but we have to get the hell out of here. If any of Sinclair's men heard those gunshots, they'll come running. And once they find Malcolm, he'll tell them we came this way."

He shrugs off his pack and tosses it into the canoe. "Get in!"

"Wait," I say, unzipping my pack. "First, life jackets."

"There's an army of minions after us, Edwards!" Ryder cries. "We don't have time for life jackets!"

I scowl at him. "There is *always* time for life jackets."

He rolls his eyes but slips his on when I toss it to him, and I grab my pack and carefully step into the boat.

"Do you know anything about canoeing?" I ask, watching as he pushes the vessel into the water and hops in.

He looks at me. "Don't ask questions you don't want answers to."

I sigh and take a paddle, dipping it into the water as Ryder grabs the second one.

"Go, go, go!" he says, rowing furiously. "Push, Edwards, push!"

I don't know what he means by push—surely I'm not supposed to literally push the water away from the boat with the paddle?—and so I just paddle as hard as I can, my arms ablaze with exhaustion.

"You're doing it wrong!" Ryder says, yelling at me like he's Jason and I'm the underperforming kickball teammate who cost us the big game. "You're doing it wrong, and we're going in circles!"

"*You're* doing it wrong!" I counter, water splashing in my face as I realize that we are indeed turning the boat in circles.

"Steer with me, not against!" he cries, his arms working the paddle vigorously.

"I don't know *how* to steer!" I tell him. "I couldn't steer against you if I tried!"

"Why would you try to steer against me?" he asks, his tone aggrieved. "We're supposed to be a team!"

"Can you chill out?" I ask, my ankle throbbing and my head pounding from where Ryder pelted me with the rock. "I can't think when you're like this."

"No, Emily, I cannot chill out!" Ryder says, spiraling. "Because we both just almost died *again*, and I'm exhausted, and I'm hangry, and I think I got stung by a bee or something on my calf, because it really fucking hurts! Oh, and also, I lost my pack. I slid it off so we could run faster."

Well, that effing sucks, considering his pack had most of our food, but we don't have time to wallow.

"Here," I say, setting my paddle down. "You steer. I'll look at your leg." I scoot toward him and gently lift his right leg, placing it in my lap. "Is this the one that hurts?"

He nods, and I glance at his calf expecting to see a bugbite or a beesting. Instead, I find a one-inch wound that, despite not being very deep, looks gnarly as hell.

"Is it a beesting?" Ryder asks, grimacing. "I hate bees."

"Um, Ryder?" I ask. "Did you *feel* something sting you?"

He shakes his head. "I just felt a sharp pain when we were running back there. Why?"

I bite my lip, not sure exactly how to deliver this news. "Because you appear to have been, shall we say, a little bit grazed by a bullet."

Dazed, Ryder drops his paddle into the water, and I rush to grab it back.

"*A little bit grazed by a bullet?*" he repeats, going alarmingly pale. "Holy shit. That fucker shot me!"

"It's not so bad, really," I say, trying to comfort him. "The bullet nicked your skin and then kept on zooming past." I make a cute zooming sound, hoping that will ease some of the tension, but it doesn't.

"Zoomed past, my ass!" Ryder says, retching when he glances at the wound on his calf. "I have been shot! I have been *wounded*. We don't even have any bandages left! Which means we can't cover my *gunshot wound*. Which means it might get infected, and my leg might swell up, and I might die."

I watch as he grows increasingly flustered.

"That seems to be an unlikely escalation—" I say, but Ryder cuts me off.

"Who will watch Hallmark Channel Christmas movies with Lulu?" he asks, his chest heaving. "Who will give Tara Caleb's boat? I never even got to catch up on *Breaking Bad*, Emily! I mean, I know how it ends, because how could anyone not, but I hadn't actually seen it, you know? I just started streaming season two!"

"Who's Lulu?" I ask. "Caleb had a boat?"

He doesn't seem to hear me. Instead, he runs his hands through his hair, panting.

"Ryder," I say gently, placing a hand on his chest, "look at me. You're going to be okay. But I think you're having a panic attack."

"No, it's blood loss," he insists, gripping the sides of the canoe so tightly that I can see his knuckles blanch. "I'm feeling faint from all the blood I lost from my *gunshot wound*—"

I glance at the wound again, which is small enough that two Band-Aids could cover it. "No, I don't think that's it."

"I can't breathe," Ryder wheezes. "Malcolm *shot* me, and now I can't breathe."

He looks at me, his expression haunted, and I can practically see the stress of the last few days bubbling up inside him.

"Hey," I say, keeping my voice steady and calm. "Look at me. You're okay."

"I'm not okay—"

"You're okay," I repeat, cupping his face in my hands. "Feel my hands. Look into my eyes. Hear the sound of my voice." I pull him down to rest my forehead against his, hoping physical touch will calm him in a way my words cannot.

I take one of his hands in mine and place it on my chest, letting him feel the rise and fall of my rib cage.

"You got this, Ryder," I say, telling him the same thing Dad used to tell me when I would get myself too worked up over a spelling test or a mean girl at school telling me my curly hair looked like a lion's mane. "Just breathe. I'm here. You're okay. I'm here."

He does as I say, breathing in and out, trying to match his inhales and exhales to mine.

"Thank you," he says after a few minutes, when his hands have stopped shaking and the hollowness leaves his voice.

"You're welcome," I say quietly, his hand still on my chest and mine still cupping his face. And I know he's okay now, that I can pull away and scoot back and find something in my pack that's halfway sterile enough to use as a makeshift bandage.

But I don't. Because nothing that's happened in my life in the last eleven months—Dad dying, my work performance slipping, surviving run-ins with a moose and a wolf pack and a henchman named Malcolm—makes any sense. And I've spent the last few days feeling cold and tired and frightened, and the months before that feeling guilty and heartbroken. But now, my forehead resting against Ryder's as we huddle together in a canoe that neither of us knows how to paddle, I don't feel lost or lonely, even though I should. I feel something brighter, something stronger.

I feel loved.

SIXTEEN

RYDER

When Emily finally pulls away, it's like someone ripping a warm blanket off me on a cold winter morning.

My first instinct is to pull her toward me again, but I resist the temptation. The sun is beginning to set, the bursts of pink and purple reflecting off the water signaling that nightfall is almost here, and we need to come up with a plan.

"I can't find our compass," Emily says, checking her pockets frantically. "I think—shit, I think I dropped it when Malcolm popped out from behind that tree." She searches her pack quickly, then smacks it in frustration. "Please tell me you know something about celestial navigation."

"Uh," I say, trying to shake off the lingering embarrassment I feel from my meltdown. "I know a tiny amount."

She perks up. "Tiny's better than nothing. What do you know?" she asks hopefully.

"Just that old saying: red skies at night, sailor's delight, red skies in the morning, sailor's warning," I say, grabbing my paddle.

Emily glances up at the sky. "What about pink skies at night?"

I shrug. "That wasn't in the poem."

She closes her eyes, as if willing her soul to leave her body, and when that doesn't work, she opens her pack and takes out a granola bar, tearing it into two pieces and handing one to me.

"Thanks." We both chew quietly for a minute, probably trying not to think about the fact that we're out on the open water near nightfall with no compass, no plan, and no more than half a day's food in her pack. I didn't have much of a strategy when I directed us to the canoe, except to put as much distance as possible between us and Malcolm, and the new prospect of being caught by henchmen in open water makes my skin crawl. At least on land, we had someplace to run and hide. Out here, surrounded by algae and fish, we'd be screwed.

Trying not to focus on the heavy fatigue weighing down my arms, I force myself to keep paddling. With each row, I concentrate not on my burning muscles but on how Emily's lips parted when I stepped toward her earlier and grabbed her by the waist. I think about the way she looked at me when she said *I'm yours*, her expression earnest and open. I know now isn't a great time to tell her that I wasn't just acting for Malcolm's benefit, that I meant every word I said, but whether we get off Isle Royale alive or not, I'll probably never be alone with her in a canoe again, the pastel hues of the setting sun giving her an ethereal glow.

If I'm gonna shoot my shot, I need to do it now, before Sinclair or a wild animal has another chance to take me out.

"So," I say, swallowing my nerves, "I wanted to talk about what happened between us. With Malcolm. I mean, not *with* Malcolm, but in front of Malcolm." My words are not at all coming out as smoothly as I hoped, and I wish, just this once, I could say what I mean and sound halfway intelligent doing it.

"I want to answer the question you asked me earlier," I explain, the burning in my shoulders no match for the burning in my heart. "About how I look at you."

"Wait," Emily says, and the bubble of hope bouncing around inside me pops.

"I'll wait if you want me to," I say. "It's just that we may not have much time—"

"No, I mean, wait as in *look*," she says, pointing at something in the distance. "There's some kind of tower over there. See?"

I follow her index finger to the shoreline, where a black steel tower sits nestled among the trees.

"It could be a radio tower, Ryder," she says, her tone suddenly energized. "A radio we could use to call for help. Let's go!"

We paddle quickly, which is a mistake, because we start accidentally going in circles again, and it takes us a minute to get our rhythm. By the time we reach the rocky shoreline and bank the canoe, dragging it uphill and stashing it behind a tree to keep it out of view, my arms ache like they haven't since the time Caleb and I challenged each other to a pull-up contest. I whip out my flashlight to do a quick sweep of the area, and when I'm satisfied that no one's lurking in the bushes, ready to jump out and murder us, I take Emily's hand and we hurry toward the tower. If by some miracle it has a functioning radio and we manage to signal the rangers for help, maybe they'll rescue us with a helicopter and we'll get to watch while they arrest Sinclair for murder, attempted burglary, and the universal crime of being an absolute douche. After all, it would be a damn good ending to *Cover of Darkness*.

"Dammit!" Emily says when we reach the tower. "It's closed."

She points to the NO ENTRY sign posted at the bottom of the stairs, her face crumpling like she's on the verge of tears.

"And?" I say, climbing over the sign.

Her jaw drops. "We can't just ignore the sign, Ryder!"

I don't even try to hide my grin. "Watch me. I live on the edge, remember?"

I jog up four flights of creaking metal stairs, Emily cursing under her breath as she clambers up after me. When I reach the top, I attempt to throw open the door leading inside, but the knob doesn't budge.

"See?" Emily says, breathless from the climb. "It's closed."

Shielding my face, I use the flashlight to break a window, and then I stick my hand through and reach around to unlock the door.

"Will you look at that," I say dryly. "It's open."

I open the door and step inside a small, dank room, where the intense scent of mildew assaults my senses.

"Homey," I say, pausing to study the dusty ceiling and sticky linoleum flooring.

But Emily has no time for that.

"The radio!" she says, brushing past me to marvel at a dusty panel of buttons and switches. She glances sideways at me. "Any chance you know how to work this thing?"

There's as much chance of me knowing which buttons to push as there is of her taking up skydiving as a casual hobby. I shake my head.

"Okay," she says, biting her lip as she studies the equipment. "Let's see."

I watch as she brushes a curl out of her face and gets to work, her jaw flexed in concentration as she flips switches and turns knobs.

"My dad used to tinker with old radios sometimes," she says, picking up a small handheld microphone and tapping it. "He liked taking broken things apart and figuring out a way to make them work again. I only wish I'd paid more attention when he talked about it . . ."

She trails off, frowning, but her expression transforms into a smile when she hits a series of buttons, and a blinking red light comes on.

"Is it working?" I ask, my pulse racing as the sound of radio static fills the tiny space.

"I think so." She taps the mic again. This time, a low-pitched echo fills the airwaves, and she smiles at me.

"How'd you do it?" I ask, staring at her like she just solved the problem of world hunger.

"It was incredibly difficult. You see, I determined the location of the power button." Grinning, she points to a red button labeled ON and taps her temple. "Never forget that you once kissed a genius, Ryder Fleet."

I shake my head, but I'm not grinning. "I never could."

"Okay," she says, lifting the mic toward her mouth. "Here we go."

I nod at her, and she takes a deep breath before speaking.

"Hello," she says politely, as if she's greeting a friendly pass-erby on the street and not blasting out a call for help. "This is Emily Edwards and Ryder Fleet—"

"*Dr.* Emily Edwards," I cut in, and she gives me a look.

"We require emergency assistance," she continues with a calm, even demeanor of someone well accustomed to dealing with the chaos of the ER. "We witnessed a homicide near the wreckage of the *Explorer* on the northwestern side of Isle Royale. The victim was Dr. Benning Sharp. The perpetrator was Dr. Killian Sharp, chair of Science of the Human Past at Harvard."

"He'd love that you mentioned Harvard," I mutter, but she shushes me.

"We have sought refuge inside the radio tower from which we are broadcasting this message," she continues. "I repeat, we require emergency assistance. We are not injured—"

"I was grazed by a bullet!" I correct her.

"—but we are being pursued by Dr. Sinclair and an un-known number of armed men. We require emergency evacua-tion off the island. Our lives are in imminent danger."

She holds the mic toward me and nods in case I want to add anything.

"This is Cover of Darkness signing off," I say, not able to pass up my one opportunity to live out my action movie fanta-sies. "Please help us. Over and out."

Emily raises an eyebrow. "Cover of Darkness signing off? Really?"

"Sounded cooler in my head."

She sets down the microphone and sighs, rubbing a hand over her weary eyes. "Okay. So now we just hang out and wait for someone to rescue us, I guess."

"I'm sure the rangers will be here before you know it," I say confidently. And even though the thought should fill me with pure relief, it doesn't. Because yeah, I want to get the hell off this island as much as anyone—hearing the words *a little bit grazed by a bullet* took at least ten years off my life—but leaving Isle Royale means heading home to an empty apartment and a soul-sucking existence spent doing mundane odd jobs for flirty housewives. It means no more heart-pounding excitement, no more chances to prove that I'm more than the dim-witted he-man people think I am.

It means no more Emily.

"So," I say as we hunker down to wait for our rescuers, the last rays of sunlight disappearing over Lake Superior. "I was thinking . . ."

I trail off, searching for the words to say what I mean. I want to revisit the conversation I started in the canoe, but it seemed simpler out on the water, where we were surrounded by fresh air and the risk of imminent death. Now that we're cloistered together in a tiny room that reminds me of my grandpa's creepy basement, I feel like a nervous kid gearing up for a round of seven minutes in heaven with his longtime crush.

But before I can swallow my nerves and figure out a smooth

way to tell her that my feelings for her are as strong as my navigation skills are incompetent, she shrugs off her backpack and drops to her knees in front of me.

"Holy shit," I say, the words coming out of me before I realize that she's bent down to examine my calf wound.

"Sorry," she says, drawing her hand back even though she hasn't touched my leg yet. "Does it hurt?"

"Oh. No. I mean, yes. It does. Sort of."

She looks up at me, and her gaze meeting mine is not at all helpful to the wild fantasies running through my mind right now. "Are you okay?"

"Fine," I say gruffly, forcing myself to look anywhere but at her. The last thing I need right now is a hard-on, considering I should be more focused on getting the hell off this island than my growing desire.

Easier said than done.

"I'll get us something to eat," I say, turning away from her, but she rises to her feet to stop me.

"Hold on. I need to clean your wound. An open one is a breeding ground for bacteria. Sit, please."

Letting her touch me right now seems like a bad idea, but I don't have the strength to argue. Instead, I sit down and stretch my injured leg out, watching as she switches on her lantern and pulls out her first aid kit.

"So, do you want the good news or the bad news?" she asks, sliding the light closer to my calf.

"Uh, the good news," I tell her. "And only the good news."

She sighs. "The good news is, the wound isn't very deep.

The bad news is that it's deep enough that I want to give you stitches."

"Uh, no," I say quickly. "Hard pass. I don't do needles."

She raises an eyebrow. "I didn't know you were afraid of needles."

"I'm not *afraid* of needles," I say tersely, pulling my leg away. "I just don't like them. Kind of like how I'm not *afraid* of the dark, I just prefer sleeping with a night-light."

She looks at me for a long moment.

"It's a very small night-light," I add. "Almost infinitesimal."

"Look, Ryder," she says, rifling through her medical kit, "you don't have to let me stitch you up if you don't want to, but it is the clinically appropriate course of action."

"Well, I hardly ever take the appropriate course of action," I remind her. "In case you haven't noticed."

Emily smiles. "Oh, I've noticed." She glances around thoughtfully. "Hey, what if I find something that will distract you while I'm giving you the stitches? Will you get them then?"

Unless she's going to thread my skin back together topless, I'm not going to be distracted, but I don't say that to her.

"I don't know," I say honestly. "What's the distraction?"

She combs through her pack and pulls out Sharp's notebook. "Here. Read to me."

No offense to Dr. Sharp and Captain Sebastian Evermore, but that's way less exciting than anything I envisioned.

"Oh good, a notebook about an old dead guy written by another old dead guy," I say dryly. "Riveting."

But I don't want her to think I'm a coward, and so I leaf

through the pages as Emily assembles her little tray of torture tools. I flip through maps and diagrams and Sharp's barely legible notes about the layout of the *Explorer*, and then I find one of the letters Captain Evermore wrote to his wife.

"Find anything good?" Emily asks.

"Mayb—ow!" I twitch as a burst of pain washes over my calf. "Holy shit, Edwards, can you warn me before you slice me open?"

She stares at me. "That was the alcohol swab."

"Right. Well, the alcohol swab sucks."

She pulls the wrapper off a syringe, and I feel my head getting woozy before she even does anything with it.

"I'll inject you with numbing medication, and after that you won't feel a thing," she says. "Now read to me. Read me one of Evermore's letters."

I study the page in front of me. "I don't know if you want me to read this one."

"Why?" she asks, adjusting the fingertips of her gloves.

I watch her work, appreciating how calm and focused she is. It's easy to imagine her doing this day in, day out, helping her patients feel better with her expertise and caring demeanor, and I marvel at her talent.

"It's a love letter, Edwards," I explain.

She doesn't look up from her work. "So? They're all love letters."

"Yeah, well," I say, "this one's different. Steamy, if you will. I'm not sure you can handle it."

She inserts the syringe into a small vial and draws out liquid. "Anything you give me, Fleet, I can handle. Promise."

Her words, paired with the very recent memory of her crouching in front of me, turn my throat dry, and I grab my flask and sip desperately.

"Read," she says, eyeing the liquid in the syringe and holding it up to the lantern. "For me."

The last part just about kills me, and I return my attention to the page and force myself to focus only on Captain Evermore's words and not the memory of Emily's lips parting to make way for mine.

"'My dearest Katherine,'" I read, squinting at the captain's neat, sloping cursive, "'I dreamed of you last night. I dreamed of you in my bed, your dark hair strewn over my pillow and you underneath me.'"

"You think that's steamy?" Emily asks, leaning over my calf. "Bless you, you sweet summer child."

"No," I say, turning the page in Sharp's journal. "I think *this* is steamy: 'I dream of kneeling over you and spreading your legs open, of pressing my mouth to your most tender, aching part. I dream of the soft, sweet gasp you make when you come, of the way your fingernails claw at my back and the way that when I am inside you, there exists only us and the insatiable passion that has consumed me since we first met.'"

A sharp sting lights up my calf, and I suck in my breath.

"That's the anesthetic," Emily says. "The worst part. Don't stop reading, 'cause that shit is juicy."

I force my attention back to the page as the stinging peaks, stabbing my calf like a tiny bolt of lightning, and then, slowly, eases.

"'At night, my dearest Katherine,'" I continue, my gaze

flitting between Evermore's words and Emily's face, "'when I cannot sleep, I grip myself and think of you, only of you, of your raven hair and sweet mouth and nimble hands. I think of you underneath me, and on top of me, and beside me. I think of how, were the world to meet its end, I know exactly where I would want to spend my final hours: inside you, our bodies rising and falling together, one last time and forever.'"

Emily glances up from my leg, and I could lose myself in her soft gray eyes, but the look she gives me implores me to keep going.

"'You are my home,'" I read, glancing from the page back to her. "'And with those thoughts of you, desperate for the next time I shall look upon your face, I erupt.'"

Emily doesn't say anything, and neither do I, but I cannot continue to look at her and think about *erupting* without giving in to the intense longing taking over my body, and so I close Sharp's notebook with a thud.

"So yeah," I say finally, extreme sexual tension practically radiating off me. "Pretty spicy stuff. How's the old calfy-calf?"

I would love to throw myself off the top of the tower right now as punishment for saying *calfy-calf*, but I can't help that I ramble when I'm nervous, and if it takes uttering ridiculous words to get my imagination to stop pairing *Emily* and *erupt* together, so fucking be it.

"Oh, it's uh, it's finished," Emily says, clearing her throat. She removes her gloves and sanitizes her hands, looking everywhere but at me.

"That's it?" I ask, and if I'm being honest, I'm kind of

disappointed. It's not that I want more stitches—I'm not *that* stupid—so much as I want the chance to keep reading to her.

"Yep," she says, glancing at the notebook on my lap and then at my face. "That's it." She smiles. "See, all you needed was a little nineteenth-century sexting to distract you."

"I'll admit, Evermore had some serious swagger," I say. "Not many men can talk about erupting and make it sound halfway decent."

She laughs. "Right? One can see why Katherine chartered a ship to find him." She tucks her first aid kit away and crosses her legs, scooting closer to me. "They were such a brave couple. I mean, he had the courage to stay aboard a sinking ship to save his crew, and she risked her life to sail across the sea to try to find him. The sex must have been insaaaaane."

What's insaaaaane is how badly I want her right now, but I only make a noncommittal noise in reply.

She tucks a hand under her chin. "Can you imagine loving someone that much? So fiercely that you'd lay down your life for them?"

"Yes," I say without thinking, because I don't need to think. I don't even need to imagine. "I can."

"I—" Emily pauses, wrapping her arms around herself. "Can I ask you a question? A personal one?"

I shrug. "Our lives are in imminent danger, remember? If there was ever a time to ask personal questions, it's now."

The lantern casts a shadow across her face. "Will you tell me about Caleb?"

I suck in my breath, because asking me to tell her about my

brother is asking me to tell her about the rawest, most tender part of me. The darkest part of me.

"Tell you about him?" I ask. "Or about what happened to him?"

She reaches out like she wants to touch me before hesitating and pulling her hand back. "Either. Both. Whatever you're comfortable sharing. And if you're not, I understand."

I run a hand through my hair, contemplating her request. I'll pretty much give Emily anything she wants—I let her stick a needle in my leg, for Christ's sake—but I've barely talked about Caleb to anyone since he died, and even though I want to tell her, I'm still trying to figure out how. I tried joining Tara at her grief support group once, but the facilitator mispronounced Caleb's name, and that was enough to make me leave before anyone even touched the free donuts at the refreshment table. I didn't even talk to Hannah about him much when we were still dating; I was too busy drinking, and she was too busy getting on with her life as though nothing had happened at all.

"He was my best friend," I say finally. "Don't get me wrong, we drove each other insane sometimes, but he was the one person in the world who liked me just the way I was. Our dad wasn't exactly a winner, and our mom busted her ass with two jobs, so Caleb was the one who took care of me a lot of the time. He's the one who taught me how to swim and ride my bike. He used to give me pocket money from his paper route so that I could buy something at the school book fair. I didn't even like books—I'd waste the money on something stupid, like a yo-yo or bookmarks I'd never use—but he gave it to me anyway, because he didn't want me to be the only kid in the class who couldn't afford to go."

I pause, tapping Sharp's notebook against my knee. Emily doesn't say anything as I gather my thoughts, doesn't try to rush me or change the topic. She just waits patiently, silently, as if we have all the time in the world. But we both know time is a fickle thing—one second you have plenty of it, the next you'd do anything to rewind it—and so I take a deep breath and tell her how my kind, industrious big brother grew up to be a kind, industrious man, and how Fleet Outdoor Adventures was the culmination of everything he loved: family, adventure, and the great outdoors. I tell her how I tried to keep things running after he died, but trying to fill his shoes was like trying to fit a dumb peg into a smart hole, and I spent more time drinking and being angry at everyone and everything than doing anything useful. I tell her what it was like when the agency finally tanked, to walk alone through the silent, empty office that had once thrummed with people and activity.

I tell Emily about the beginning, and I tell her about the middle. She doesn't ask about the end, and maybe that's why I find the balls to tell her about that, too.

"He died three weeks before his wedding day," I say, and it shocks me now, even two years later, as I say it out loud. "He wanted to do a vertical camping trip for his bachelor party, so he and a few of his buddies—guys who were experienced tour guides at the agency—went climbing." I swallow, remembering Tara's voice on the other end of the line when she called me at four a.m., remembering how I kept waiting and waiting and waiting to wake up and realize the whole thing had been a terrible dream.

"Caleb was always careful," I tell Emily. "Intentional. He never took unnecessary risks. But there are accidents in nature you can't always predict. They got caught underneath a rockslide, and—well." I pause, trying to stop my brain from forming the images it always tries so hard to create. "Four of them made it out. But two of them, Caleb and his buddy Charlie, didn't."

I go quiet, thinking of how the medical report listed his injuries as *unsurvivable*. I couldn't get the word out of my head for a long time after reading it, because it was the only word that seemed to adequately describe my grief. Surely losing Caleb would be *unsurvivable*; the earth, without him on it, would stop spinning. Surely my heart, without him there to love me and tease me and kick my ass in *Mario Kart*, would stop beating. Surely I could not bear this pain for the rest of my life.

But surely never came.

"Ryder," Emily says, taking my hand, but I haven't even told her the worst part yet.

And suddenly I have to. I have to tell her, because if by some crazy miracle she does want me after all of this is over, she can't know that without knowing this. Because it's not just Caleb's death that's haunted me for two years and turned my life unrecognizably upside down; it's that I wasn't there for him when he needed me the most. I wasn't there for the brother who'd taken care of me from day one, and every day I wonder why I'm even here at all. It's why I can't sleep, can't date, can't channel some energy into finding a new career I give half a shit about. Because I failed Caleb, and so the rest of it is meaningless.

The rest of it is dust.

"I was supposed to be there," I tell Emily. "At his bachelor party. I was the best man. I missed my flight because I slept through my alarm, and I had to schedule a new one for the next morning."

"Oh, Ryder," she whispers, squeezing my palm.

I wait for her to say something to stop me, like *Everything happens for a reason* or *Time heals all wounds* or some other politely cruel way of saying *Please take your misery elsewhere, because you're really killing my vibe.* I wait for her to say *He's in a better place now* or one of the two dozen other trite phrases people throw out when they don't know what to say in the face of unnerving, all-encompassing grief, but she doesn't. She only sits, and waits, and watches.

She only listens.

"If I had been there," I tell her, my voice breaking, "if I had fucking shown up like I was supposed to, maybe I could have done something."

And because I promised Emily honesty, I close my eyes and say the other thing, the darkest thing, the thing that Hannah screamed at me the night she left and that I scream silently at myself all the time.

"It should have been me instead," I confess, my eyes burning. "But I let him down, so I wasn't there, and I will never forgive myself for it."

It's dark in the tower, but not so dark that I can't see Emily's eyes shining with tears.

"It should not have been you," she says. "And it shouldn't have been *him*, either, but it's not your fault, Ryder. Has anyone told you that? That it's not your fault? Because it wasn't. It isn't. It will never be your fault, no matter how many times your grief tries to tell you that it is."

Her words are a gift, but I'm not sure that I can accept them.

"I wish I could believe that," I tell her.

"I wish you could, too." She frowns, still clutching my hand. "You know, earlier you said that I think I'm better than you, but I want you to know that's not true. I don't think that at all."

"It's okay if you do," I tell her. "Truly. I mean, you *are* better than me. You're someone who heals people for a living. I'm someone who knows way too many *SpongeBob* episodes by heart. Honestly, sometimes it's okay to call a spade a spade."

She shakes her head. "You're not the only one who feels like you let down the person you love. I'm not better than you, Ryder. I'm exactly the same."

"What are you talking about?" I ask, mystified at the distorted way she views herself. "You describe yourself as someone who's scared of practically everything, and you still came to a remote national park to honor your dad. That's the opposite of letting him down."

"Remember how I told you my dad asked me three times if I'd go to Isle Royale with him before I said yes?" she asks, her hand shaking. "*Three times*. He raised me and loved me and set aside his own wants to take care of me, and I was still too selfish to go do the one thing he asked me to do. The only reason I'm here to honor him now is because I didn't do it while he was alive. I missed my chance, and just like you'll never forgive yourself, I'll never forgive myself, either."

"That doesn't make you selfish, Emily," I tell her, wishing I could make her believe it. "It just makes you human."

"No, you don't understand." She sniffles and wipes her eyes with her sleeve. "I thought my dad was happy with the way his life turned out. I thought he was content, you know. Like maybe he couldn't go hike the Swiss Alps or parachute into the rainforest, but he was happy enough with running the local paper and walking his dog and listening to my stupid little diatribes about Judith. But he wasn't. I was wrong."

I don't know who Judith is, but I'm pretty sure that's not important here, and I squeeze her hand to comfort her.

"Why would you think he wasn't happy?" I ask. "Did he tell you that?"

She wipes away a tear. "No. Not me. After he died, I found these journals full of letters he wrote to my mom after she died. I hadn't even known he wrote to her, but I guess it was his way of trying to stay connected to her. I thought I would glance at them, you know, and maybe they would bring me comfort."

"I understand," I say. "After Caleb died, I missed him so much that I read some of his college term papers just to feel closer to him."

"Did it work?" Emily asks.

I shrug. "Not really. They were super boring. It just made me appreciate how he never used a run-on sentence."

She smiles briefly, and then it fades. "I found one letter

Dad had written to Mom when Brooke and I were in middle school."

"What did it say?" I ask.

"It said, and I quote, 'Dear Jenny, I dreamed of a life of adventure, and instead, I got minutiae.'"

"That doesn't sound so bad," I say. "He was probably just stressed out being a single dad."

"It gets worse," she says miserably. "He wrote about how he'd gotten a job offer at a news desk in New York, but he didn't take it because he didn't want to uproot my sister Brooke and me. And about how he wanted to travel to Europe for the summer, but I was so scared of planes he knew I'd never set foot on one. He talked about a whole lifetime of things he dreamed of doing, things he wanted to do but couldn't because I was holding him back."

"You weren't holding him back," I argue. "You were just a kid."

She shakes her head. "He gave up so much for me, so much joy he could have had, and I couldn't even make time in my schedule to go on a damn hiking trip with him. And now he's gone, and I'll never have the chance to honor the sacrifice he made for me."

"Hey." I lean forward to grasp her arms gently. "I bet if your dad was here right now, he'd tell you that it wasn't a sacrifice. That it was a freaking gift. But come on, Emily, you didn't miss your chance. We're here, aren't we? You said it yourself, your dad loved adventure, and look at you. You're having the craziest fucking adventure of all time on his behalf."

She nods and sniffles. "It really is crazy. And I haven't even gotten the chance to use my solar shower. Or my glow-in-the-dark toilet paper."

"I know," I say. "But look, even though the odds are stacked against us—since, you know, we're terrible at being outdoors and our adversaries have guns and we have no idea if anyone heard our desperate radio plea for help—"

"I think you've listed enough odds," Emily cuts in. "You can probably stop there."

"Right. Well, even though the odds are stacked against us, we're still alive. We've still got the Evermore. And as long as we're still fighting, your dad's story isn't over," I tell her. "And maybe, I don't know. Maybe Caleb's isn't, either."

"Do you really believe that?" she asks.

"I have to," I tell her. "I have to believe that we can get off this island with the diamond, and that you can spread your dad's ashes like you wanted. And I have to believe that one day, whether it's on this island or in court, I'll get the chance to punch Sinclair in the face and take Caleb's Discman back."

"I don't think they let you punch people in court."

I shrug. "A guy can dream, Edwards."

She studies me, her expression thoughtful. "I've never told anyone that before. About my dad's letter. Not even Brooke."

I hold her hand a little tighter, grateful that she trusts me enough to share something so private.

"You can tell me anything, Emily."

She nods, and then she pulls her hand back to tuck a curl behind her ear.

"You were trying to tell me something," she says. "Earlier. In the canoe."

I swallow, trying to summon the courage to explain that I want to keep being the person she tells things to, even after we leave Isle Royale. That I want to know everything that makes her tick, from her favorite feel-good movie to the worries that keep her up at night. That I want to know *her*, through and through, in every sense of the word.

"I was trying to answer the question you asked me in front of Malcolm," I explain. "I was trying to tell you how I see you."

"Oh," she says softly, her gaze locked on mine.

"Do you want me to tell you now?"

I pray that she'll say yes, but she only watches me for a long moment, like she's trying to read something in my expression.

"No," she says finally. "I don't want you to tell me."

Then, her cheeks flushed and her mouth slightly parted, she leans forward to loop her arms around my neck.

"I want you to show me."

SEVENTEEN

EMILY

Those six words are all the encouragement Ryder needs, and he moves toward me like he did when he pretended to kiss me in front of Malcolm. But this time, it's not just for show, and my legs tremble as his face nears mine. I expect him to go straight in for a kiss, and my lips are ready, eager, but instead, he takes a loose curl in his fingers, tucking it gently behind my ear.

"Emily," he says, his voice gruff. He lowers his face to press a kiss to my collarbone, one hand gently gripping the back of my head, and I swear to God that I will die if he doesn't kiss me soon.

"If we do this," he says, kissing my neck, and then my jaw, and then pulling me forward so that I'm in his lap, "it can't be because we're in a life-or-death scenario. I don't want you to want me because I might be your last chance to get off. So if that's what this is to you, tell me now."

"It's not," I say, wrapping an arm around his neck and leaning into his chest. "It's not, it's not, it's not."

"Good." He runs his hands up my back, kneading the sore muscles under my T-shirt, and then down to my ass. "Because I've been wanting to do this since you yelled at me on the ferry."

"I didn't *yell* at you," I protest, but I forget the rest of what I was going to say, because Ryder finally has mercy on me and presses his mouth to mine, and suddenly I don't care that my legs aren't shaved and my curls are a mess and my body is rife with exhaustion. I don't even care that there's an insanely valuable diamond burning a hole in the bottom of my backpack. Because there's only him, and there's only me, and there's only us together, his strong hands on my waist and my mouth on his mouth and—

I pull away from him when a low-pitched rumbling sound interrupts our impassioned bliss.

"What was that?" I ask in a whisper. "That sound?"

He blinks like he has no clue what I'm talking about. "Huh?"

I shush him when I hear it again, and then I leap up and run toward the window, grabbing my binoculars on the way.

Ryder follows closely behind me, one hand on the small of my back as I peer out toward Lake Superior.

"It's a speedboat," I say, squinting at the approaching vessel. "Ryder, it's a boat! Someone's coming to help us! We're saved!"

"Fuck yeah!" He pumps the air with his fist and sweeps me off my feet, twirling me around in the dark, dank room before setting me down again. His eyes glint with mischief as he smiles at me. "I suppose this means we don't have time to—"

"Ryder!" I hiss, swatting his arm playfully, but he only shrugs.

"Just kidding. Sort of." He motions for my binoculars. "Mind if I take a look? I need to capture every detail I can for my *Cover of Darkness* screenplay."

I laugh, handing the binoculars over, and I wrap my arms around him from behind as he peers out the window. I'm exhausted and hungry and my ankle hurts like no other, but we're almost out of here. We're almost safe. And we're one step closer to being someplace where we can kiss and touch and caress each other without interruption.

Except, apparently, we're not.

"Hey, Emily," he says, a note of worry in his voice, "are the park rangers usually armed?"

"Armed?" I ask. "Huh?"

I grab my binoculars back rudely and stare out onto the water, my pulse racing. The boat, probably a minute or less out from the shore, has picked up speed, and I squint as I try to make out the three men aboard. There's a scowling guy in a beanie—which, hey, I wouldn't be thrilled if I were a park ranger and had to interrupt my sleep to go rescue two idiots from a tower—a dark-haired man with a mustache, and a grim-faced dude with a buzzcut. The kicker is that all three have firearms clipped to their waistbands, and I watch, my stomach clenching, as the dark-haired guy pulls out a knife the size of Ryder's arm.

"Ohmiiiigod," I say, jumping back from the window. "Machete! One of those guys has a fucking *machete*."

"Maybe the rangers use machetes to cut down trees," Ryder

says hopefully, clearly clinging to some shred of hope. "You know, to clear their paths or whatever."

"Those are not the fucking rangers," I tell him, my voice barely a squeak as the boat nears the shore. "Killian's men got our message. We need to get the hell out of here, now."

"For fuck's sake," he seethes, grabbing my pack from the ground, "if I get cockblocked by a henchman one more time—"

"Ryder, move!" I insist, my heart pounding.

He grabs my hand and flings open the door leading toward the stairwell, and I gasp as we spot the men jumping off the boat and hurrying ashore. There's no way we can make it down the stairs without being shot at, much less seen, and my throat goes dry as I realize that we're trapped.

"This way," Ryder says, pulling me away from the door. He grabs my flashlight and uses it to smash the back window, covering his head to block the shards of glass.

"What are you doing?" I ask, suddenly dizzy as I realize just how far we off the ground we are. "There's only one set of stairs—"

"Forget the stairs." His tone is blunt, urgent. "We're climbing down."

"We're *climbing* down the tower?" I ask, breathless. "Listen, I'm not sure what *Indiana Jones*–style stunts you think I'm capable of, but we can't just parkour our way out of this!"

"Fine. Then I'll climb down first and catch you."

"Catch me?" I repeat, panic turning my voice shrill. "Surely you don't expect me to *jump*—"

"I expect you to trust me." Ryder's voice is calm, steady, even in the midst of Operation Cover of Darkness going very,

very wrong, and he gives my hand a reassuring squeeze. "I promised to protect you, Emily Edwards, and protect you I will."

His voice is gruff, determined, like he thinks he's Jason Statham in a high-stakes action movie, and I watch as he climbs through the window and steps cautiously out onto a narrow steel platform. My head spinning, I peek out the broken window to survey the scene and very much wish I hadn't. We're even higher up than I remember, and without access to the stairs, the only way someone could make it safely to the ground would be to jump from the platform to the metal beam one story below and then somehow repeat that three more times without losing their foothold and crashing to their death.

I flinch as Ryder drops my pack to the ground, where it lands with a sickening thud.

"Now, I need you to stay calm," he says, glancing back at me. "Because we're gonna Cirque du Soleil it."

The wave of nausea that comes over me is anything but calm, and I suck in my breath.

"That has got to be the single worst sentence I've ever heard."

"I'll climb down first, and when I say jump, you jump," he directs. "I will catch you."

"But what if you don't?" I ask, my voice trembling. "What if you don't, and I break my neck or hit my head or at the very least break both legs so that I can't run from—"

"Stop." Ryder leans forward to touch his forehead to mine, placing his hands on either side of my face. "I *will* catch you."

There's no time to say more, and I watch, terrified, as he takes a deep breath and prepares to jump to the next beam.

"Be careful, please," I plead, curling my hands into such tight fists that I'm certain I'll draw blood.

I hold my breath as he lowers himself off the platform, holding on to the steel lattice for literal dear life. Then, his jaw clenched, he grunts and leaps downward, landing on the narrow scaffolding with surprising athleticism.

"See?" he calls to me. "Not so bad."

But it is bad, very bad, because when I glance back toward the lake, I see the henchmen rushing toward the tower, guns at the ready.

"They're almost here," I say in terror, and Ryder grunts and jumps again.

This time, his landing is shaky, and I swear that if we get out of this alive, I'm never leaving the ground again.

The henchmen are so close now that I can hear their voices in the not-so-distant distance, and I utter a silent prayer as Ryder makes his third dangerous jump. When he slips on the last beam, stopping his fall only by grabbing hold of the scaffolding with one hand, I have to cover my mouth with my hand to stop myself from crying out. It's Cirque du Soleil with all the danger and none of the fun—or the kill switches—and my heart pounds like it's going to burst out of my chest.

Finally, Ryder makes his final jump to the ground, where he tumbles onto the grass and hurries to his feet. My terror mounts as I hear the clang of boots against metal and realize that the henchmen have reached the stairs. They'll be here in seconds, and if I don't jump, there's not a chance in hell we make it out of here.

Then again, if I do jump, there's a chance I won't make it out of here anyway.

Ryder waves his arms wildly at me, indicating that it's go time, but my feet are frozen in place. I shut my eyes, trying to focus, but all I see are broken bones and fractured skulls and blinding, unremitting pain. Gritting my teeth, I open my eyes and shake my head at Ryder, because no matter how desperately I know I need to jump, I can't do it. I, the woman who has an extra smoke detector in her kitchen and actually studied the evacuation safety map on the door of every hotel room she's ever stayed in, cannot jump to my possible death.

But Ryder, his expression calm, believing, only nods at me.

I will catch you, he mouths, motioning a catch with his arms. *I will catch you*. And then he places one hand against his chest, against the knot of skin and bone and muscle beneath which his heart beats.

I will catch you, he mouths again, and as the henchmen's footsteps get closer and the Lake Superior wind howls and every terrible injury I've ever treated in the ER flashes through my mind, I clench my fists and force myself to keep my eyes open and look only at Ryder, at his steady gaze and beating heart and waiting arms. And then, against all reason and logic and everything I know about fall prevention protocols, I suck in my breath and jump.

EIGHTEEN

RYDER

"You caught me," Emily whispers when she lands in my arms.

"Always," I whisper back, my pulse racing.

I want to dip her and kiss her and drop a clever one-liner like the main character would in a movie—*Fancy meeting you here* or *Come here often?* might work—but there's no time for that. There's not even time for us to sprint through the darkness and into the woods, because the henchmen have reached the tower room.

So instead, with Emily in my arms, I dive sideways to duck under the tower. Hoping tall weeds and inky darkness will be enough to keep us unnoticed, I lay on top of her, covering her with my body lest a henchman spot us and decide to shoot first and grab the diamond later. I can feel her heart pounding against my chest, and mine must be, too, but I can only focus on the fact that she slips an arm around the back of my neck and holds on like there's no tomorrow.

Which, if we're unlucky, there might not be.

We barely breathe, barely even blink for seconds, a minute, maybe two. Finally, after a whole lot of grumbling and even more F-bombs, Sinclair's men jog back down the stairs and do a sweep of the area, the brightness from their flashlights bouncing off the trees and the tower. Emily digs her nails into the back of my neck, petrified, and I will these unrepentant assholes to fuck off and go crawling back to Sinclair.

At long last, they return to their boat and speed off, the motor gunning, and I roll off Emily and let out a long, shaky exhale.

"Thank you, Ryder," she whispers, squeezing my hand, but the kiss she gives me when she rolls on top of me, her curls falling over her shoulders and tickling my cheek, is all the thanks I need.

We spend the night huddled together under the radio tower, our teeth chattering as we fade in and out of sleep. We're both too exhausted to move, much less come up with a plan, and we're holding out a shred of hope that a park ranger or the Girl Scouts or a friendly, nonmurderous hiker might respond to our call for help.

But when morning comes, the pastel sunrise reflecting off the gleaming waters of Lake Superior, we decide it's better to move on than to linger too long in one spot. Strong wind gusts make the lake choppy and rule out any chance of safely traveling by Malcolm's boat, and so we set off by foot, surveying the little food we have left.

"We're down to three freeze-dried ice-cream sandwiches

and one Cosmic Brownie," Emily says, scowling. "And it doesn't even have many sprinkles."

We don't talk much when we hit the trail, hiking in what I sincerely hope is east toward the ranger station, because we're both exhausted and hungry and the strong wind gusts make it hard to hear each other anyway. I keep whipping my head around to look behind us, terrified I'll see one of Sinclair's men, but the forest is quiet except for the sound of birds chirping and waves crashing against the shore, and it would be a serene scene if we didn't look like the bedraggled survivors of a zombie apocalypse.

We're trying to figure out how long we can go without tearing into the freeze-dried ice cream when I spot a blur of something blue hanging from a thicket of bushes in the distance.

"Hey, is that . . ." I jog toward the bushes, some of my energy bouncing back as I realize this might be a stroke of good luck. "Holy shit. Blueberries!"

I sound like an absolute maniac, crying out with joy for a couple of fucking berries, but I can't help myself.

"Emily!" I cry, waving for her to catch up as I grab a handful of blueberries and hold them up like they're the Evermore diamond. "Look! Motherfucking BLUEBERRIES!"

"Uh, Ryder," she says, hurrying toward me as I gaze at the rich blue berries in my hand and pop one into my mouth. "Are you sure those are—"

But she doesn't finish her sentence. Instead, she lets out a gasp, and I do, too. Because as soon as the berry touches my tongue, a hand emerges from behind the bush and smacks me in the jaw.

"*Ow!*" I cry, gripping my jaw as none other than Killface, the haggard-looking man we encountered at Washington Creek, stares at me with unblinking eyes.

"Spit it out, you goddamn idiot!" he says, slapping me roughly on the back. "Spit it out!"

Too startled to protest, I do as I'm told while Emily catches up to me, watching wide-eyed as Killface smacks the everloving shit out of me.

"What the hell, man," I grunt, spitting the blueberry out and coughing when he thumps my back again. "What's your problem?"

His scraggly white hair hanging loosely around his face, he shakes his head in disbelief. "I don't have a problem. You do. *You* just tried to eat a blackthorn berry! Are you a goddamn idiot, son?"

I glance from him to Emily and back to him. "Honestly, yeah. Kind of."

He rolls his eyes and hands me a flask of water. "Blackthorn berries are poisonous, you nitwit. I sure hope you didn't swallow any. Here. Drink."

I'm terrified to drink anything he gives me, considering he looks exactly like the dude from *Tales from the Crypt*, but I'm even more terrified that some of the berry juice trickled down my throat, and so I accept his flask and drink thirstily.

"Why in the hell are you kids out here eating poisonous berries?" Killface asks, his face permanently locked into a deep scowl.

"Well," I say, "it's kind of a long story, one that involves a diamond and a madman and me not being as familiar as I thought I was with how blueberries look."

His scowl intensifies. "Son, are you high?"

"I *wish* I were high," I mutter as Emily steps forward and extends a hand toward him.

"Sir, hi. Hello. My name is Emily Edwards. You might remember me from when you were sort of, uh, looking at me in the ferry cabin? And then we saw you at the creek?"

She glances at me. "This is Ryder Fleet. And I know we're complete strangers, but we desperately need your help." She takes a deep breath and clasps her hands together like she's about to deliver an important speech. "You see, I have my dad's ashes in my backpack. And I hired Ryder here as my tour guide to help me navigate Isle Royale and spread those ashes. But it turns out he's not actually a qualified tour guide, which might have been okay except that we almost got stomped by a moose, which led to us stumbling upon one guy pushing another guy off a cliff. And we helped the guy who got pushed off the cliff, which we thought was very Good Samaritan of us, but it turns out that *that* guy was the real bad guy and a crazed archaeologist. And then he shot the guy who'd pushed him off the cliff in an attempt to steal a super valuable diamond, and then he tried to kill us, too, but we escaped with the diamond, and then we ran into some wolves, and also a guy named Malcolm, and I had to jump off a radio tower. A *radio tower*!"

Killface blinks at her. "Who the hell is Malcolm?"

"Oh, that's one of Sinclair's henchmen," I explain, glad to have something to contribute. "But not the one who's probably going to execute us. That one is named Butcher, and she's a henchlady."

The lanky hiker looks at me for a long second before turning his gaze toward Emily.

"Is that all?" he asks gruffly.

"*Is that all?*" I repeat. "Are you serious? She tells you that we stumbled upon a jewel theft, witnessed a murder, and are currently being pursued by a crazed archaeologist with a burly team, and all you can say is *Is that all?*"

"I've been to all sixty-three national parks, son. I've seen some shit." He glances at Emily. "And I wasn't staring at you on the ferry, missy. I was reading the map on the wall behind you."

"Oooh, she's not gonna like that you called her missy," I mutter. "She yelled at me for calling her ma'am."

"This crazed archaeologist," Killface says, ignoring me entirely, "what's he look like?"

"Like a hot professor." Emily glances sideways at me, biting her lip. "I mean, like a professor. He's got auburn hair and glasses and a tweed jacket. You might have seen me talking to him in the cabin on the ferry."

"Oh, that's right," Killface says, nodding. "Real tall, handsome fellow? Looks a bit like a young Robert Redford?"

"He's not that handsome," I grumble, annoyance prickling my skin. "Not that tall, either. And Robert Redford would never steal someone's Discman."

"Son, I'm gonna ask you this one more time," Killface says. "Are you *sure* you're not high?"

"I can assure you that neither of us are high," Emily says quickly. "We're just exhausted and hungry and very, very out of our element here. If you could help us find our way to the ranger station so we can contact the police—"

"No can do, sorry," the old man says, shaking his head. "I go into the wilderness to get away from people, not get roped into somebody else's business."

"But you have to help us," I protest. "Come on, man. We're hapless and adorable!"

"I think you're hapless and annoying," Killface says.

"Well," I say, "that seems like something you should say in your head and not out loud—"

"Look, Mr. Killf—" Emily freezes. "Mister . . . sir man person, I know you don't know us. And at first, I know I might come across as clueless and Ryder as an oafish buffoon—"

"Hey!" I object.

"—but we're begging for your help," she continues. "I promise that we're good people, albeit completely misguided, and all we're trying to do is stay alive and stop a diamond from landing in the hands of a greedy madman. Please don't let the bad guys win. Please help us."

Killface sighs, but much like me, he seems unable to resist Emily.

"Fine," he says after a long silence. "But only because my wife, Edith, would roll over in her grave if she knew I turned you kids away. And because I saw that professor yelling at his assistant on the ferry, and he seemed like a real jackass." He frowns. "Never trust a man who doesn't carry his own pack."

"See, that's what I'm talking about!" I cry, clapping at

Killface's words. "That's exactly what I said! This guy knows what's up!" Beaming, I raise my hand for a high five, but he only glares at me in return.

"Never mind, then," I say quietly, lowering my hand. "So, what should we call you, sir?"

"Biff," Killface says. "My name's Biff."

"Pleased to meet you, Biff," Emily says, shaking his hand.

"I'm sorry, did you say that your name is *Biff*?" I ask without thinking. "Is that short for, like, Bifford? Biffington? Biffley?"

He shakes his head at me. "What kind of idiot is named Biffley? Use your brain, son."

I really don't know what to say to that, but he doesn't give me a chance to reply anyway.

"Now, the closest ranger station is about nine miles that way." He points to his right, which I think is east, although I can't be sure. "If you're looking to stay hidden, you'll want to stay off the coastline and cover your tracks. I can show you how to do that, but what do you kids have in terms of weapons?"

"Well, we had a slingshot," I tell him, cringing as I remember pelting Emily in the head with a rock. "And I made daggers, too."

I yank my homemade dagger out of my sock, holding it up proudly, and Biff stares at it for a moment before bursting into laughter.

"You couldn't pop a balloon with that thing," he says, laughing so hard his eyes tear up, and he grabs my dagger and snaps it in half like it's a Popsicle stick. "Now, if I'm going to help you, you'll need to follow a couple of rules."

"Of course," Emily says. "Just name them."

"One, don't eat any berries or mushrooms you find in the wild," he says, narrowing his eyes at me. "You're not Bear Grylls. You will get poisoned, and you will die. Two, if I tell you to run, you run. If I tell you to hide, you hide. And three, speak to me as little as possible. Edith was the chatty one. I prefer to hike in silence."

"Edith was a saint," I whisper to Emily.

But as our strange new helper leads us into the forest, my hand wrapped around Emily's, I find myself feeling more than grateful for his intervention. After all, we need all the help we can get.

Biff may be a bit of a curmudgeon, but he knows his shit. He shows us how to move stealthily through the woods, covering our tracks by walking on rocks whenever possible. When there are no rocks to walk on, he uses a stick with leaves to sweep the forest floor clean behind us. He teaches us how to select a good throwing rock and keep it at the ready in our pockets, and he lends us each a small hunting knife with a blade so sharp it makes my homemade dagger look like a joke.

"Are you a retired spy or something?" I ask as he shows us how to leave decoy footprints in the direction we're not going, then demonstrates how to make our footfalls as quiet as possible.

"No."

"Well, what did you do?" I ask, ducking under a low tree branch.

He glares at me. "Rule three, son. Rule three."

Hiking in silence is incredibly difficult for me—actually, doing anything in silence is—so I'm relieved when we stop at dusk to set up camp for the night. I'm pretty sure Biff almost has a stroke when he watches me try to get the campfire going, but in the name of his beloved Edith, he shows me how to create a pit, then pile a few handfuls of tinder in the middle and crisscross kindling over top. Using as few words as possible, he explains the different ways to layer the kindling— teepee, lean-to, cross, log cabin—and how to blow lightly at the base of the fire to encourage the flames. It's all stuff Caleb could have taught me had I only paid attention, but it feels good to learn it now, and when we gather around the campfire to eat the bean soup Biff cooks over the flames, I feel more hopeful about our chances of survival than I ever have.

I watch as Biff sets up two red camping chairs side by side, then meets my gaze with his.

"This is Edith's chair," he says, pointing to the empty one beside him. "You try to sit in it, and I'll hand you over to the hot professor myself."

"Once again, he's not that good-looking," I insist. "And of course. I wouldn't dream of sitting in Edith's chair."

"I think it's nice that you still bring her chair along," Emily says, smiling at Biff and pulling her fuzzy blanket over her shoulders.

He shrugs. "Wouldn't be right not to. We were married for forty years. She was the one who got me hooked on back-packing."

"Can I ask how long ago she passed?" Emily asks.

"Nine years this November," Biff says. "Lymphoma."

"I'm sorry," I say, listening to the campfire pop. "I'm sure she was a wonderful woman."

Biff nods, and it's the first time he hasn't looked like he wanted to punch me in response to something I've said.

"She put up with me, so you know she was."

I'm sure she has an absolute mansion in heaven for tolerating Biff for forty years, but I don't say that out loud.

"Can I ask you something?" Emily says, sipping from her canteen. "Does it get easier? Living without her? Missing her?"

Her question brings a lump to my throat, and I reach over to take her hand.

"No," Biff says after a beat. "And yes. It took me years to find a new rhythm, a way to go on without her. I swore I'd never visit a national park again after she died, because the thought of doing it without her was . . ." He looks into the fire, scratching his beard and searching for the words.

"Unsurvivable," I say quietly.

He nods. "Yes. Exactly." He blinks, as if surprised that I'm capable of producing a sensible answer. "The older you get, the more people you see die. People you love, people who love you. And everybody tells you that you have to find a way to move on eventually, to keep going, but I don't think anybody really moves on. I don't think anybody should."

"What do you mean?" I ask, thinking of the words Hannah hurled at me the last time we spoke: *You need to move on, Ryder. Caleb's life ended, but yours doesn't have to.*

"I mean, Edith was my best friend," Biff says. "I spent forty years of my life living with that woman. She was the best thing that ever happened to me. Why would I want to move on from that? From her?" He taps the arm of the empty chair. "I don't. So I just move forward, and I bring her with me as best I can."

"That's really lovely, Biff," Emily says, sniffling, and our wizened rescuer shrugs.

"I don't know if it's lovely," he says, the fire crackling before him. "But I know that it's love."

It might be the most profound thing ever uttered by a man named Biff, if there are any other Biffs in the world, and I find myself thinking of my brother, of how much he would have liked Biff, and liked Emily. Of how much they would have liked him. And for the first time in a long time, maybe for the first time ever, I don't try to push away the thought of Caleb when it comes to me. I don't try to chase it away with beer—though I couldn't right now even if I wanted—and I don't scramble to blunt the pain with *Calvin and Hobbes* or junk TV. I just sit with it, imagining that Caleb was here right now, huddled around the fire with the three of us. I know exactly what he'd do, after trading backcountry camping tips with Biff and toasting a marshmallow to a perfect crisp for his s'more. He'd put in a good word for me with Emily, find a way to bring up some endearing story from our childhood that made me look like the hero. And then he'd grin at me, his dimples on full display, and I'd know that even out here in the middle of the wilderness, I wasn't alone. That my brother had my back, always, no matter where we went.

I think of how Biff still sets out Edith's chair and how Emily ventured into a wilderness she was terrified of to pay tribute to her dad. I think of how I took this gig in the first place so that I could help pay for Caleb's boat, so I could carry a piece of my brother's past into the future. I think of how Katherine Evermore chartered a ship to go find her husband with no promise of success. I think of all the things people do for love, all the everyday acts of courage I'm surrounded by if I would only open my eyes and see them.

If only I would be brave enough to open my heart.

NINETEEN

EMILY

Biff doesn't camp with strangers. I don't blame him—the *Bloodsport* podcast is still fresh in my mind, not to mention what happened with Killian—and after Ryder and I set up our tent, he bids us goodnight and says he'll be back at dawn.

"Don't get yourselves killed overnight," he instructs, and there's a moment when Ryder jokingly asks for a bedtime story where I think Biff might murder him personally. But then he hikes off to his own campsite, wherever that may be, and it's just Ryder and me in our tent. It's drizzling rain outside, and the eerie cries of a loon and occasional howl of a wolf in the distance give me goose bumps.

"You okay?" Ryder asks as I slip into the sleeping bag.

"Yeah. The loons just creep me out."

"Here," he says, lying down next to me and pulling me close. He smells like firewood, and I wonder what he smells like in his regular life, and if I'll ever get the chance to find out.

"Question," he says, running a hand over my hair. "If you could be anywhere right now, where would you be?"

"Hm." I pause to think. "You're gonna think my answer's boring."

"I don't find anything about you boring, Edwards."

"I'd be home," I say, smiling against his chest. "Where there's a shower and clean clothes and a proper bed."

He presses a kiss to my forehead at *proper bed*, and I really wish we had one right now.

"And what would you be doing?" he asks. "At home?"

"Honestly? Baking cupcakes, probably. The Funfetti kind. And reorganizing my home library in my PJs."

"I like the sound of PJs," he says, brushing my arm with his fingertips.

I laugh. "You won't when you realize the PJs are a ratty T-shirt and loose sweatpants."

"Loose sweatpants are my favorite. They're easily removed."

I smile into his skin. "What about you? Where would you be, if not this absolute paradise? What would you be doing?"

"Uh, probably ordering a burger and fries at my favorite diner," he says. "I'd even ask you to join me."

"You would?" I ask playfully, wishing the layer of cotton T-shirt between my face and his chest would disappear.

"Yep. I think we could have a lot of fun sharing a meal that wasn't freeze-dried or dangerously poisonous."

"What about after the diner?" I ask.

Ryder rolls away and onto his back, tucking his hands behind his head as he ponders the question. "Well, that would be up to you."

"Maybe you could take me to your favorite dive bar," I suggest.

He smiles. "A dive bar? Sticky floors, dim lighting, neon beer signs everywhere you look? Doesn't seem like an Emily Edwards type of establishment."

"No, but it seems like a Ryder Fleet type," I say. "And considering you were grazed by a bullet helping me escape Malcolm, I think I owe you a divey night out."

"Fair enough," he says. "I hope you know I'd kick your ass at darts."

I don't argue with that, because we both saw my aim when I attempted to throw my binoculars at Killian.

"And after darts?" I ask. "What then?"

"Then we'd drink whiskey, and I'd secretly wish death upon every guy who even thought about hitting on you."

I blush at the thought of Ryder getting jealous and turn toward him, propping myself up on my elbow. "What would we do after the dive bar?"

"I'd see you home, of course."

"What if I didn't want to go home?" I ask. "What if I wanted to come back to your place?"

He rolls onto his side to face me. "Then I'd take you back to my place. I'd take you anywhere you wanted."

"And what would we do?" I ask, practically melting at the thought of being alone with Ryder someplace safe and warm and quiet, someplace where we could do anything we wanted without being bothered by life-threatening dangers.

"Honestly? I'd probably try to sneak you past my neighbor Lulu's door, because she's nosy as hell. And then I'd scramble to hide my very embarrassing Funko Pop! collection."

"Is that your usual MO?" I ask, laughing.

His smile disappears. "I don't have an MO, Emily. Especially not for someone like you. I'd just try to follow my instincts."

"And what do you think your instincts would tell you to do?"

It's an invitation as much as it is a question, and Ryder's gaze meets mine in the dark.

"Touch you," he says, his voice rough.

The gruffness of his tone makes my knees weak, and I'm grateful that we're already horizontal.

"Touch me how?" I ask softly.

Ryder studies me for a moment, his hand brushing a stray curl from my face.

"I'd take you into my arms and pull you tight against me," he says. "The way we were after we rolled down the hill. I'd feel your heartbeat against my chest. I'd run my hands over your hair, your wild, beautiful hair, and I'd pull your face toward mine, and—"

"Show me," I whisper, my body desperate for his touch. "Show me."

He doesn't need to be told a third time, and Ryder, his arm already wrapped around me, grunts as pulls me on top of him. It's delicious, the sensation of his body beneath mine, and I breathe in sharply as he tucks a hand behind the back of my head and brings my face toward his.

"Kiss me," he says, and I do, eagerly, desperately, grinding against him as our tongues meet and part and meet again.

"I would kiss your neck," he says, pressing his lips to my neck and the hollow of my throat, "and your breasts, and I would kiss my way down your belly and stop at your thighs, and then I would spread your legs apart—"

"Show me," I whisper, and he rolls me over onto my back so that he's on top, his strong arms on either side of me. He reaches underneath my shirt and lifts it up to plant soft kisses from my hip bone to my rib cage, and then he tugs my shirt over my head and tosses it aside.

"I would marvel at you," he says, lowering his mouth to my stomach again as his hands find their way to my breasts. "I would marvel at how fucking gorgeous you are, even more gorgeous than I could have imagined." He slides his tongue over my nipple, his hips responding as I rub against him, wanting.

"Touch me," I tell him, unable to wait any longer for his touch where I need it the most. "Touch me, and let me touch you."

He tugs my pants down and uses his palm to massage the space between my legs, and then he kisses the soft flesh of my inner thighs and returns his mouth to mine.

"I want to touch you," I whisper, and he slides his boxers off and lies down next to me, his lips meeting mine again.

His hands slide down beneath the band of my underwear, and his fingers find the soft place where I crave him the most.

"Emily," he says at the breathy moan I make as he touches me, and I wrap my hand around his hard shaft and grip him tightly, reveling in the rock-hard evidence of his desire for me. I grind against his hand, showing him that I want him on top of me. That I want to take him inside my body, just as I've taken him inside my heart.

"Let me see you," he murmurs. "Let me look at you. Please."

The *please* is a desperate half whisper, and the urgency of it just about undoes me. I have never been wanted like this. I have never *wanted* like this, never desired someone so badly that every part of me burns with a fever that only his touch can cure.

I push myself into a sitting position, and Ryder watches, his jaw tight, as I unhook my bra and let it fall away.

"Now you," I say, my voice barely a whisper, and he doesn't tear his gaze away from me as he takes his shirt off.

And I always knew he was beautiful—knew it from the moment I saw him sprinting down the dock toward the ferry, knew it when I saw him shirtless and glistening in the pond— but here he is *beautiful*, not just because of his broad chest and solid arms and strong hands but because of the way he's looking at me right now. Because of the way he leans over me and presses a kiss to my ear, then my mouth, and then lower, burying his head into my chest and letting out a groan of unbridled want when his thumb brushes my nipple.

I reach for him, reach to curl my fingers around the place where I so badly want to touch him, but he stops me.

"I want to say something," he says. "Before words fail me."

I'd respond, but my words have failed me already, and so I just watch him as he swallows hard, one hand cupping my cheek.

"If I die on this island," Ryder whispers, his thumb stroking my ear, "it'll have been worth it for this fucking moment. To see you like this. To have you like this."

His eyes are blazing but his expression is soft. Vulnerable. "It will all have been worth it."

And then I can't wait anymore, and so I lean forward to kiss him, to savor him, to let go of all the worry and fear and revel in each other instead. He grips my hips, pulling me into his lap, and I know that the moan that escapes his lips will play in my dreams for the rest of my days.

"I want you inside me," I whisper, gasping as he lowers me to the ground and presses his tongue between my legs. "Do you have any condoms?"

He grunts a no, and I hate myself for packing glow-in-the-dark toilet paper but not condoms.

"We can just do this," Ryder says, his words warm against the delicious ache between my thighs. "I can just do this. I want you, Emily, and I'll take you any way I can get you."

He licks me again, fervently, expertly, and even though it kills me to do it, I reach down to grab his hand and pull him up next to me.

"Then we do it like this," I tell him, guiding his hand toward my clit and then reaching out to grasp his length. "Together."

"I was really just getting started down there," he protests, but his words give way to a low groan when I begin to stroke him.

His mouth finds mine as we touch each other, our breaths warm and ragged and verging on the edge of collapse.

"Let me see you," he whispers into my skin. "Let me see you unravel."

And his words, like his hands, are magic. Because he increases the speed and pressure of his touch, grunting as I run my hand along him, and just when I think I can't take it anymore, that I would sacrifice life and limb and throw all caution to the wind just to feel like this for one moment longer, the sensation welling up inside me erupts. His touch unearths me, destroys me, and puts me back together again, and I can only rock against his palm, biting my lip so as not to scream.

"Fuck," he whispers, grinding into my hand. "Fuck. Watching you like that, hearing you like that . . ."

But now, I want only to watch *him* like that. To hear *him* like that. And so I press my mouth to his, increasing the pace and pressure of my touch until he rocks against me, letting out an unbridled cry of pleasure when he comes. He kisses me ardently, desperately, and I want to live in this moment forever.

I want him, forever.

He holds me as our breathing slows and our pulses normalize, pressing kisses to the top of my head.

"That was everything I ever imagined it would be," he says, dazed. "And it was everything I never could have known to imagine."

I smile and run my hand through his hair. "Imagine what we'll be able to do when we have condoms."

"I already have," he whispers into my skin. "Trust me, one day soon, we'll be off this island, and we'll be able to do anything we want together. Including you giving me a tutorial on how to organize your home library."

I laugh. "I'm already naked, Ryder. You don't have to sweet-talk me."

We hold each other for a moment, my body and heart buzzing, and it's not long before my eyelids start to grow heavy.

"It's weird, isn't it," I mutter, fatigue setting in. "That we found each other this way."

"What do you mean?" His breath is warm against my skin, and I wish I could make this moment last longer—could bottle up how safe and secure I feel right now and uncap it the next time I feel frightened.

"I mean, out in the real world, we never would have crossed paths," I tell him. "And if we had, we wouldn't have given each other more than a passing glance."

Ryder runs a hand over my hair and presses a kiss to my temple. "You're a very smart woman, Emily, but you're dead wrong about that one."

I want to ask him how I'm wrong, but sleep makes my head fuzzy, and I close my eyes and let it take me away.

"I would have given you more than a passing glance," he says, his words carrying me into slumber. "You would have stopped me in my tracks."

TWENTY

RYDER

The next day, after a silent breakfast of cold oatmeal and weak coffee during which Biff, who is clearly not a morning person, threatens to feed me blackthorn berries if I ask him one more time what Biff is short for, we resume our hike across Isle Royale. I'm exhausted and stressed and incredibly sexually frustrated, but Biff promises we'll reach the ranger station in just a few hours, and sure enough, after an hour and a half spent trekking across rocky ground in a serpentine formation—harder to track, Biff explains—a small, rustic cabin comes into view.

"Oh my God," Emily says, clapping her hands gleefully, "is that the ranger station?"

"Sure is," Biff says, and for the first time since he terrified us at Washington Creek, he smiles. It changes his whole face, making him look like a skinny Santa instead of a crypt keeper, and it warms my heart to see Emily wrap him in a hug.

"Woohoo! We did it!" I cry, then cover my mouth when Biff shoots me a dirty look.

"Sorry," I whisper, remembering that we're trying *not* to get caught. "I got excited." I raise my hand toward Biff, hoping he'll high-five me this time, but he only rolls his eyes.

"There's no time for getting sentimental," he says, as though I was asking for his hand in marriage instead of a high five. "We're not in the clear yet."

But we are awfully close, and I'm practically skipping with relief as we reach the ranger station and bang loudly on the door. Within thirty seconds, a middle-aged man in a khaki outfit ushers us inside, and Emily wastes no time in getting straight to the point.

"You need to call the police," she says. "Now."

The ranger, whose gold name badge bears the name RICK, reaches for a radio on his desk.

"Okay. Mind telling me why?"

"Sure," she says. "Basically—and this is a very long story with a lot of twists and turns that I'm really watering down for the sake of brevity—I have a diamond in my backpack, and we witnessed a murder, and this national park is teeming with bad guys."

"Did you not hear us on the radio?" I ask, gritting my teeth in frustration. "Cover of Darkness, signing off?"

The ranger stares at me but presses a button on his radio at the same time. "I'm not following any of what you guys said, but I'll call for emergency personnel right away."

We watch, still panting from our run toward the station, as Ranger Rick calls for backup over the crackly line. Within two minutes, a knock sounds on the door, and I sigh in relief. Finally, we can get the hell out of Isle Royale and put the stress and violence of this whole ordeal behind us.

"Police!" a deep voice shouts.

"Wait a second," the ranger says, glancing toward the door. "They shouldn't be here that quickly—"

But the next instant, someone kicks the door in and rushes inside, gun up and ready.

"Malcolm," Emily says in horror, her jaw dropping as Sinclair's burly henchman bursts through the door.

Rage fills my veins as Malcolm points his gun at her. I haven't hiked across Isle Royale for days, running from wolves and armed men and my own self-doubt, just to lose everything when we finally made it to safety. I haven't found the girl of my dreams in the craziest way imaginable just to let some douchebag with a weapon intimidate her. And I haven't finally started to examine my own grief at losing Caleb just to multiply it by losing someone else I love.

Love.

It's love and fury and an endless desire to destroy anyone and anything that threatens Emily that causes me to spring into action, and I reach instinctively for a wooden chair placed at one of the ranger station's two small tables. Simmering with rage, I hoist it into the air and bring it down as hard as I can over Malcolm's head. He fires but misses, and I lunge for him, kicking him in the family jewels like all our lives depend on it. He cries out in pain, and I shove him into a souvenir display rack, sending postcards and miniature moose figurines flying everywhere. Malcolm falls to the ground, sputtering, and in a move I learned from the countless WWE WrestleMania matches Caleb and I watched as kids, I execute a near-perfect leg drop on his chest.

"Emily!" I yell, scrambling to my feet as Malcolm drops his gun. "Grab it!"

She's already diving for the weapon, her jaw clenched in determination, but someone else gets there first. I watch in horror as two more of Killian's men sprint into the ranger station, one squat and muscled and the other blond haired and lanky. The muscular one grabs Malcolm's gun just as the other presses a boot to Emily's back, pinning her to the ground.

"Get off of her, you sack of sh—" I start, but Malcolm's fist meets the back of my head in a violent sucker punch, and I groan in pain, my head throbbing.

"Get up," Malcolm commands as his fellow blockhead returns his gun to him. "Now."

I do as instructed when I feel the cold metal poking my back, my head pounding as I desperately scan the room for anything I can use as a weapon.

"The police are on their way," says Ranger Rick, his gaze shifting quickly between our three enemies. "So let's all take a breath and—"

But the breath he takes is a sharp inhale of pain, because in a flash of noise and motion, the stout, muscular henchman shoots Biff and then the ranger in rapid succession.

I let out a cry of fury, and Emily screams and covers her head instinctively. Her captor presses his boot harder into her back, causing her to whimper in pain, and suddenly I don't give a shit about the throbbing ache in my head or the gun pointed at my back. I only care about her, about getting my hands on the guy who has her so I can tear him limb from limb. I lunge for him, managing to encircle my hands around his throat just as Malcolm kicks me hard from behind, causing my knees to buckle. I hit the ground with a thud as Emily screams out for me, and before I can gather my bearings, someone wrestles my hands behind my back and yanks me to my feet.

"Another peep out of you and I'll kill her," Malcolm says through gritted teeth. "Sinclair told us to bring you both in alive, but I have my limits. So stop fighting before I lose my temper."

Fury courses through me as I hear Biff moaning in pain, but Malcolm only twists his gun into my side.

"Ryder, listen to him," Emily says desperately.

That's the last thing I want to do, but I don't have any other choice. My head pounds so badly I can barely stay conscious, let alone come up with a new plan of attack, and with Malcolm gripping my arms so tightly I think they might break, I can't reach for the wooden chair or the knife Biff lent me.

I grit my teeth as the lanky henchman pulls his boot off Emily's back and tugs her to her feet, wrapping an arm around her neck in a tight chokehold. She resists instinctually, elbowing him roughly in the gut, but it's not enough to free her. Instead, the third henchman handcuffs her hands and then mine behind our backs with zip ties, and I'm half-blind with rage as they usher us out of the ranger station.

"Biff!" Emily calls frantically over her shoulder. "Biff, hang on!"

But Malcolm's partner pokes his gun into her side, and she shuts up quickly. They guide us across the rocky shore and toward Lake Superior, where a speedboat waits idly.

"All aboard, lovebirds," Malcolm says, motioning to the boat with his gun. "Chop, chop."

"Uh, no way," Emily says, shaking her head as if we have any choice in the matter. "I'm not getting on that thing without a life jacket."

"There's no time for life jackets," Malcolm mutters, and it's all I can do not to spontaneously combust with anger.

"There is *always* time for life jackets, motherfucker!" I shout, and I'm punished for my outburst by a quick pop to the chin from Malcolm's buddy.

Malcolm gives me a hard shove so that I have no option but to stumble onto the boat, and he leads Emily aboard just as roughly. The engine roars to life as Blockhead Number Two shifts the gears, and I wrap my legs around Emily to keep her from flying off as we launch into the water.

"We're gonna be okay," I tell her. "I'm gonna make this okay."

But the motor is so loud that I don't think she hears me, and we fall sideways as the boat zooms through the waves. I close my eyes, growing nauseous with each passing minute, and I don't know whether I'm more relieved or terrified when I sit up and see that we're passing the wreckage of the *Explorer*. But when we near the shore and I spot a smiling Sinclair standing on the edge of the dock, eagerly awaiting our arrival with Caleb's headphones looped around his fucking neck, I don't feel relief or terror. I feel only fury. Pressing a gun to our backs, the henchmen usher us off the boat and onto the dock, and Sinclair greets us like the mustache-twirling villain he is.

"Emily, darling," he says, spreading his arms wide in greeting. "Welcome back!"

She glares like she'd spit on him if she got the chance, but he only chuckles.

"You do look less happy to see me than I hoped, but I warned you about going to the rangers, did I not? And here I thought you were the clever one." He laughs, and the sound of it makes me want to rip off a piece of the dock and smash it over his evil head.

"And that stunt you pulled at the radio tower? Well, that wasn't your brightest move, darling," he adds. "Did you not think we'd be monitoring all possible avenues of communication?"

"She's not your darling," I say through gritted teeth.

Sinclair laughs again, more cruelly this time. "And I suppose you want her to be yours? Tell me, Fleet, can you even spell 'archaeologist'?"

I'm not sure that I could—I know there's a lot of vowels, and I mix them up in my head sometimes—but I don't need to be a great speller to be a better man than Killian Sinclair could ever dream of being.

"Sure I can," I say easily, staring him down. "F-U-C-K-Y-O-U. Do you want that in a sentence?"

Malcolm and Blockhead Number Two laugh, and Sinclair smiles tightly. "Careful, Fleet. You wouldn't want anyone getting hurt, would you?"

"It's a little late for that," I say, thinking of Dr. Sharp, Ranger Rick, and poor Biff, who went into the wilderness for peace and quiet and ended up in a nightmare because of us. "You hurt people. Good people."

He shrugs. "An outcome that could have easily been avoided, had you two not absconded with my diamond."

"It's not your diamond," Emily tells him, her eyes flashing. "It belongs to the people, not to you."

Sinclair rolls his eyes. "Emily, I like you, I do, but I find your rigid view of morality highly irritating. So please do shut up and hand over the Evermore."

She glances at me, and I can see the fear in her eyes. She knows as well as I do that the second we give him the diamond, we're as good as dead.

"Bad news," she says suddenly. "We can't hand it over. Because one of us swallowed it."

"Well, that's not an issue," Sinclair says, crossing his arms over his chest. "I'll just shoot both of you now, and my men will slice you open to retrieve the stone. Problem solved, eh?"

I can't help the groan of annoyance that escapes my lips. "C'mon, Sinclair. Don't you do anything yourself?"

"Well, I'm not about to comb through intestines," he says in his lilting accent. "That's disgusting."

"What's *disgusting*," Emily says, "is your blatant disregard for the core values of your profession—"

"Anyone know where Butcher is?" Sinclair asks, yawning in boredom.

The mere mention of Butcher sends my pulse skyrocketing, and I remember the vow I made to protect Emily.

"Hang on," I insist, my heart pounding. "There's no need

for anyone to get Butcher involved." I take a deep breath, steeling myself. "*I* swallowed the diamond. Not Emily. So you only need to slice me open."

"Ryder!" Emily cries, shaking her head at me. I understand the message she's trying to convey—*Don't sacrifice yourself*—but at this point, I don't see another way out.

Sinclair, on the other hand, beams at me. "Excellent. Good on you for showing some courage, Fleet. Malcolm, I'll let you handle this one."

Malcolm, grinning like the cat that got the cream, moves toward me, and Emily tries to block him by jumping into his path. He swats her aside easily, and if I could just get these damn zip ties off, I would rip his head off in retaliation for laying hands on her.

"Stop!" she cries, fighting against her own ties. "Leave him alone!"

"Emily," I say, refusing to let my voice waver. "Emily, it's okay."

"It's not okay," she says, her voice breaking as her eyes flood with tears. "None of this is okay."

"It is," I tell her. "I'm okay. Because I know what it's like to care for someone so much that you'd give your life for them, and this time, I actually have the chance to do it."

"Just let us go!" Emily tells Sinclair, who observes our emotional display with the bored disinterest of someone watching grass grow. "We'll give you the diamond, and you'll never hear from us again."

"I'd love to, darling, I really would, but the problem is, you saw me shoot Dr. Sharp," he says, biting his lip like he sincerely regrets this unfortunate turn of events. "And even if I spared you, I'm not going to spare him." His gaze flickers toward me. "He's intolerable."

"And you're a prick," I tell him. "I should have let you drown."

"But you didn't, because you wanted to be the hero." Sinclair smiles coldly. "How's that working out for you?"

"Well, I'm not wearing a tweed fucking jacket," I say, spitting the words out. "So I'm still doing pretty good."

"It's pretty *well*, sport," Sinclair corrects me. "Not pretty good. Bravery doesn't get you any IQ points, I'm afraid."

"Leave him alone," Emily says, glaring at Sinclair. She looks at me, her eyes pleading. "Ryder, don't do this. Don't give up."

But it's not giving up to lay your life down for someone you love, and as Malcolm reaches me with his gun ready, I realize that's exactly what this is. If they kill me and search me for the diamond, Emily will at least have a fighting chance of survival. She's smart; maybe she'll be able to make a quick escape, or maybe the real authorities, upon finding poor Biff and Ranger Rick, will somehow track their killers here in time to rescue her. Whatever happens, at least I'll go out knowing I did everything I could to protect her. To give her a chance.

"I'm not giving up," I tell Emily, meaning every word. I wasn't there for Caleb when I should have been, and I refuse to let her down the same way. "*Diamond bright, diamond strong, forever you and I belong.* Remember?"

"Ah, somebody read the Evermore letters," Sinclair says, adjusting his glasses. "I'm impressed, Fleet. I wasn't aware you could read."

I ignore him, looking only at Emily, at her untamed curls and the rosy pink of her lips and the curves of her body that I was lucky enough to touch.

"I've fallen for you, Emily," I tell her, my heart swelling with emotion. "And I know that sounds crazy, to think you can fall for someone in five days, but here I am. And I wish things had turned out differently. I wish I could help you finish your dad's bucket list. I wish I could take you to Yosemite and that sticky dive bar and show you my favorite *Calvin and Hobbes* strips so you can see what makes them special. I wish I could kiss you and touch you and make you believe that these five crazy days together are just the start of something amazing, and that what I lack in wilderness survival skills, I make up for with heart."

I take a deep breath and focus only on Emily, not on Sinclair or his men or the fact that we're only meters away from the spot where Captain Sebastian Evermore went down with his ship.

"I love you," I tell her, relishing the fact that at least for this moment, the sun is shining down on me and the wind is at my back and the woman I love has a chance of survival because of me. "I thought love was a poison that inevitably led to grief, but I was wrong. Love isn't poison. It's the fucking antidote."

And Emily, having listened to my declaration of love with an earnest, heartbreaking expression, says the last thing I—or maybe anyone—expects.

"He's lying."

TWENTY-ONE

EMILY

I will not watch Ryder die in front of me. I will not let him die, period, even if that means ruining his heroic attempt to take the fall for both of us.

"I'm sorry," I tell him as his expression turns crestfallen, "but this is completely ridiculous."

Steeling myself for whatever comes next, I direct my attention toward Killian. "Ryder doesn't have the diamond," I confess. "I do."

The archaeologist crosses his arms over his chest, one eyebrow raised. "You wouldn't lie to me, would you, Emily darling?"

His repeated use of *darling* makes me want to chop off his balls and fling them into Lake Superior, but I know better than to try that when I've got guns pointed at me. Instead, I shake my head, a curl falling loose from my bun.

"No, I wouldn't. I'm a terrible liar." I take a shaky breath, my gaze flitting from Ryder to Killian. "I have the Evermore, and I'll give it to you. I refuse to watch anyone else get hurt over it."

"A wise choice," Killian says, nodding approvingly. "You always did strike me as an intelligent girl."

"She's not a girl, you jackass," Ryder interjects, his tone incensed. "She's a *doct*—"

But Malcolm shuts him up quickly with a quick tap of his gun against the back of Ryder's head, and my stomach turns at his grunt of pain.

"For once, you're not entirely wrong, Fleet," Killian says, watching Ryder in bemusement. "Stupid, yes. Wrong, no. You are indeed a doctor, Emily. A lovely one at that."

He smiles at me, and it's a wonder that I once found him even halfway charming.

"You deserve someone who's your equal," Killian explains, taking a step toward me. "Someone who challenges you. Surprises you. Someone who's clever and ambitious and knows how to handle a rare jewel when he finds one."

He casts a disgusted look at Ryder, who's practically foaming at the mouth to throttle him. "Why settle for a knuckle-dragging tour guide when you could have someone powerful? Driven? Wealthy beyond imagination?"

"Oh my God, how many times do I have to tell you that I am not a tour guide?" Ryder seethes, his jaw clenched. "I am a goddamn *ambassador of adventure!*"

Killian ignores him, his attention focused solely on me.

"I know you think I'm the villain here, Emily. And sure, from a certain perspective, I am."

I'm pretty sure he's the villain from every perspective

imaginable, but I keep my expression neutral, because there's nothing an egotistical man loves more than the chance to hear himself talk.

"You say the diamond belongs to the people, but which people do you mean?" he continues. "If Sharp had gotten his way, the Evermore would sit in a glass case in a shiny museum thousands of miles from where it originated. Is it really so terrible that I, the person who discovered the diamond's existence, should stand to make a profit from it?"

I don't answer, because I know Killian's not actually looking for one.

"Yes," Ryder says flatly, not caring what he's looking for one way or another.

"The Evermore diamond should belong to someone who knows its worth," Killian says, moving toward me. "All beautiful jewels should."

He smiles when he reaches me, extending a hand to brush away my loose curl. His hand lingers on my temple, his gaze on my mouth, and a shiver of revulsion runs through me.

"Where is the diamond, darling?" he asks, his voice velvet.

"I'll tell you on one condition," I say, even though I know his word is as useless as the glow-in-the-dark toilet paper I wasted twenty bucks on. "If I give you the diamond, you let both of us go."

Killian rolls his eyes in exasperation. "You? Perhaps. But the tour guide . . ."

"Both of us," I insist, his fingers still grazing my face.

He shrugs. "Fine. I could use a little good karma. But a word of this to anyone, ever . . ."

"We wouldn't," I promise. "We just want to go home and forget any of this ever happened." I nod toward my bound hands. "Cut me free, and I'll give you the Evermore."

Killian brushes a hand down my cheek and sighs. "You are quite irresistible, Emily. Fine. We'll do it your way."

My heart pounds as he drops his hand from my face to remove a Swiss Army knife from his pocket. I don't need to look at Ryder to see every muscle in his body stiffen as Killian raises the knife toward me, and I breathe a sigh of relief when he slices my zip ties off in one swift cut.

"The diamond," he says, still clutching the knife. "Now."

Nodding, I unzip my backpack and slip it off, the henchmen's guns trained on my every movement.

"Emily!" Ryder cries as I unzip my backpack. "Stop!"

But I don't stop. A stupid gemstone, valuable as it might be, is not worth Ryder's life. "Sorry, Dad," I whisper as I dig out the urn, then twist the cap open and retrieve the Evermore diamond.

"For you," I say, handing it to Killian, and he accepts it eagerly, cradling it in his hands in adoration.

"For *you*," he says in turn, and I recoil as he suddenly moves in for a frenzied kiss, his tongue wet and unrestrained and reminding me a great deal of my childhood dog, Rocket.

"Like I said," he says when he comes up for air, grinning at me. "Irresistible."

The henchmen laugh as I wipe my mouth, my skin crawling, and I don't need to look at Ryder to know that he's shaking with anger on my behalf.

Killian, wearing a smug look I'd love nothing more than to

smack into oblivion, beckons to the lanky henchman who kept me pinned at the ranger station.

"Have Butcher take care of Fleet," he instructs before turning to his third lackey. "You, go find the champagne and drop it off at my tent."

The henchmen—sans Malcolm, who's still looming over Ryder—scurry off to do his bidding, and Killian casts a backward glance at me as he strides down the dock toward base camp. "Feel free to join me for a drink, Emily, if you want. I'd love to celebrate the return of *two* beautiful jewels."

I'd rather spend the rest of my life traipsing around this island alone than pop champagne with him, and I know if I'm going to save Ryder, it's now or never.

Still holding Dad's urn, I try to appear calm as I walk down the dock after Killian. Of *course* I've had a change of heart and suddenly want to wash away the memories of the last few days with expensive champagne. Of *course* I'm not silently scrambling for a way to save the day.

The placid expression I force myself to adopt must convince the henchmen that I'm harmless, because no bullets come flying at me as I near Killian.

"Wait up!" I call, and when he turns to face me, I raise the urn as high as I can and bring it down, hard, over his annoyingly well-coiffed head. *Bam!* He falls to his knees with a holler of pain, then collapses onto the dock.

"Fuck," I whisper, because I wasn't trying to *kill* him, but I don't have time to plan my next move. Because when I turn away from Killian to look at Ryder, I see Malcolm moving toward me, his gun raised and ready.

I can't stop the scream that escapes my lips as he fires, and it's by pure luck that I dive left and his bullet misses my leg by inches.

An enraged Ryder, his hands still bound, lets out a cry of fury and rushes the henchman from behind, tackling him to the ground.

"I will fucking *end* you," Ryder seethes, but he lets out a gurgle of pain when Malcolm thrusts an elbow backward into his face.

My hands trembling, I grab Biff's knife from my sock and sprint toward the grappling pair, lunging toward Malcolm just as he clambers to his feet. He's got strength, size, and a complete lack of morality on his side, but I've got the element of surprise and an exact precision for locating the carotid artery.

I manage to slash his arm before he raises his gun toward me, and when he fires, the bullet pierces a hole straight into the dock below us.

I cry out as Malcolm reaches for my knife, his hand ensnaring my wrist and squeezing so tightly that I can only wait for the bone to snap. But Ryder, struggling desperately to his feet, rushes Malcolm again just as the pain turns blinding. He kicks the henchman as hard as he can in the stomach, sending him flying backward, and when Malcolm's back hits the dock with a thud, he drops his gun. Gasping, I sprint toward it and kick it into Lake Superior before he can grab it back.

"Emily!" Ryder yells, exasperated. "Pick *up* the gun next time!"

It's an excellent point, but one I don't have much time to consider as I hurry to cut Ryder's zip ties.

"Faster!" he says, glancing warily down the dock as Malcolm clambers to his feet.

"I'm going as fast as I can," I mutter, my fingers trembling. "This dagger isn't that sharp."

"You're a doctor! You're supposed to be good at cutting things!"

"I'm not a surgeon, Ryder!" I retort, slicing his ties frantically. "It would be different if I had a scalpel—"

"Move," Ryder barks, and I leap aside as an enraged Malcolm approaches. I gasp as my tour guide, his hands still clasped, headbutts Malcolm in the chest so hard that the henchman falls off the dock and into the water.

"Oh my God," I marvel, watching Malcolm sink below the surface. "You headbutted him!"

"I know," Ryder says, wincing as he tilts his head left and then right. "It was like running into a wall."

"Hands," I say, grabbing Ryder's, and it only takes a few more cuts of the knife to sever the ties.

"Come here," he says when his hands are free, pulling me to his chest and wrapping his arms around me. "Are you okay? Are you hurt?"

"No."

He leans back to get a good look at me. "What were you thinking? You should have been focused on saving yourself!"

I look at him in disbelief. "No way. I'm not about to leave this island without you, Ryder. I'm not about to lose you now."

I think back to what Jason told me when he broke up with me, that there wasn't a linear relationship between love and time spent together. He might have been wrong about a lot of things, but he wasn't wrong about that.

"I love you, too, Ryder," I say, cupping his cheek in my hand. "I never imagined I could fall in love in five days, either, but I have."

"Oh, Emily," he says, brushing his lips against mine. "I could have done it in two."

His kiss is fast and furious, and I sigh against him, inhaling as much of him as I can. Our embrace only lasts an instant, though, because I hear the sound of boots smacking the dock, and I look behind me to see that Killian has clambered to his feet.

"Emily, *darling*," he says, his face twisted into a menacing scowl, "don't worry about leaving this island without Fleet." He squints at me, raising his gun. "You won't be leaving it at all."

I scream when he fires, and Killian laughs cruelly as Ryder dives valiantly in front of me. The bullet misses, but that doesn't ease my rage. Incensed, I pull one of Biff's throwing rocks from my pocket and hurl it at Killian as hard as I can, but I miss by a mile yet again, and he only laughs bitterly and points his gun at Ryder.

"No!" I shout in protest.

I watch breathlessly as Ryder dives into Lake Superior, his only chance of escape, while Killian fires at him mercilessly.

"Alright, then," Killian says, shrugging when Ryder disappears beneath the water's surface. "Your turn."

He turns toward me, his gun level with my chest, and I step backward, hands raised, as he advances.

"It's too bad, really, that you have such terrible taste in men," he says bitterly, laughing at my terror. "We could have really been something. But instead, you've chosen to die with a hapless buffoon who has too much testosterone and not enough brain cells."

I glance around frantically, looking for anything I can use as a weapon, but there's only him and me and miles and miles of open water.

Killian might think Ryder lacks brain cells, but no one could think that he lacks balls. Because just then, Ryder emerges from the water and heaves himself onto the dock in one smooth motion, his shirt clinging to his chest like he's the badass hero in an action movie. He lunges toward Killian, who darts sideways to escape him. But Ryder's high school long jump prowess finally pays off, and he manages to grab hold of Killian's tweed jacket sleeve, causing the archaeologist to lose his grip on the diamond.

"No!" Killian cries as the Evermore falls to the dock, and I watch as Ryder sprints to retrieve it.

"Enough fucking around," Killian says, and pain sears through me as he grabs me by the hair, snaking an arm around my neck and pointing his gun at my temple.

"Give me the Evermore, Fleet," he spits, pressing the gun into my skull so hard I see stars.

"Ryder, don't!" I scream, but he only looks at me remorsefully.

"I have no choice," Ryder says, opening his fist to reveal the bright, sparkling diamond that started all this bullshit. "I'm sorry."

He extends the jewel toward Killian. "Here. Take it. Fucking take it and let her go."

My heart sinks as Killian snatches the diamond from Ryder's outstretched hand.

"Thank you, sport," he says, closing his fingers over the gem. "Now say goodbye."

I don't hear what Ryder says next. I hear nothing except for the thud of something hard and metallic slamming into my head, and then all that exists is pain. I cling to consciousness for a moment, my vision blurring as I witness the rage and heartbreak on Ryder's face. And then everything slips away, and the world goes dark.

TWENTY-TWO

EMILY

I'm underwater, but I'm not swimming or struggling. I'm float-ing in Lake Superior, or maybe I'm dead. Maybe I'm some-where between life and death, someplace where the fuzzy edges of my vision blur and the sounds of Ryder and Killian fighting on the dock above me fade to nothingness.

I tell myself to open my eyes, to fight, but instead I'm sink-ing, weightless. I hear something—a voice, deep toned and desperate, calling for me, and then it disappears, replaced by the distant sound of my mother's voice, as tinny and warm as if it were pulled straight from a memory.

"Emily," I hear, and I swear I feel the warm pressure of my mom's hand in mine, squeezing me tight like she did when I was a little girl and got spooked by a thunderstorm.

I knit my fingers through hers, even though I know I'm just *remembering*, or hallucinating, like a halfway-conscious lucid dream. Because of course Mom's not here, but she was once, and I remember it. I feel her, the same way I feel my brain aching and swelling and responding to the all-consuming pain of Killian hitting me with his gun.

"Emmy," another voice sounds, and it's deeper than my mom's. Closer. "*Emmy.*"

My eyes are still closed, I know it, and yet I can see, not just underwater but everywhere. I can see Dad, right in front of me, smiling at me like he always did, with that wide, easy grin that reaches all the way up to the corners of his eyes. It makes no sense, of course it doesn't, but my neurons keep firing and resting and firing again, and there he is, plain as day.

Dad.

My heart cracks open at the sight of him before me, and I know he's not *here*, not really, because I remember picking the outfit he would wear for his funeral, and crying with Brooke as we organized his belongings, and burying my head in my hands as I sat in the recliner where he always listened to baseball on the radio, wondering how I was ever going to make it in a world where he no longer existed.

But here he is regardless, whether through a memory or my imagination, and relief floods me as I realize that everything is okay now. I don't have to be afraid; my dad is here. My dad is *here*. And there's so much I want to tell him—I love you, I miss you, I'm *sorry*—but trying to say the words aloud is like trying to cartwheel through quicksand. So I just think them instead, think about how I wish Dad had found the diamond instead of me, because he would have known what to do with it and how to protect Ryder. I think about what I read in Dad's letter—*I dreamed of a life of adventure, and instead, I got minutiae*—and how I wish I had been different so that his life could have been different, too. I think about how deeply I regret letting him down when he asked me to come to Isle Royale, how badly I wish I could reverse time and give him his big adventure.

"Emmy," he says, and I know this is all my brain trying to make sense of my grief and my fear and Killian hitting me over the head, but I don't care. Because Dad is smiling at me, that warm, everything's-okay smile, and all that exists is him and me and the endless love that binds us together, the love that lives on beyond death.

"Emmy," he says, his tone bearing the same quiet patience it did when he helped me memorize my multiplication tables and taught me how to drive and listened to me describe, in excruciating detail, my ranking of every Disney Channel Original Movie from worst to best. "You don't need to be sorry. Because I got to be your dad. I *get* to be your dad. And that's the greatest adventure anyone could hope for."

I know I'm delirious, hallucinating, whatever description my medical textbooks would give the intricate cascade of synapsing neurons happening inside my brain right now, but it doesn't matter. I know I'll cling to those words for the rest of my life, for all the days I live on after this and all the adventures I have until I see Dad again.

The sounds from above the surface of the water get louder, sharper, and an aching tightness fills my lungs. I know without knowing that I'm going to come to, to return to reality, and the realization is both a relief and a tragedy.

"Listen to me, Emmy," Dad says, his voice getting so fuzzy and faint I have to strain to hear it. "Focus on what's real. Okay? *Focus on what's real*."

I want to ask him what he means, want to tell him all about Sharp's last breaths and Killian's cruelty and the devastated look on Ryder's face when Killian hit me with his gun. But of course I can't, not really, because this is all just a strange, beautiful trick my brain's playing on me as it tries to rewire itself back to consciousness.

"Emily!"

And I don't understand what Dad meant, because my head is swirling and I can't tell what's real or imaginary any more than I can use the stars to find my way home.

"Emily!" the voice repeats, and the tightness in my chest aches, peaking, just as someone wraps an arm around me from behind and yanks my head out of the water.

TWENTY-THREE

RYDER

"Breathe, Emily!" I command, pulling her out of the water and onto the dock. "Breathe. Please!"

Watching her collapse after Sinclair's blow fueled me with a rage so intense it scared me, and I grabbed him and threw him into the lake, then dove in after Emily.

Now, as I settle her onto the dock and press my palms against her chest, begging her to wake up, Sinclair fires at us from the water, swimming toward us like the little cockroach he is.

"Where is the diamond, Fleet?" Sinclair screams, pulling himself onto the dock.

I ignore him, focused only on getting Emily to breathe again. The bastard had the diamond in his hand when I lunged at him, and for all I care, it's on its way to the bottom of Lake Superior as we speak.

Sinclair sprints at me, delivering a swift kick to my ribs as I crouch over Emily, and I yell out in pain and stagger to my feet to fight him off. I watch, panicking, as Malcolm and two more of Sinclair's henchmen stride toward us, guns and scowls out, but I breathe a sigh of relief when Emily opens her mouth and coughs, spewing up a mouthful of lake water.

"Here's your diamond, motherfucker," she croaks, reaching for something on the deck just beyond her grasp.

She closes her fingers over the Evermore, which must have fallen from Sinclair's hand when I shoved him into the water, and clambers to her feet.

"Enough!" Sinclair shouts, incensed. He points his gun at Emily, fury flickering in his eyes. "Give me my diamond, you bitch!"

I want to sever his head from his body with my bare hands, because I'll be damned if someone calls Emily a bitch right in front of me and lives to see another day. But she only shakes her head, staring at the diamond in her hand like she's seeing it for the first time. She mumbles something to herself, the lines of her forehead furrowed in thought, and then the concentration on her face gives way to a flicker of something else: relief, maybe, or realization. Whatever it is, I don't understand it, and I can only watch in confusion as she laughs the slightly maniacal laugh of someone who's barely slept or eaten in days.

"Give me the diamond," Sinclair repeats, his tone venomous.

But she only grins at him. "I can't," she says simply, not anxious or afraid. "I can't give you the diamond."

She laughs at the stone in her hand, actually doubling over in amusement, and I wonder if I didn't move quite fast enough to get her out of the water before a few of her brain cells started dying off.

"Focus on what's real," she says, looking not at me or Sinclair but only at the diamond. "Focus on what's real. Of course."

"Emily," Sinclair says, "this whole Mad Hatter routine is highly unattractive, darling. Now give me the diamond before I kill you."

She smiles at him, her gaze steady, focused.

"No," she says. "I can't. Because there is no diamond."

"Stop playing around," Sinclair snaps, his tone venomous. He pauses, as if registering the fact that Emily is standing near the edge of the dock and could easily toss the diamond into the lake if she wanted, and takes a deep breath.

"I mean, of course there's a diamond," he adds, his tone less acidic. "It's that big, gleaming thing in your hand right there." He extends an open palm toward her and whistles softly, as if she's a stubborn labradoodle refusing to return the ball she was supposed to fetch. "There you go, love, give it here."

"I can't give you the diamond," Emily repeats, shaking her head, "because the diamond isn't real."

Sinclair's jaw drops for an instant, and then he laughs, grinning at his henchmen.

"Good one, darling. You sounded so serious you almost had me there for a second."

"I am serious," she says, lifting the gemstone up to squint at it. "It's not real. It's a fake."

"What the fuck are you talking about, Emily?" Sinclair asks, no longer amused and waving his gun.

"Ryder dropped it into a puddle," she says, tossing the Evermore into the air and catching it like it's no more significant than a softball. "But it didn't sink."

"That's impossible," Sinclair says, his eyes widening. "Diamonds don't float. Of course it sank. It's a simple principle of density." He sneers at me. "Physics. You wouldn't understand."

"Maybe not, but I do," Emily says. "I reacted so fast when Ryder dropped it that I barely had time to realize that it floated. But now I see." She curls her fingers over the gem, shaking it. "Now I know what's real."

"You misinterpreted Captain Evermore's letters to Katherine," she continues, pacing back and forth across the dock. "He's not talking about a literal diamond. He's using the stone as a metaphor, as a symbol." She looks at me, her gray eyes bearing no trace of fear or hesitation. "A symbol of his love."

Sinclair's face twists in rage and confusion, but I can only laugh uproariously, because holy shit, this is fucking hilarious.

"Damn, you got fucking played," I tell him, the glee almost too much to handle. "It's a metaphor, *bitch*!"

"No," Sinclair says, watching as I let out a series of victorious whoops. "It's not. It can't be."

"It can be, you preppy little murderer!" I say, doing a little jig in his honor. "And it is."

"You're lying!" he cries, pointing at Emily. "She's lying!"

She smirks, and without a word, she tosses the stone off the dock and into Lake Superior.

"No!" Sinclair shouts, sprinting toward the water, but he stops when he sees that Emily's right. The diamond—or rather, the nondiamond—floats on the surface like a magnificently shiny fishing bob.

"Uh-oh," I say, watching as Sinclair's face turns from red to purple. "I don't think you're gonna be wealthy beyond imagination anymore."

The archaeologist lets out a scream so loud and primal that the seagulls on the shore take off in flight, and I cover my ears until he's finished.

"I sure hope you have a backup career plan," I say, watching as he dry heaves. "I don't think they'll let you be an archaeologist anymore, on account of, you know, the fact that you murdered your boss and can't tell a real diamond from a fake one." I grin at him. "Hey, maybe Taggart needs an assistant."

He lets out a cry of fury, his face so purple I'm actually kind of worried for him, and he points his gun at me. But before he can fire, Malcolm and the other henchmen advance on him, their expressions incredibly unamused.

"If there's no diamond," Malcolm says, cracking his knuckles as he moves toward Sinclair, "how are we going to get paid?"

"There *is* a diamond!" Sinclair cries, pulling at his hair. He points to Emily and me. "They must have switched the real Evermore diamond with a fake!"

"But how could we manage to pull that off?" I ask, relishing in Sinclair's panic. "Emily's not that clever, remember? And I'm just a hapless buffoon."

"Listen to me!" Sinclair cries, spittle flying from his mouth as he screams at his advancing henchmen. "They're lying! They know where the real diamond is! Apprehend them, you fools!"

"Are you really going to believe them over me?" he asks, his face crumpling in disbelief. "I'm a Harvard archaeologist! I have *tenure*, for fuck's sake!"

My stomach churns at the memory of what he did to Dr. Sharp, of what his men did to Biff and Rick the ranger.

"You're no archaeologist, Sinclair," I say, crossing my arms over my chest. "Archaeology is the noble art of preserving history, and you're nothing more than a murderer."

Emily beams at me, then narrows her eyes at Sinclair as his angry henchmen approach.

"It's too bad," she says with a shrug. "They might have liked you better if you'd carried your own pack."

Sinclair spits at her. "Get back to the ship!" he tells his men. "The Evermore diamond is down there somewhere, and you're going to find it for me!"

"Amazing," I whisper to Emily. "It's like he doesn't listen at all."

"Get back to the ship, or I'll shoot you myself!" Sinclair warns Malcolm, but he doesn't get the chance.

Because Malcolm, in a move that would surely displease his wife, Miriam, shoots Sinclair right in the chest.

"Fuck," I say, shocked, watching as Sinclair collapses and falls into the lake.

Emily's horrified expression matches my reaction, and I reach for her hand and squeeze it. Granted, we weren't huge Sinclair fans—what with the stealing and the murder and the way he smashed Emily over the head with his gun and almost killed her—but we're not on board with murder.

"So," I say, giving the henchmen my friendliest smile when

they turn toward Emily and me, "would you guys be willing to give us a ride back to the ferry, or . . ."

I pause, trailing off as they move toward us without lowering their weapons.

"Gotcha," I say, reading the room. "No worries. We'll find our own way. I just wasn't sure if this was a 'the-enemy-of-my-enemy-is-my-friend' situation."

But it's clearly not, and Emily lets out a squeak of fear when none of them move to lower their weapons. As I scramble for a way to get us the hell out of here, a wolf howls suddenly in the distance, drawing the henchmen's attention.

"Emily, run!" I tell her. "Swim to the speedboat!"

For once, by some truly astonishing miracle, she listens to me. Sort of. She makes a pit stop at the edge of the dock to grab her dad's urn, and then she jumps into the lake, swimming toward the boat with all her might.

"Not so fast," a glowering henchman says, but I've got a plan. Using the cord of Caleb's headphones, which Sinclair dropped in the scuffle, I wrap them around the nearest man's neck from behind, then hurl him toward his friends. All three tumble into the water, and I really hope Emily saw that, because it was cool as hell. I dive into the lake, reaching the boat a fraction of a second behind her.

"Hey, Ryder?" Emily asks, her tone desperate. "Please tell me you know how to drive this thing."

"Uhhh," I say, watching as she frantically turns the key. The motor purrs, coming to life, and we both let out a cheer as she glides the boat over the water.

But our escape isn't that easy. Because just as Emily manages to pick up speed, one of the henchmen leaps out of the water and fires one last shot at her. Desperate, I dive in front of Emily to protect her, because just like the Evermores, I really do know what it means to love someone so much you'd give your life for them.

For her, I'd give anything. I crash to the floor of the boat, hot pain searing through my foot.

"Holy shit, Ryder, they shot you!" Emily cries, glancing down at me in alarm.

"I noticed," I say, grimacing as blood pools around my leg.

"Oh my God," she says, the boat jerking as she watches me instead of the water.

"Keep your eyes on the road!" I tell her. "Or the lake, or whatever. Don't worry about me. I'm not gonna die on you now."

"Promise?" she asks, hitting the gas, and I do promise, I really do, but I'm a little distracted by the unbelievable pain in my foot and the fact that Emily's dangerously close to capsizing the boat and killing us both.

She speeds up the coastline for miles, and I do my best to fight against the dizzy lightheadedness creeping over me. I'm not going down without a fight, and certainly not before I get the chance to take the woman I love on a real, henchmanless date.

"Campfires!" Emily cries finally, steering the boat roughly toward the coast. "Campfires! There!"

She points to the shoreline, but the boat floor and I are one being now, and I make no effort to look.

"Whose campfires?" I ask, grunting. "Please don't say more henchmen."

"No, it's . . . oh my God, it's the marriage retreat group!" Emily cries, waving wildly toward them. "Help! Help us, please!"

I hear voices yelling back at her, concerned and confused, and she breathes out a sigh of relief as we near the shore.

"We're saved, Ryder," she promises. "We're saved."

And she's right. We are saved.

"Holy hell, it's the hot long jumper from the ferry!" a woman's voice exclaims, and I swear I hear more than one husband groan in displeasure. "And his Debbie Downer friend."

If Emily's annoyed by that description, she doesn't show it, and all is forgiven anyway when the hikers from the retreat sprint toward our boat, helping us ashore once she manages to bring it to a shaky stop.

"What the hell happened to you, honey?" a middle-aged woman asks me, noticing the blood on my leg.

But I don't know where to start, and I wouldn't have the energy to explain even if I did. I wince as the woman and her husband usher me toward their campsite, where others wrap us in blankets and press thermoses of water into our hands.

"We'll be okay now," Emily promises, wrapping her arms around me and pressing a kiss to the top of my head.

And she's right. Because whatever marital strife led the couples swarming around us to sign up for a relationship retreat in the middle of Lake Superior, our urgent need for help supersedes it. United in a shared mission, they work together to slow the bleeding from my wound and treat Emily's dehydration, and the retreat leader uses a personal locator beacon to send out an emergency distress signal.

"You are my heroes," I tell the retreaters as they apply fresh bandages to our injuries and hand us steaming mugs of hot chocolate, and Loretta, the woman who briefly pretended to assume Emily's identity on the ferry, shrugs at me.

"We're not heroes, we're just prepared," she says, looping her arm through her husband's. "Who the fuck goes into the wilderness without a radio?"

Emily widens her eyes at me, trying not to laugh.

"Touché, Loretta," I tell her. "Touché."

While we wait for emergency personnel to arrive, someone passes us a sleeping bag, and I huddle with Emily inside it.

"I guess it's getting serious now," I observe, wrapping an arm around her. "Since we're spooning and all."

She laughs, snuggling her butt into me. "Of course it's serious, Ryder. You're the only man I know who brought a Discman to a gunfight and lived to tell the tale."

I do sound pretty impressive when you put it that way, but there's still one important thing I couldn't get done for her.

"You know," I say, relishing the feeling of lying next to her in a soft sleeping bag and not being shot at, "I wanted to tell you that I'm sorry for—"

"Ryder Fleet," she scolds, rolling over to face me, "don't you dare. You have nothing to apologize for. You took a literal bullet for me."

She leans forward to kiss me, her mouth soft and wanting, and I kiss her back for a moment before pulling away. I'd love to kiss her all night—hell, I'd like to do a lot more than kiss her—but I can't afford to get distracted from what I want to say. It's too important.

"I just want you to know how sorry I am that we didn't get to scatter your dad's ashes," I say, brushing my thumb over her temple. "I know how important that was to you."

She places her hand over mine and brings my fingertips to her mouth for a kiss.

"It's okay, Ryder," she says, wrapping her hand around mine. "We'll do it at the next national park."

"The *next* national park?" I ask in disbelief, wondering if her head injury is more severe than I thought. "You want to do all this again?"

"Well, no, not all of it. I could do without the murder and the trauma and the constantly having to run for our lives thing." She squeezes my hand. "But I promised myself I would finish my dad's bucket list, and I still intend to. Besides, you're not such bad company after all."

I laugh, and she smiles at me, but then her expression turns serious. Thoughtful.

"You could be a really great ambassador of adventure, Ryder," she says. "You could be a really great anything, you know. You're strong and brave and you never give up, and that's the stuff nobody can teach you." She shrugs. "The rest of it, you can learn. If you want to."

Her fierce belief in me fills me with pride, and I don't fight the urge to press my mouth to hers.

"But next time," she adds, her lips brushing mine again, "we're definitely bringing a GPS."

TWENTY-FOUR

EMILY
Houghton, Michigan
Two days later

I will never, for the rest of my life, take a hot shower for granted. Nor will I forget to count my blessings every time I eat a warm meal or curl up to sleep in an actual bed. Don't get me wrong, eating chicken soup in a hospital cot while nurses assessed me for signs of severe head injury wouldn't ordinarily be my idea of a good time, but it was leagues better than what Ryder and I endured on Isle Royale. Luckily, I was discharged after a few hours with instructions not to operate heavy machinery anytime soon—an easy recommendation to follow, considering I never plan on driving a speedboat again.

Ryder, who was listed in stable condition after a minor surgery on his ankle, is due to be discharged any time now, a thought that fills me with joy and relief. In fact, I think the only person who'll be happier than me to see Ryder leave the hospital is our heroic helper, Biff, who had the good luck of being rescued from the ranger station by emergency personnel—and, in his view, the grave misfortune of being Ryder's in-hospital roomie. Ryder and I cried with relief when we got to the hospital and realized that both Biff and Ranger Rick had survived, and perhaps the only thing that pissed Biff off more than Malcolm shooting him was Ryder enveloping him in a bear hug.

I've only left Ryder and Biff for brief periods to grab food and shower at the nearby hotel, and now, as I stand in the steamy shower and relish the sensation of being warm and clean, I'm already itching to get back to the hospital. Switching off the water, I step out of the shower and wrap myself in a towel, cherishing the fact that I don't smell like dirt or dead fish. As I wipe the foggy mirror and scrunch water out of my hair, trying to decide what to grab Ryder and Biff for dinner, I hear a knock at the door.

Startled, I quickly slip on a robe and glance around the hotel room, searching for a weapon just in case. I settle on the complimentary iron, holding it with two hands like a baseball bat as I tiptoe toward the door and glance warily through the peephole. I'm not sure who I'm afraid it could be—Killian's long gone, and law enforcement rounded up the henchmen after our evacuation—but from here on out, I'm ready for anything.

My fear vanishes, however, when I see that the person standing outside my door is none other than my handsome ambassador of adventure.

"Ryder!" I cry, flinging the door open and wrapping my arms around him. "What are you doing here?"

He smiles, tracing a line down my cheek with the back of his hand.

"I got discharged early," he says. "Thought I'd surprise you."

"Are you sure you're supposed to be walking?" I ask, glancing toward his ankle. "No, there's no way you should be walking. You just had *surgery*—"

"Always playing it safe, Edwards," he says, shaking his head. "*Don't jump onto a moving ferry. Don't camp in a wolves' den. Don't walk around on your bad ankle.*" He grins. "When are you finally gonna accept that I live on the edge?"

"Probably around the time you start living to shop at HomeGoods. But I have to say, this is an incredible surprise."

I can't help but marvel at the sight of him in the real world, standing at my threshold like we're normal people who didn't just survive an insane journey through the wilderness.

Ryder laughs. "Oh, my presence is not the surprise."

I raise an eyebrow. "What is it, then? Did you make me a fingerpaint version of a Foxamura painting?"

He rolls his eyes. "No. The surprise is that I'm going to recite a poem for you."

"Really?" I ask, leaning against the doorframe. "A poem by who?"

"By me."

I do a double take. "You wrote me a poem?"

Ryder shakes his head. "No. I wrote you *ten* poems. This was just the least terrible of the bunch, and that's saying something." He takes a deep breath and rolls his shoulders back. "Are you ready?"

Ready for the man in front of me, who I now know is beautiful not only on the outside but on the inside, too? Hell yes.

"More than ready," I tell him.

"Okay." He clears his throat. "I should warn you before I start: it's short and very pathetic."

"Ah, yes," I say, crossing my arms. "Just what every girl dreams of hearing when a man comes to her hotel room."

His cheeks flush, but he presses on. "Here we go. Don't laugh."

I smile. "I make no promises."

"Emily," he says, the humor in his tone replaced by bashful earnestness, "roses are red, violets are blue, I want to get dinner, and I want it with you."

I wait for him to continue, but he exhales as if he just delivered a lengthy monologue.

"That's it. That's the poem."

"Oh!" I say brightly, knowing he could stand at my door and recite the periodic table for all I care. All that matters is that we're here, together, safe and sound and with the rest of our lives to look forward to. "Wow. Thank you."

"I know, I know, I'm no Captain Evermore, but I'll keep working on it." Smiling, Ryder takes my hand in his. "What I'm trying to say is, I meant everything I said on Isle Royale. I want a future with you. I want to learn your favorite ice-cream flavor, and your favorite day of the week, and everything that makes you tick."

"Strawberry," I tell him. "Friday, obviously. Weekly planners and venti caramel lattes."

He laughs and strokes his thumb over my palm. "In the words of the one and only Shel Silverstein, I don't want our sidewalk to end."

I can't help but smile. "I don't think Shel Silverstein said that, exactly."

"A minor detail," Ryder says, lowering his lips to mine, and then all thoughts fade away, and there's only him and me and the fact that we're together, with all the time in the world to explore each other.

"So what do you say?" he asks when he comes up for air. "Can I take you to dinner?"

"No," I say, leaning into his chest. "But you can definitely take me to breakfast."

Ryder and I might not agree on everything—we still have very different views on documentaries, for example—but we can both agree on this: my robe is a perfect outfit for this long-awaited moment.

As soon as I utter the word *breakfast*, he steps into my room, one arm scooping me up like it's nothing. I wrap my legs around his waist as he presses his free hand to the back of my head, guiding my mouth toward his. His lips are somehow softer than I remember, his touch hungrier, and suddenly I'm grateful for every wrong turn we took on the island, for every foolish mistake and misread map that brought us to this moment.

We reach the bed in only a few strides, and I wait for him to drop me onto it and tear my robe off like there's no tomorrow, but he doesn't. Instead, Ryder sets me down just before the foot of the bed, his eyes blazing as he tears his mouth away from mine. He takes one of my robe ties in each of his hands and pauses, studying me like he's trying to commit this moment to memory.

"Emily," he says, his tone reverent. He says my name like it's a wish, a promise, and I wrap my hands around his.

"Ryder." It's a promise, too, an answer to a question he didn't need to ask aloud. It's an *invitation*, and I pull his hands back so that they untie the robe, leaving me exposed. Open.

He steps toward me, his kiss deep and wanting as he slides the robe off. It lands at my feet, and even though I should probably feel at least a little bit nervous as Ryder gazes at my face, my breasts, my bare skin, I don't. I feel wanted, truly and desperately, and I want, too.

"Fuck," he whispers, taking in every inch of me, and it's the shortest, most erotic poem I've ever heard.

I tilt my head up to kiss him, my hands reaching for his T-shirt, and he removes it swiftly, leaving his torso so beautifully bare that I can hardly believe he's real. But of course he is, because these are the arms that carried me to safety, and the chest I curled into when we rolled down the hill, and these are the hands that reached out to catch me when I jumped blindly from the radio tower. I run a hand from his shoulder to his hip, feeling every muscle tighten beneath my touch, and Ryder sucks in a breath as I press my mouth to every bruise I see, every visceral reminder of what we endured and how we took care of each other. How he took care of me.

I kiss him from his chin to his navel, and my hand wanders lower, cupping the place where I want to touch him the most. I unbutton his pants, our mouths meeting again, and he moans as I grip him through the fabric, wishing for it to disappear. He takes over for me, removing his jeans and boxers as smoothly as he can without breaking our kiss, and when I finally pull away so I can look at him, at all of him, I'm hit with a wave of unrelenting, uncompromising need.

Ryder must be, too, because he picks me up again, his hands kneading my bare ass, and sets me on the edge of the bed, nudging my legs open with his knee. I run a hand through his hair as he leaves a trail of kisses from my mouth to my thigh, pausing at my breasts to run his tongue over my nipple. I can't help but let out a soft whimper as he presses his mouth to my inner thigh, working his way toward my most wanting, aching part. I gasp when he slides this thumb down my clit, his touch responsive to my every moan, and his name leaves my lips again when he lowers his mouth between my legs, his tongue licking and coaxing and savoring with an intensity that leaves me perfectly and utterly wrecked.

"Come here," I say before my ability to speak escapes me. "Come be with me."

He licks me again, slowly, lavishly, and then he climbs onto the bed and positions himself above me. I reach for him, stroking him as his mouth finds mine, and the uncontrolled moan he makes when I grip his shaft is delicious in its coarseness.

"Emily," he says, his hand cupping my face, "I've wanted you so badly. I *want* you so badly."

His eyes search mine, and I revel in the way he looks at me, like I'm more precious than any diamond that ever existed. And I want him, too, today and forever, in whatever adventures await.

"I'm yours," I tell him, wrapping a leg around his waist, and he kisses me deeply as he enters me, letting out an unbridled grunt of pleasure that will leave me wet and wanting every time I think of it.

He murmurs my name into my skin, whispering his love for me, and I whisper it back as everything fades away except for Ryder on top of me, inside me, riding me until every nerve and cell and muscle in my body coils, tight, tight, tight, and then peaks and releases, rocking me with an orgasm so intense I press my teeth to his broad shoulder. Spurred on by my pleasure, he thrusts faster, deeper, all his reservation and self-restraint cast aside. And when he comes, moaning as he presses his mouth to mine like he'll die if he doesn't, I hear his rapture as a vow, a pledge, a culmination of everything we promised each other on the island.

A recognition that we might not have found everything we initially set out looking for, but we found something better. Something bigger. We found love.

Afterward, I sprawl out in the bed, enjoying the blissful combination of soft, clean sheets and Ryder's warm body next to mine.

Suddenly ravenous, I reach for my phone to scroll through the hotel's room service options, and Ryder grabs Sharp's notebook from the bedside table and flips it open.

"Maybe we can find another steamy Evermore letter," he says, grinning at me. "To get you in the mood for round three."

I swat him. "You don't need to read me a poem to get me ready for round three."

"Well, then," he says, kissing the top of my head, "round four, maybe."

I'm trying to decide between pasta or a cheeseburger, and I elect to get both when Ryder lets out a gasp so loud and sudden that I drop the menu.

"Jesus, how steamy of a letter did you find?" I ask, clutching my chest.

"I didn't find a letter," he says, sitting up straighter. "I think I found something else."

He holds up Sharp's notebook and takes my fingers to run them over the back cover, where I feel a small lump hidden under the leather.

"If that's a giant Isle Royale bug," I say, "I'm gonna need a whole lot of therapy."

"I don't think it's a bug," Ryder says, fishing something out of a hole in the leather.

"Ohmiiiiigod," I say when he pulls out a shimmering gemstone so shiny it makes me blink. "Is that what I think it is?"

"There's only one way to find out," Ryder says, and I follow him as he runs to the bathroom to fill the sink with water and plug the drain. Then we clutch hands, our hearts pounding, as he tosses the rock in.

"Holy shit, it sinks!" he says, laughing in disbelief.

"The Evermore diamond is real," I whisper, staring at the gem. "The Evermore diamond is real!"

"Forget room service," Ryder says, taking me into his arms. "We gotta call the Smithsonian."

EPILOGUE

RYDER
Yellowstone National Park
1 year later

September was, in Caleb's opinion, the best time to visit Yellowstone. By early fall, the massive summer crowds thin, leaving the park significantly less packed, and the green leaves of the aspen trees start to change, popping with bursts of fiery red and eye-catching gold. Not to mention, of course, that most of the bugs are gone, a fact that made Emily smile so widely you'd think there was a half-off sale at HomeGoods.

And as Emily and I look out over a lush green valley, a soft breeze gently mussing her curls, I'm starting to think that Caleb was right—Yellowstone in September is beautiful. And Yellowstone in September with her? Well, it's pretty damn perfect.

I watch as she packs dirt over the small hole where she just finished spreading some of her dad's ashes, then stands up and brushes off her knees.

"Happy birthday, Dad," she says, leaning into me, and I slip an arm around her waist. "I wish you were here."

"We sure do," I say, pressing a kiss to the top of her head.

"So a lot's happened in the last year," Emily continues. "Which you might know already, if you can check in on me from wherever you are now, but I'm obviously not sure about that, seeing as how I'm not, you know, dead myself, and therefore have no clue."

She sighs and glances up at me. "This is clearly going great."

"It is going great," I assure her. "Just say whatever feels right."

I'm sure as hell not going to judge her, just like she didn't judge me for crying like a baby when Tara, the proud new owner of *The Little Adventure*, took the two of us on the first of many rides on Caleb's beloved boat. That's one of the best things about my relationship with Emily: because we both understand grief, it makes it easier for us to understand each other, and she doesn't ask questions when I tear up at the opening credits of *The Sandlot* or spend an hour listening to mundane voicemails Caleb left me just to hear his voice. She only grips my hand and understands, just like I understand why she listens to Cleveland Guardians games on the radio even though she doesn't give a damn about baseball. Just like I get why she still won't go into bookstores, even though she's a big believer in buying local, and so I stop in for her, loading up on cozy mysteries and Nora Roberts and ridiculous how-to guides on reorganizing every room in your home.

Emily doesn't try to get me to move past my pain; she helps me live with it, and I try to do the same for her.

"Okay, so," she continues, trying again, "Brooke had her baby. A son. They named him Lucas Roger, in tribute to you, but don't hate me for thinking Roger is a rough middle name for an infant." She smiles, her voice less reluctant now. "I've been to *four* national parks, all of them with Ryder, and after Isle Royale, we've encountered nary a henchman or angry wild animal."

I can't help but raise an eyebrow at *nary*, and she elbows me gently.

"We were VIP guests at the Smithsonian," she says, "which is not a sentence I would have ever imagined saying, but it's true. There was a gala for the opening of the Evermore diamond exhibit, and we were the guests of honor."

"It was a fancy gala," I add. "There was a harpist and everything."

"I'm sorry to say that the Browns still haven't appeared in the Super Bowl," says Emily. "Though to be fair, if you'd lived to be three hundred, that would still be true."

I nod as she clasps her hands together, thinking.

"I work less these days," she says. "I still work a lot, but it's less, and I still see you in every patient who comes through the door. And I think that actually makes me a better doctor. Kinder, you know. More observant."

"Don't forget to tell him about Cedar Point," I whisper.

"Oh. Right." She grins, her cheeks flushing with pride. "I rode a roller coaster at Cedar Point."

"Not just any roller coaster," I clarify. "She rode Millennium Force! It's a giga-coaster. Over three hundred feet."

"It was horrible," she admits. "I screamed so loudly going up the hill that I made some little kids cry."

"But you did it."

She smiles. "Yeah. I did it."

I watch as she bends to the ground again, giving the dirt a firm pat.

"I miss you, Dad," she says, "and I love you even more. I always will. Happy birthday."

"Happy birthday, Roger," I echo.

I reach for Emily, and she burrows her head into my chest, and we stay like that for a moment, together. Then she steps back, smiling, and smooths the front of her forest green Fleet Outdoor Adventures T-shirt.

"Ready?"

"Ready as I'll ever be," I tell her, adjusting the straps of my pack.

"Good." She grins at me, reaching up to brush my cheek with her hand. "I'm really proud of you, Ryder. And I think Caleb is, too."

And for the first time in a long time, I don't want to laugh at the thought that the second part might be true. And not just because I've rebuilt Fleet Outdoor Adventures from the ground up—a feat that required me to take many, many survival and backpacking courses, and one made easier by the fact that national press over the discovery of the Evermore garnered the agency a lot of attention and a chance to start over—but because I've found something that makes me happy. I love helping people, and I love being outdoors, and once I stopped trying to be just like Caleb and started aiming to be a better version of myself, I succeeded.

In fact, I didn't just succeed. I kicked ass. Not only can I now use a fuel canister without almost causing an explosion, I can also identify which nonedible plants could instantly kill me. And thanks to Emily, who's always up long before any sane person should be, I haven't slept through an alarm clock in ages.

Thanks to her, and the obstacles we faced on Isle Royale together, I'm starting to realize that I might never stop grieving, but that doesn't mean I have to stop living. And sure, there are nights when I still toss and turn with guilt, my mind playing the what-if game it loves to torture me with. *What if* I hadn't missed my flight to Caleb's bachelor party? *What if* I could have done something to help him? But those nights are becoming less frequent, and when they happen, Emily wraps her arms around me and presses her cheek to mine and whispers, "*What if* we just lay here like this?" and I feel better. Less alone.

"We'd better get back to the group before Biff terrifies any more of your clients," Emily observes. "I heard him warning everybody about what happens if you're dumb enough to touch a geyser. There was a lot of talk about fourth-degree burns and the stink of boiled flesh."

"For fuck's sake," I mutter, shaking my head as we turn to hike back toward the group.

Despite the fact that Biff isn't so great with people—and that I have yet to discover what *Biff* is actually short for—asking him to join the agency as a wilderness expert was a no-brainer. The fact that he actually accepted the invitation, albeit in a grumble, surprised me, but what can I say? I guess our adorable haplessness grew on him. Besides, nobody likes to be alone all the time. Not even Biff, who still packs Edith's camping chair and glowers at anyone who dares to look at it.

"So," I hear him telling the tour group as Emily and I return for the end of the hydration break, "as I said this morning, I will answer three questions per hour, max."

A worried-looking teenager who signed up for the tour with her parents bites her lip. "Can we borrow questions from future hours? So like, can I ask you four questions from five to six o'clock if I only ask two from six to seven?"

"No," Biff says flatly.

"He's joking, Callie," I tell the dejected-looking teenager, casting a sideways glance at my ill-mannered friend. "You guys can ask me or Biff as many questions as you want, whenever you want. We're all here to learn, right? And to have an adventure."

"To adventure!" Callie's dad cheers, punching the air with his fist, and I ignore Biff's piercing glare as I prepare my dozen fearless clients for the next leg of our hike.

Finally, when everyone is hydrated and ready to go, their hiking boots laced and their backpacks on, I turn to Emily and extend my hand.

"Ready?" I ask her, grinning at the woman who took my broken heart and helped me piece it back together.

She smiles, slipping her hand into mine. "Ready as I'll ever be."

And then, together, we set off to explore the beauty of Yellowstone. Because whatever challenges we face on the trail before us—rocky terrain, or the deep, sometimes overwhelming grief of missing someone gone too soon—I know the two of us can handle it. Because we've got love, laughter, and enough high-SPF sunscreen to hike all the way to the sun and back.

"I love you," I tell her, squeezing her hand, and the tender look she gives me in return is worth more than any diamond.

"I love you, too."

Adventure awaits.

ACKNOWLEDGMENTS

Writing a book is its own kind of adventure, and I'm very grateful for the people who supported me in making this one happen.

Many thanks to agent extraordinaire Jessica Watterson and her team at Sandra Dijkstra Literary Agency, my insightful (and incredibly patient!) editor, Angela Kim, and the entire Berkley team.

I am forever grateful for the support of my husband, Chris, who is swoonier than any book boyfriend I could ever dream up and who loves me no matter how loudly I type.

Thank you to my son Ciaran for making me brave, and to Finn and Junie for filling my days with so much joy and laughter. Loving you three will always be my greatest adventure.

Many thanks to my sister, Kelly, who has been my best friend since 1989, and to my mom, whose help made it possible for me to write a book with a toddler and a newborn at home. Thanks to my dad for his endless support, and to my brother, Josh.

Special thanks to the friends and family who make up my village, especially Audrey Roncevich.

Kellan McVey, here's your shout-out!

Finally, thank you to nine-year-old me, who vowed that she would 1) publish a book and 2) marry a Hanson brother. You don't end up marrying a Hanson brother (see Chris, your husband, mentioned above), but you've published three books and built a life you love, and there's no ending in the world happier than that.

IMAGE BY SIMON YAO

Kerry Rea lives in central Ohio with her husband and children. In the rare moments when she's not writing or wrangling her baby and toddler, you can find her reading, listening to bookish podcasts, and looking up new recipes that she probably won't get around to trying. She believes that happily-ever-after is always possible and considers herself to be outdoorsy-ish—meaning she's happy enough to go on a hike as long as she gets baked goods and a bubble bath afterward.

VISIT KERRY REA ONLINE

AuthorKerryRea.com

AuthorKerryRea

KerryMRea

Ready to find
your next great read?

Let us help.

Visit prh.com/nextread

Penguin
Random
House